blue
rider
press

THE WITCH

and other tales
re-told

ALSO BY JEAN THOMPSON

NOVELS

The Humanity Project

The Year We Left Home

City Boy

Wide Blue Yonder

My Wisdom

The Woman Driver

COLLECTIONS

Do Not Deny Me

Throw Like a Girl

Who Do You Love

Little Face and Other Stories

The Gasoline Wars

BLUE RIDER PRESS

a member of Penguin Group (USA)

New York

THE WITCH

and other tales re-told

JEAN THOMPSON

blue
rider
press

Published by the Penguin Group
Penguin Group (USA) LLC
375 Hudson Street
New York, New York 10014

USA • Canada • UK • Ireland • Australia
New Zealand • India • South Africa • China

penguin.com
A Penguin Random House Company

"Three" originally appeared in *Southwest Review*, Vol. 98, No. 4

ISBN 978-0-399-17058-4

Printed in the United States of America
1   3   5   7   9   10   8   6   4   2

Book design by Michelle McMillian

CONTENTS

AUTHOR'S NOTE

When I was a kid, I went to a dentist with a practice limited to children. Her office was downtown, in a building with claustrophobic elevators and long, echoing, deserted hallways.

In my memory, it was always raining. The dentist's door was made of dark wood and frosted glass, with a transom. The dentist herself was a stately woman who wore her hair pulled back in a bun. She kept her dental instruments in a tall cabinet of many drawers, painted and carved to look like a grand house. She'd fix a piece of cotton ball on the cable of her old-fashioned drill and tell you to watch the rabbit as it zipped back and forth. There was no such thing as novocaine, so you set yourself to endure, and concentrated on the cotton rabbit, or the dollhouse with the drawers full of picks and drill bits, or the windows gray with rain. I had many fillings, and I spent a lot of time in that chair.

The waiting room was small, enclosed, and lit with ordinary table lamps. It was stocked with books and games and puzzles that mothers used to distract their fretful children. But the best thing was the big full-color framed picture that hung on the wall at child's-eye level, a map called "The Land of Make Believe."

The map is a landscape of winding paths, streams, waterfalls, bridges, lagoons, mysterious forests, improbable mountain peaks where castles perch. "The Land of Make Believe" admits all manner of imaginary figures. Here are Mother Goose characters, like Little Miss Muffet, here also the Emerald City of Oz, the Water-Babies, and the Little Lame Prince's tower. It is East of the Sun and West of the Moon, it is equipped with a magic carpet flying overhead, and with mermaids bathing at the water's edge. Here too are many landmarks from the classic fairy tales: Bluebeard's castle, the cottage where Red Riding Hood's grandmother lives, Hansel and Gretel in front of the witch's gingerbread house, and Jack the Giant Killer climbing his beanstalk.

It was a wonderful thing, as a child, to trace the curving paths with a finger and imagine yourself inside the stories. Many years later I bought a print of the map. It is the work of Jaro Hess, a Czech immigrant who settled in Michigan. He drew it, in a number of different versions, around 1900, and sold the rights to it in the 1930s, when it was first published. It hangs on my wall, and sometimes I stand in front of it, wondering about the Enchanted Wood, or the City of Brass, or the dark cave marked, Do Not Go In Here.

Whatever you grow up with triggers nostalgia, and I suppose that *Teletubbies* or *Sesame Street* or any other televised production can serve that purpose. But the great tales connect us not only to our childhoods (to the dentist, that kindly witch) but also to an earlier era in human history, when they were not necessarily designed for children. Instead they serve as repositories for primeval fears, such as being devoured. They remind us of a time when getting lost in a trackless forest was not just a risk of outdoor vacationing. They encompass our wish that the usurper and the evildoer be found out and punished in satisfyingly gruesome ways. The downtrodden will triumph. The little-regarded youngest son will find his fortune. The terrifying giant can be outwitted. There are magical transformations and visitations and chances to change our luck. Appearances deceive, but humility and virtue will guide us. We learn that, given a choice of three caskets, we are to bypass the gold and the silver and select the one made of lead. The bear at the cottage door, seeking shelter from the storm, must be let in and allowed to sleep on the hearth, for rendering aid to any needy creature will be rewarded. And goodness always manifests itself as beauty. (Unless, of course, that beauty is the product of an enchantment.)

All you need to do to remind yourself of the persistence of these stories is to browse the Disney catalogue or other current entertainment offerings. Fairy tales are regularly dusted off, retooled, and retold for new audiences. Often enough sentimentalized and colorized, but the old structures, their darkness and their glories, are still present beneath. And so our collective human past makes its imperfect way into the present, trailing its rumors, talismans, and memories of memories. Amid the wicked fairies and wish-granting fish, some actual events are dimly visible. It has been argued that "The Pied Piper of Hamelin" recounts the loss or removal of some number of the town's children during the thirteenth century.

I have tried here to write a cycle of stories that are not recountings or versions of the old tales but something looser. I wanted to recapture their magic, but in a way that used them only as a kind of scaffolding for new stories. The old ones tantalized with questions. Why might a young woman be persuaded to marry Bluebeard? How, exactly, might an animal come to have the power of human speech? And in what circumstances might Cinderella really have lost that glass slipper? Sometimes the answers led me in lighthearted directions, but just as often not.

I must admit that I have often turned up my nose at what seemed to me weak, inauthentic, bowdlerized versions of the tales. But authenticity is a relative and mutable concept here. Even if you take the Brothers Grimm or Perrault as authorities, they did not serve only as faithful scribes. They too edited, suppressed, and embroidered. Folklorists have found different versions of the same stories in China, India, Malaysia, Persia, Arabia, Greece, all across the globe. So that stories once told around ancient campfires in dead languages, passed down by way of dreams and nightmares, are now reincarnated as animated cartoons. In the inclusive spirit of "The Land of Make Believe," we should celebrate them all. For the tale belongs not to the teller but to those who hear and remember it.

THE WITCH

My brother and I were given over to the Department of Children and Family Services after our father and his girlfriend left us alone in the car one too many times. The reason we were put in the car had to do with some trouble when we were younger, in some of the different places that we lived, when we were left home by ourselves. Neighbors had made calls and DCFS had come around, turning our father into a concerned and head-nodding parent, at least while the interview lasted. Once the investigator left, he had things to say about people who tried to tell you what to do with your own goddamn kids. They should just shut their faces. "Let's go," he said. "In the car, now. Vamoose." He wasn't bad-tempered, at least not as a rule, but people who thought they were better than us, by way of criticism or interference, brought out the angry side of him.

At the time when everything changed for us, my brother Kerry was seven and I was five. We knew the rules, the chief one being: Stay in the car! We accepted that there were complicated, unexplained adult things that we were not a part of, in places where we were not allowed. But sometimes we were scooped up, Kerry and me, and brought inside to a room with people and noise and the wonderful colored lights of cigarette machines and jukeboxes, encouraged to tell people our names, wear somebody's baseball cap, and drink the Cokes prepared for us with straws and maraschino cherries.

And sometimes Monica, our father's girlfriend, drove. Then she'd stay in the car with us and keep the engine running while our father went inside some unfamiliar restaurant or house. These errands made Monica nervous, made her speak sharply to us and turn around in her seat to keep watch, some worry in the air that filled Kerry and me with the uncomprehending anxiety of dogs. And when our father finally returned, we were all so glad to see him!

But mostly it was just me and Kerry, left on our own to wait. We were fine with being in the car, a maroon Chevy, not new, that drove like a boat. We knew its territories of front and back, its resources, its smells and textures. We always had something given to us to eat, like cheese popcorn, two bags, so that there would be no fighting. We had a portable radio, only one of those, so that we did fight over it, but the fighting was also a way of keeping busy.

Most often we fell asleep and woke up when our father and Monica returned, carrying on whatever conversation or argument was in progress, telling us to go back to sleep. The car started and we were borne away, watching streetlights through a bit of window, this one and this one and this one, all left behind by our motion, and this was a comfort.

Normal is whatever you grow up with. Sometimes Monica

made us French toast with syrup for breakfast, and so we whined for French toast whenever we thought it might pay off. We had television to watch, and our intense, competitive friendships with kids we saw in the hallways and stairwells. All of this to say, we didn't think anything was so bad. We knew bad right away when it showed up.

Kerry was a crybaby. Our father said so. Kerry was a candy ass. This was said in a spirit of encouragement and exhortation, since it was a worrisome thing for a boy to be soft, not stand up to teasing or hardship. People would keep coming at you. When Kerry tried not to cry, it was just as pitiful as the crying itself. He had a round chin and a full lower lip that quavered, or, as our father used to say, "You could ride that lower lip home!"

The expectations were different for girls, and anyway, I didn't need the same advice about standing up for myself. Our father's name for me was Little Big Mouth. I didn't have a portion of Kerry's fair good looks either; everything about me was browner and sharper. I don't know why we were so different, why I couldn't have been more sweet-tempered, why Kerry didn't have more fight in him. Throughout my life I've struggled with the notion of things that were someone's *fault*, of things that were done *on purpose*, and it was a relief when I finally came to understand that one thing we are not to blame for is our own natures.

Monica hadn't always been with us. I knew that from having it told to me, and Kerry claimed he could remember the very day we met her. I said I did too, even though I didn't. My baby memories were too confused, and how were you supposed to remember somebody not being there? Or maybe she had been around us but not yet living with us as she did now. I think she was a little slow, with a ceiling on her comprehension. She had a round, pop-eyed face and limp black hair that she wore long, and she favored purplish lipstick that coated the ends of her cigarettes. If Kerry or I did something we weren't supposed to, she waved her hands and said, "You kids! Why you don't behave? I'm telling your dad on you!" We never paid attention. Monica wasn't entirely an adult, we sensed, and could be disregarded without consequences.

Our father didn't like to sit home. He'd done something that involved driving—a truck? a bus?—until he hurt his back and couldn't work regular hours. His back still pained him and we learned to walk wide of him when it put him in a mood. But if he was feeling good enough, or even borderline, he needed to get out and blow the stink off, as he called it, see and be seen, claim his old place among other men of the world. And since Monica wasn't going to be left behind, and since now we could not be left behind either, we all went.

One problem with staying in the car was when we had to go to the bathroom. Sometimes either Monica or our father came to check on us and carry us to some back entrance or passageway where there was a toilet. At other times they didn't come and didn't come, and we tried not to wet ourselves, or sometimes we did and were shamed.

Once, whimpering from urgency, Kerry got out of the car and stood behind some trash containers to pee. I watched, unbelieving and horrified. And jealous at how much easier it was for boys to manage these things. "I'm telling," I said, when Kerry let himself back in and relocked the car door.

"You better not."

"I don't have to, they can see right where you peed."

He looked out the window to see if that was true. "No you can't," he said, but he didn't sound so sure.

"You are going to get beat bloody." It was one of our father's occasional pronouncements, although so far we had not been made to bleed.

"Shut up." He kicked me and I kicked back.

When our father and Monica returned, they were fizzy and cheerful. "How are my little buckaroos?" my father asked. "How's the desperadoes?"

We said, faintly, that we were okay. Monica said, "They look hungry."

"Now how can you tell that by looking? Let's get a move on."

"You know what sounds good right about now? Chicken and waffles. Where's a place around here we can get that?"

"Some other time, Mon."

"That's not fair. I bet if you was the one wanted chicken and waffles, we'd be halfway there by now."

"Shut it, Monica," our father said, but not unpleasantly, because he was in such fine spirits. "If you were the one with the car, you could drive yourself to the moon." He turned on the radio and started singing along with it.

Kerry and I kept quiet in the back seat, and I didn't give him up. Like it or not, we were stuck together in some things.

So the next time I had to go, I told Kerry, "Move." He was sitting next to the door on the sidewalk side. On the street, cars passed by us fast, with a shivery sound of rushing air.

"You better not."

I popped out and made a face at him through the car window. I walked a little way, looking for a good place. But everything was out in the open, and it wasn't fully dark yet, and I didn't think I could crouch down and pee on the sidewalk, in front of everyone. I didn't know where our father and Monica had gone. None of the buildings looked likely. I kept walking.

Behind me, a car door slammed, and Kerry ran to catch up with me. "You're gonna be in trouble."

"Well so are you now."

Kerry walked backward in front of me. "Where are you going?"

"Home."

"Uh-uh!"

I ignored him. He didn't have any way to stop me.

"You don't know where it is."

"Yes I do." I didn't think we were that far away. And both Kerry and I wore house keys around our necks on shoelaces, just in case.

Kerry looked back at the car. It wasn't too late for him to return to it, but he kept walking with me, looking all worried. "Candy ass," I said.

"You're a candy ass," he said, but that was so lame, I didn't bother answering back.

If I'd found anyplace I could have peed, or if we'd managed to get ourselves home, things would have gone differently. But we walked and walked, and the street didn't offer anything like a bathroom, and we came to an intersection I didn't recognize, though I set off with confidence in one direction. Walking, I didn't have to go so bad. I thought I could keep on for a while.

Kerry lagged a pace or two behind me. He thought I was going to get in trouble and he was trying to stay out of the way. It was dark by now and the lights around us, from cars, streetlights, store windows, were bright and glassy, and the shadows beyond the lights were a reaching-out kind of black.

I'd been lost for a while. I knew it but I didn't want to come out and say it, and anyway, I had the idea that I could find our building if I only looked hard enough. At least I think that's how I thought. I was five, and it was a whole world ago.

The street was becoming less and less promising. There were vacant lots with chewed-looking weeds, and the gobbling noise of loud music from a passing car. I wondered if our father and Monica had come back yet and found us missing, or if they were still inside having their important fun. I was holding on to my pee so tight, I was having trouble walking. We came to a big lighted storefront, a grocery, with people going in and out of the automatic doors, and we hung back, afraid of getting in the way.

A lady on her way out of the store stopped and peered down at us. "Harold," she said to the man with her, "look, two little white babies."

Because we were white, and the lady and the man and everybody else around us was black.

"Where's your mamma?" the lady said, and we just stared at her. We didn't have one of those. "Awright, no matter, we fine her for you. You-all lost? Harold, you go put them bags up and come right back." She squatted down in front of us. "Can you talk, honey?"

"I have to go to the bathroom," I announced. Now that there was somebody to complain to, I was tearing up.

"Yeah?" She took my hand. "Come on with me, then. Brother too." She held out her other hand to Kerry, who was sniffling now. We were both moved by our own piteousness.

She led us through the store, back to the place with gray

mops resting in buckets, jugs of blue industrial cleanser, and a small, walled-off toilet. The lady asked if I needed any help, and it shocked me to think of some strange lady watching me pee, though she was just being nice. After I came out, Kerry said he had to go too, and then the lady directed us to wash our hands, lifting us up so we could reach the utility sink. She took us back through the store again, and we were set on a bench in an office where a radio played, and given cartons of chocolate milk and a package of cake doughnuts to eat.

And shouldn't everything have been all right then? We had been found, tended to, soothed. Our father and Monica should have come in, full of remorse and relief, to bear us away, and promise never to let us out of their sight again. Or maybe we could have gone home with the lady who found us. She seemed to know a thing or two about children. She and Harold could have taken us in, two strange little white birds hatched in a different nest, and we would have begun a new, improbable life.

Instead the police were called, and protective services, and different adult strangers herded us this way and that, talking in ways that were meant to be reassuring, I guess, but the enormity of what was happening made us both cry. Of course they had all seen crying children before, and children who had been beaten, burned, starved, violated, in much worse shape than Kerry and I. They were, perhaps, a little brusque with us, a little impatient. We sat in a room decorated with crayon drawings, with books and puzzles and rag dolls and toy trucks, and these were meant to distract and amuse us, but none of them were our toys, and we hung back from them.

Because it was already so late, too late to do anything else with us, Kerry and I spent the night in a kind of dormitory with blue night lights on the walls, wearing clean, much-laundered pajamas, each of us tucked in with some other child's stuffed bear. We were the only ones sleeping there, though we heard adult feet passing the open door and, from other rooms, different shrill or urgent sounds. I must have slept. But I kept waking up and seeing the blue lights and then I would remember everything that had happened, the weight of it sliding onto me in an instant.

I heard Kerry in the next bed, moving and restless. "Are you awake?" I whispered.

"Why did you get out of the car?" he said, and his voice was thick and full of snot from all his crying.

"Shut up."

"You weren't supposed to."

"Well you did too."

"You started it!"

Some noise beyond the doorway made us stop talking, and fall back into uneasy sleep. This was exactly the weight bearing down on me: the knowledge that I had set a terrible thing in motion.

In the morning we thought that we'd be going home now. But after breakfast (juice, apple slices, oatmeal that curdled in our mouths), it was explained to us that we would be going to stay at a lady's house for a while. There were some things that had to be discussed with our father. He was fine, he said to tell us hello, and that he missed us. (Kerry and I looked down at the floor at this. It was not a thing our father would say.) Meanwhile, we would be with Mrs. Wojo (her name was longer and more complicated, but that is what we heard), a lady who helped out with children when they needed a place to stay.

I said that we didn't need a place to stay, we just needed to go home. But we would not be going home. Explained and repeated to us by adults who had so much practice in telling children unpleasant things. We were going to Mrs. Wojo's.

Was our father mad at us, was that why he wouldn't come for us? Did he really know where we were, or were they making that up?

In the car on our way to Mrs. Wojo's, I tried to memorize landmarks so that we could find our way back to somewhere familiar. One of the DCFS people, a woman, sat in the back seat between Kerry and me so I couldn't talk to him. Another woman drove, and I guess they had names but I've forgotten them. It was one of those spring days that freezes up and turns water in gutters to oil-covered sumps, and a scouring wind pours out of the sky. We passed blocks and blocks of old warehouses, black-windowed buildings of dark red brick where nothing had happened for a very long time. A fenced-off park with a baseball diamond, chill and empty. Some streets of ordinary commerce, little shops and car lots and motels.

I wasn't crying now. I was too sore-hearted and tired. I watched the cold world slide by outside, and it seemed like there was nowhere in it for me. The car turned and turned, and here were streets of small houses. They were shingled in white, green, or gray, each with some kind of porch or stoop, each with its own small square yard set off with board fences. The car slowed and pulled over to the curb. "Okay, kids," the DCFS woman in the back seat with us said, in the voice adults use to try to head off any trouble, cheery and energetic but full of lurking strain. "Here we are!"

At least the house looked nice. It was white with red trim, and frilly curtains in the windows. It was too early in the season for flowers, but the window boxes were filled with red plastic geraniums. Someone was at least making an effort. Kerry and I were led up the front steps and the DCFS woman rang the bell. The front door was gated off with an ironwork barrier, painted white, and beyond that was a glass panel, and beyond that, a lace curtain.

The curtain stirred and there were a great many sounds of locks unsnapping and bolts sliding before we were admitted. The DCFS woman put a hand on each of our shoulders and propelled us forward. "This is Kerry. And this is Jo."

Too many things were happening at once for me to take everything in, but later I learned the details of that room by heart: the reclining chair, exclusive to the use of Mrs. Wojo, with the protective plastic doily across the back. The television table alongside where the remote control lived, and the different items necessary for the comfort and convenience of Mrs. Wojo. Kleenex, ashtray, eyeglasses case, crossword puzzle book with the small gold pen hitched to its spine. The television itself, furniture-like and old-fashioned even for that time. The line of African violets on the windowsill, each of them set on top of a cottage cheese carton with a wick made of nylon stocking. The plaid sofa with the clear plastic hood laid over the back cushions, the lamp with the base in the shape of a ceramic fish balanced on its tail. The carpet, a dank green. The air had a thickened quality, different layers of smells. Cigarettes, something yeasty, something burnt, and many cleaning products.

Mrs. Wojo stooped to get down close to us. "Hello, children." She had a powdery face, with powder under her lipstick too, so that her red mouth was worked into paste in the corners. She wore eyeglasses with pink frames and her hair was gray and puffed out. Like the house, she had layers of smells: soap, hair spray, undergarments, Pond's hand cream. And in the moment her face was closest to mine, she breathed out, and I smelled not just cigarettes, but something black, dead, fouled in her, and I knew her for what she was, and she saw that I knew it and her eyes glittered even as her mouth still smiled.

"Can they have candy?" she asked the DCFS woman. "Would you like some candy?" She held out a glass bowl with a mound of lemon drops stuck together. Kerry and I each picked one loose. "What do you say?" Mrs. Wojo prompted us, and we each said thank you.

The candies were hard and they stayed in a lump under our tongues for a long time.

Then we were taken upstairs to see the bedroom prepared for us, two little beds made up with checkerboard quilts, one blue, one yellow, and a dresser and a closet for all the clothes we didn't have. (These arrived later, collected from our home and transported in paper bags.)

The bathroom was downstairs, tiled in green, with a shower curtain patterned in seashells. Mrs. Wojo's magisterial bedroom was next to it. We caught a glimpse of dark wood and a white chenille bedspread. Mrs. Wojo and the DCFS woman had a number of things to discuss, while Kerry and I stayed silent. Kerry kept rubbing his eyes like he was sleepy, but it turned out there was something wrong with them, pinkeye, and I caught it too and we both had to have ointment squeezed into our eyes, which we fought as hard as we could, our hair yanked back to make us submit and stay still.

But this was yet to come. The two adults finished their talking, and the DCFS woman prepared to leave. She said that she would be back to see us soon, and that we should behave and do everything that Mrs. Wojo told us to. Mrs. Wojo escorted her out, saying goodbye in a musical voice. Then she redid all the locks and bolts and turned to face us.

"Kerry," she said. "That's a girl's name. Are you a little girl?" She lifted a piece of his long, fair hair. "We'll get this cut so you don't turn femmy."

Then she looked at me. "Joe, that's a boy's name. Did somebody think that was funny? Both of you named queer?"

"I'm Joanne," I said, not knowing what queer was, except that I didn't want to be it.

"That's not much better, is it? My name is Mrs. —" And here she spoke her full name, that impossible sequence of tangled consonants. "Say it."

"Mrs. Wohohohoho," Kerry and I came up with. She shook her head.

"Not the sharpest knives in the drawer, are you? Never mind. Go play in the back yard while I get your lunch ready."

We still had our coats on. She took us through the kitchen, with its enormous gas stove and more of the African violets set on a window ledge, and a smell of dishrags, out to a landing. Stairs led down to a basement, and opposite, the back door. "Go on," she said. "What are you waiting for, Christmas? Scoot."

The door closed behind us. The back yard was not as nice as the front. It was fenced off in chain link, with wood slats set into it for privacy. One bare tree, staked down with wires, grew in a plot of gravel. A sidewalk along one side led to some garbage cans and a high gate to the alley, padlocked. The wind was shrill and cold. Kerry rubbed at his eyes. I sucked on the collar of my coat for warmth. What were we supposed to do? Not just, what were we supposed to do in the cold yard, but for the whole of a day, or many days, in Mrs. Wojo's house?

After a while she called us back inside. We took off our shoes at the door, and then we washed our hands in the bathroom. She sat us down at the kitchen table and brought out two glasses of milk and two plates with sandwiches cut into quarters. Kerry and I tried them. They were filled with a thin, fishy paste, and we put them back down again.

"What's the matter with you?" Mrs. Wojo demanded. She was watching us from the doorway, smoking a cigarette and tapping the ashes into the lid of a jelly jar. "What do we got here, picky eaters?"

"I don't like it," I said. I didn't see any reason not to say so. I was that young. Kerry kept looking at his plate. He was scared for me.

"It's tuna fish. Don't tell me you don't like tuna fish."

I didn't know what to say to that. The tuna we had at home was mixed with mayonnaise and sweet pickle relish. This wasn't the same. "How about milk?" Mrs. Wojo said. "You all right with milk?"

"I like chocolate milk."

"Do you now," Mrs. Wojo said, agreeably. She reached the end of her cigarette, put it out in the jar lid, and set the lid on the kitchen counter. "Well, when you're old enough to get a job and earn money, then you can go buy chocolate milk. If you don't want to eat, that's your business. You look like you could miss a few meals and not suffer. You, now—" She stood behind Kerry and patted at his arms and shoulders. "You could use a little fattening up."

She turned and rummaged around in a cupboard. "Let's try, ah, peanut butter. A little good old PB and J."

We watched while she hauled out the peanut butter and jelly, spread slabs of them on bread, cut the sandwich into four pieces, and replaced Kerry's tuna fish with this new plate. Kerry and I looked at her, waiting. "Where's mine?" I asked.

"Your what? Your lunch? Sitting right in front of you. If you don't want to eat it, I can't make you."

The telephone rang then. Mrs. Wojo gave us an annoyed look, as if we were the ones interrupting her, and went out into the hall to answer it. Kerry shoved his plate at me. I took half the sandwich and shoved it back. I crammed it into my mouth and Kerry started in on his half. We heard Mrs. Wojo on the phone, her voice delighted and flirty. She said goodbye, in her fake, pleasant voice, and hung up. I wasn't quick enough, my cheeks still bulging with bread when she came back in. I froze, awaiting my punishment.

"That's better," she said to Kerry. "You need to make a habit of cleaning your plate. Get some size on you. As for you, Missy." She nodded in my direction. "If you don't like lunch, maybe you'll have a better appetite for supper."

Kerry and I traded looks, and I got the rest of the sandwich down as fast as I could.

It was a piece of luck to discover Mrs. Wojo's weakness right away—namely, she couldn't see five feet in front of her face.

After lunch we were sent upstairs for naps. "We don't take naps," I said, but quietly, under my breath.

"What's that?"

Mrs. Wojo swung around to face us. She wore capri pants that showed her red, knobby ankles, and a shirt with a pattern of pineapples. I fixed my eyes on them, pineapple pineapple pineapple pineapple, so as not to look at her. "Nothing," I said.

"Do you two know why you're here?" We didn't answer. "Do you?"

We said we did not. "It's because you have unfit parents." She paused to let that sink in.

I didn't know what that meant, unfit. Like clothes fit you?

"The state wants to keep you from turning into juvenile delinquents. That's why they took you away. You understand?"

We didn't. She exhaled, and the pineapples billowed in and out. "Now, upstairs, and keep quiet."

"My daddy says, people should keep their noses on their own faces."

I thought she would hit me. But she wasn't a hitter. Instead she gripped my wrist and squeezed hard. "And who's your daddy? A jailbird? A drug addict?" She released me. My wrist burned for a long time.

Upstairs, Kerry sat on one bed and I took the other. We heard the television going, some show with lots of laughing and applause. We didn't talk about what Mrs. Wojo had said about our father. It would have made it real. We looked out the window, a dormer at the back of the house. The view was of the yard, and the alley, and the grid of similar small, fenced yards and the houses beyond them. Where was our house? All I knew was you needed a car to get there.

Kerry rubbed at his eyes again. By morning they would be crusted over, and would have to be pried open with a warm washcloth. He said, "You shouldn't make her mad."

"I didn't." She was already mad. "Is she a witch?"

"There aren't witches."

"Are too." I knew them from television. Mostly they were green-skinned, but not always.

"There aren't any just walking around."

"I bet there are."

The argument didn't go anywhere. We didn't have enough energy to keep it up. Pretty soon Kerry fell asleep but I didn't. I poked around the room and found those things that were meant for children's entertainment: A set of alphabet blocks. A picture book, *The Golden Treasury of Bible Stories*. A jigsaw puzzle in a box spilling pieces.

I had to go to the bathroom, so I went down the stairs, as quietly as I could, waiting on each step. I crept past the door to the living room and the back of Mrs. Wojo's head as she watched her show, smoke rising from her cigarette in a question-mark shape.

I didn't turn on a light in the bathroom. The green tile and the green plastic curtains over the small window gave everything a drowned, underwater look. I peed and then spent some time investigating the different bottles and jars set out on the sink and tub and the shelf over the toilet. There were a lot of them, as if it took a great many potions and paint pots for Mrs. Wojo to make her natural self presentable to unsuspecting eyes.

I'd shut and latched the door behind me and suddenly there was a terrific rattling and commotion, Mrs. Wojo on its other side. "Open the door this instant!"

Fright made me clumsy with the latch. When I did manage it, the door flew open and smacked into me. I yelped, and Mrs. Wojo made the room echo with her rage. "WE DO NOT LOCK DOORS IN THIS HOUSE! NEVER! EVER! DO YOU UNDERSTAND? DO YOU?"

She kept yelling until I whimpered that I did. Of course it wasn't true about the doors. The front door was bolted and triple-locked, as were the back door and the back gate, and of course, the door that led to the basement.

Dinner was meat loaf, mashed potatoes, and frozen green beans that squeaked when you tried to get them on a fork. Kerry's plate had more food on it. I didn't complain. There was no point. After we were done eating, and had taken our plates to the kitchen sink, Mrs. Wojo took her own plate into the living room and ate in front of the television. We were allowed to sit on the plaid couch and watch with her, although we had to stay still. It was some old black-and-white movie with songs and dancing, a production of such vast and purposeful boredom that I wondered what I had done wrong now, that I had to sit through it. I wondered what our father and Monica were doing right now, if they were out looking for us.

Then the movie was over and Mrs. Wojo said it was time for our baths.

We didn't argue, though we might have said we didn't need a bath just then, or we didn't take baths, only showers. I don't like to admit how quick she'd beat me down, but she had.

There is no greater powerlessness than being a child. So Mrs. Wojo set out towels for us, and the pajamas we'd brought with us from DCFS, and ran water in the tub. She sat on the toilet and clamped first Kerry, then me, between her knees and picked through our scalps, looking for nits. Her hands were hard and practiced. Satisfied that we didn't have lice, she pushed the plastic curtain with the seashells to one side. "All right now, get undressed and hop in."

I found my voice. "We don't do that."

"Don't do what?"

"Take baths together."

Mrs. Wojo made a show of her exasperation. "The two of you would tax the patience of a saint. What have you got to hide? Do you think I'm going to heat up water for two baths? Does this look like the Grand Hotel? Do you want to wait until that water's cold?"

She was going to watch us too. And maybe it shouldn't have been any big deal, a child's nakedness, but it was, it felt as if we had been stripped not only of our clothes but of some last defense against her as well. I couldn't keep from looking at Kerry, his small, dangling parts and bare bottom, and he couldn't keep from looking at me. We had been made helpless. We allowed Mrs. Wojo to pour some stinging shampoo over our heads and into our eyes and scrub out our ears. The water was something less than hot. By the time we were declared clean, made to stand, and wrapped in stale-smelling green towels, I was so sunk in misery, all I wanted was to hide myself away.

Kerry started crying. His eyes hurt him, but nobody had figured that out yet. Mrs. Wojo grumbled as she got him into his pajamas, saying things along the lines of ungrateful children who didn't have anything to complain about. But when we were dressed, she shooed me upstairs and kept him with her. "Run along," she told me. "Don't worry, he's coming."

I climbed the stairs and waited. After a little while, Kerry came upstairs, accompanied by Mrs. Wojo's shouted instructions from the hallway, telling us to get to sleep, no fooling around.

The light on the stairway was left on, bright enough for a hospital. Kerry put his hand out and showed me two cookies, the packaged kind known as Fudge Ripple. "Here. She thinks I ate them."

I took one and Kerry the other, and we sucked the last bit of sweetness from them.

Oh she hated me. She really did. Because I was female, or because I had a mouth on me, or a face that showed my mistrust, or all of that. The why didn't matter. We were enemies. The next day she started in on me, giving me chores to do that I had no chance of doing right, things like going over the heavy furniture with a rag and a can of wax, or adding water to the cottage cheese cartons that fed her fussy African violets. And every time I did something wrong, I would be punished with an extra chore. "Why doesn't Kerry have to do anything?" I asked, and Mrs. Wojo said it was because he had the pinkeye, though by then I had it too, or later because he complained of a stomach-ache, or some other invention. And because we were treated this unequally, and because we were only children, after a time Kerry began to lord it over me and behave as if I deserved no better.

The DCFS woman came by that next afternoon with the paper sacks full of our clothing. We hate it here, I told her. We want to go home. But the DCFS woman was used to children who said such things, because of course the children hated these places they had been sent to, it was understandable.

Kerry and I were seated at the table in the dining room, where we had not been allowed until now. The wallpaper was a pattern of creeping vines; the tablecloth was starched and spidery lace. The DCFS woman sat with us. Mrs. Wojo was somewhere else, in the kitchen, probably. We were whispering. Mrs. Wojo might be half-blind, but her hearing was supersonic. Kerry said he wanted to see our father.

"We're working on that," the DCFS woman said, in an unnecessarily loud and cheerful voice. "Give us a few days."

We didn't say anything more. We were hemmed in at every turn by adult actions and adult dictates, pronouncements, decisions, decrees. Days and days went by, I don't know how many. Long enough for the pinkeye to clear up. Long enough for the smell of Mrs. Wojo's cigarettes to work its way into our clothes. We didn't know she was paid to feed and house us—I will not say take care of us—until she told us so.

It was that portion of the evening devoted to television watching. Mrs. Wojo was in her recliner while Kerry and I sat on the plaid couch with the plastic cover that betrayed any fidgeting. We'd found a pair of hand puppets, a dog and a cow, and sometimes we made the puppets wrestle and beat at each other in silent, furious combat. The television only got three channels and we'd given up on it producing anything interesting. Mrs. Wojo favored movies, elderly dramas about World War II soldiers and the girls they left behind them, or struggles between good and evil played out among cattle ranchers, or deeply unfunny comedies. She couldn't see much of the screen but she enjoyed following the story line, those dramas of virtue rewarded, of sacrifice and triumph.

In the breaks between shows she got up to fetch more cigarettes or go to the bathroom or make herself a highball. (She drank, but not catastrophically.) Returning from one of these, she paused and regarded us, shaking her head at whatever she saw in us that was so visibly deficient. "They need to pay me a lot more if they want me to keep taking in strays."

She rearranged herself in the recliner. Kerry and I looked at each other. I said, "Who pays you for us? Our dad?"

Mrs. Wojo laughed and raised her glass to her mouth, turning the rim cloudy with her lipstick. The drinks always put her in a more indulgently communicative mood. "Your daddy? I'm sure he doesn't have a pot to piss in. The state pays for you. You're foster children, and I'm your foster mother."

"No you aren't," I said, uselessly, not knowing what "foster" meant, but certain she wasn't any kind of mother to us.

Mrs. Wojo laughed again, and dabbed at her mouth with Kleenex. "Fine. Have it your way."

Kerry said, "Does that mean we have to stay here from now on?"

Her show was starting up, so she waved this away. "You can only stay in foster care until you're eighteen."

It was a lot to think about. No one had explained any of this to us, or if they did, we had not understood, and we didn't understand now, especially the part about being eighteen. Eighteen! We would never be eighteen! Mrs. Wojo would never let us grow up, go to school, leave the house. She'd use spells and charms and the pure evilness of her nature to keep us small, helpless, captive.

But it made sense to know that she was paid money for us. How else to explain it? And they didn't pay her enough, which was why she was always so mad.

Another television night. The show was one of the ones with dancing, a woman in a twirly skirt, violins, romance of a particularly coy, sick-making variety. Then the show ended and Mrs. Wojo snapped the television off. Getting up from the recliner, she hummed the melody and took a few gliding steps across the carpet. Her eyes were closed and her powdery face tilted upward, smiling in secret reverie. Her striped blouse, still damp in patches from the evening's dishwashing, belled out around her.

"Mrs. Wojo?" Kerry piped up then. "Do you have any kids? You know, your own?"

She stopped her swaying and opened her eyes. I waited for her to blow up with rage, but she walked past us and into the dining room.

We heard her opening and shutting drawers in the big glass-fronted buffet that held her collection of ceremonial china. When she came back in, she was holding a boxlike object in gold metal. It had a latch in the center that Mrs. Wojo worked open, splitting it into two framed portraits. She set them down on the table in front of us so we could see.

"That's him," she said. "That's my Frank. Go ahead, you can look at him."

There were two color pictures, one of a fat-faced baby wrapped in a blue blanket, the other a boy a year or two older than Kerry. He was posed in the front yard of Mrs. Wojo's house, a weedy kid in google-eyed glasses. He was wearing shorts and a peculiar shirt, buttoned up tight beneath his chin and with stiff, oversized sleeves that stood away from his thin arms. The photographer had forgotten to tell him to smile. He looked like a kid we wouldn't want to play with.

We looked from one picture to the other. What were we supposed to say about him?

"Where is he?" I asked.

"In heaven."

Mrs. Wojo coughed and sniffled. "My baby. He's an angel now."

I stared at Frank's blurry eyes behind their glasses. I felt a little sick.

"So what happened?" Kerry asked. He must not have been as afraid of her now that he was her favorite.

Mrs. Wojo picked up the portrait frame and snapped it shut. "Polio. Do you know what that is? Well, there used to be this disease. A lot of children came down with it. Every summer there'd be what they call an epidemic, children all over, one day they're fine, the next, they're cripples. You know what cripples are, don't you?

"It started out like the flu, with a fever and a sore throat and whatnot, and then pains, pains all over. And once it got bad it paralyzed them so's their legs would be all twisted up and they couldn't walk. All these little children in leg braces, using crutches. Sometimes it went to the muscles that make you breathe and they wouldn't work right and the children had to be put into what they called an iron lung machine, a big metal tube that did their breathing for them, and they had to stay inside it for the rest of their lives."

I tried not breathing. I saw the iron lung machine in my mind. The metal tube puffed in and out with a whoosh and a clang. There was a whole room of them, and inside each one was a child, and each child was pale and shriveled and growing old.

"My poor Frankie. He caught the virus from going swimming at the public pool. He came home with an earache and he didn't want his supper, and that night he woke up screaming and screaming. His stomach hurt him and then his back and then his legs. He had seizures where he went blank in the head and his poor little body almost lifted off the mattress."

Mrs. Wojo was in the grip of her story now. Her useless eyes were lifted to the ceiling, seeing the long-ago. You would have thought it was all too awful to remember, but she took some kind of energy from it, the testament of suffering. "He went to the hospital, to the ward with the other polio children. They put steamed wool blankets over him and rubbed him down with arnica. The virus went to pneumonia, his lungs filled up with water. For a night and a day he choked on his own insides. Then the life went out of him and he was at peace. He's buried up at Queen of Heaven Cemetery, with a statue of the Archangel Raphael, the Healer."

She reached the end of her story and lowered her gaze to us. "Did anybody bother to get you two your vaccinations? I'll have to ask."

That night in bed I couldn't keep myself from thinking about Frank. I saw him as he was in his picture, a dumb-looking kid forever alone, then later when he was sick, his skin white as paste, sweating under his steamed blankets, drowning from the inside out. He had lived in this very house, and might have slept in this very bed. I felt myself growing heavy, falling into the grooves of the mattress his body had made. Frank was dead but that didn't keep him from being curious about me. He came in from the cemetery, an angel with crutches in place of wings, and tugged at my pillow. "Move over," he said. "Or I'll give you polio."

I pinched my mouth together and squeezed my eyes shut so the polio couldn't get in. He was smothering me with his dead, flopping arms and legs. I was already inside the iron lung. It was rusty and echoing and it had swallowed me up and now I was trapped. I screamed, and it took me a lot of frantic heartbeats to realize the scream had not left my mouth, and my eyes had opened to the stark light of the stairway, and my brother asleep in the bed across from me.

It was witchcraft that gave me such a dream. I knew Mrs. Wojo had done it on purpose, told us a horrible story so it got stuck in my brain.

One thing we never asked her about? Mr. Wojo. It was just as well.

Our father and Monica came to see us! We had just about given up! We didn't know they were coming, but all that day Mrs. Wojo had me helping her clean, and as usual, I couldn't do anything to please her. "Does that look clean to you?" she'd demand, and there was no right answer.

We scrubbed down the front porch steps, we polished the glass of the front door. We vacuumed and dusted. I fetched rags, buckets, polish, cleansers. The bathroom got a new air freshener cone that sent out waves of industrial-strength gardenia. Mrs. Wojo set up some ancient lawn chairs in the back yard, the kind with interwoven straps. Then we were told to change clothes, wash our necks, faces, and ears, go out in the yard, sit in the chairs, and stay there.

The back door closed on us. Small as I was, the woven seat of the chair sagged beneath me. I still wasn't any good at sitting still and I kicked at the chair frame, trying to get something to break. There wasn't ever anything to do in the back yard. From the alley beyond the fence came occasionally interesting sounds of cars passing, garbage trucks, voices, but we never saw any of it. The weather had turned warm enough for flies and Kerry swatted them away. Mrs. Wojo fed him up so much, his face was getting round. He never saved cookies for me anymore. I said, "You look like a femmy girl." He still hadn't gotten his hair cut.

"Shut up. You smell like pee."

"I do not." I didn't think I did. Then the back door opened and our father stood there, with Monica crowding up behind him.

We were so unprepared for the sight of them that we just sat there staring. "Hey there, guys," our father said, jolly, but with an edge of annoyance. I guess we were supposed to rush toward him, overjoyed. "Whatsa matter with you, come here."

We did get up then and allow ourselves to be embraced and patted. Both our father and Monica looked out of breath, keyed up. She had pulled her hair back into a ponytail and was wearing a new pair of pinchy-looking shoes. Our father had shaved with so much care that his face was bright pink. They looked the way a photograph of people you know can look, familiar and strange at the same time.

One of the DCFS women came to the screen door and looked out at us. It was what they call a supervised visit.

They sat down in the extra lawn chairs and wobbled around, trying to get comfortable. Our father cursed mildly, the chair hurting his bad back. "Are we going home?" I asked. I was bouncing up and down, already gone.

"Ah, we have to work a few things out before that happens," my father said, and though I wasn't a big cryer I did cry then, and Kerry did too, out of the kind of emotional hydraulics that can lead to a whole room full of crying children, once one of them starts up. "Oh come on now," our father said, uselessly. "It's not so bad here, is it? You both look great, she must be taking great care of you."

"She's a witch," I said, and that got their attention, startled them, but I followed it up with, "She doesn't like me," and that allowed them to relax, dismiss me.

"Of course she likes you, honey," our father said. "She likes children, that's why she takes care of them."

"She's got her a real nice house," Monica said. "If I could stay in a house like this, I'd count my lucky stars."

Kerry was still crying and our father was getting impatient with him. "Come on, buddy, turn off those waterworks. Let's take a look at you. Put on a little weight, have you?"

"She's fattening him up so she can sell him to the gypsies! She locks us in the basement!"

Our father and Monica put their lips together in a way that was both tolerant and disapproving, and I knew they didn't believe me, and that there was no point in telling them about the dreams I had every night where Frank tried to smother me and give me polio, so that every night I fought hard not to fall asleep and always lost.

But they should have listened to me. They really should have.

Just then the screen door opened and Mrs. Wojo came out, carrying a tray with glasses of lemonade and some packaged cookies set out on paper napkins. "I thought you all might like a refreshment," she said, sweet as pie. She was wearing a dress made of some shiny navy blue fabric and when she lifted up her arms, you could see the white, baked-in rings of old deodorant and old sweat.

I helped myself to three of the cookies. Her eyes cut me an evil look but she didn't dare say anything in front of the others. When she had gone back inside, our father said, "See? She's real nice." But he seemed to disbelieve himself even as he spoke, his shoulders sinking.

I said, "We could leave with you. We could run real fast, they won't catch us."

"Actually, honey, you can't. It's a matter of the law now." The idea of the law seemed to take something out of him, deflate him. He shifted his weight in the miserable chair.

Monica scrubbed the cookie crumbs from her mouth with the back of her hand, and our father asked her what was wrong with using a napkin. They had themselves a little fuss about it, back and forth, and finally Monica waved her hands around and said, "Well, why do we even have to be here? It's because these kids got themselves out of the car! Why did you do that, huh? You know you wasn't supposed to!"

Kerry said, "Jo got out first. It was her fault."

The solid weight of the guilt landed on me. Everything had been my fault and always would be. I said, "I was trying to walk home."

Monica said, "The whole way to North Halsted? That would have been some trick."

"Keep your pants on, Monica. It's not like it matters now. Ah crap." Our father was trying to get himself loose from the lawn chair.

Kerry and I cried some more when they were on their way out the front door. We saw the old maroon Chevy parked at the curb, and the sight of it pierced us, the wrongness of it driving away without us. "It's gonna be fine," our father said, as we clung to his legs, wetting his knees with our tears. "Pretty soon school's gonna start, well, Ker's gonna have school. Think how smart you'll get!"

Then the door shut, and they were gone. Mrs. Wojo locked and bolted it after them. We stopped crying right away. It wouldn't do us any good.

Mrs. Wojo let the silence settle. Then she said, "So that's your father, is it? Well, that explains a few things." Then she went off to undo and dispose of the remnants of her hospitality.

I wanted to call them back and explain things better. Because it was one of Mrs. Wojo's jokes that she was going to sell Kerry to the gypsies when he was fat enough—whatever a gypsy was—and after a while we understood it as a joke, the same way our father said teasing, unpleasant things. But she did lock us in the basement.

The entire time we'd been at Mrs. Wojo's, we hadn't left the house or back yard. Still, Mrs. Wojo had her needs, her grocery shopping, her life carried on outside her four walls. And when a need arose, she herded us into the basement and locked the door to the landing. The first time we were unsuspecting. After that we tried hiding from her, and once I kicked at her shins and missed, and she clamped both hands on my shoulders and put her big powdered face next to mine and breathed death at me. "Do you want to go to the juvenile home? Do you want to live in a cell and take crazy pills? Hah? Get on down there." She slammed the door on us and slid the lock into place.

The basement was where Mrs. Wojo did her laundry. There were two squat machines and a deep tub sink, and a clothesline where she hung different horrible items of clothing. Her underpants had cuffs around the leg holes, her bras were large and heroically reinforced, a triumph of elastic. The furnace was down there too, and an old coal chute, and some half-windows up high in the walls, barred over against burglars. In a part of it, where there were no windows, the concrete floor gave out and there was only bare earth. The basement seemed to be larger than the house itself, with side passages and cupboards and a workbench with buckets of calcified paint, old coffee cans filled with nails, knuckle-shaped metal parts of unknown use, old light switches. We poked around a little but the place scared us. We had been taken away from our father because he'd locked us in a car—this had been explained to us—and now Mrs. Wojo locked us in a basement and nobody wanted to believe me about it.

Then after a while, and I suppose it wasn't ever all that long, we'd hear her footsteps overhead, and the door opened and we were summoned upstairs, to help put away the groceries or some other chore. Once, as she was leaving, Kerry begged to go with her, and you could see her hesitate, wanting to, but sorting it out. "Not today, maybe some other time."

"You suck," I informed him, once we were locked in together. It was one of my father's sayings.

"I'm going to tell you said that."

"Well I'm going to dig up worms and put them in your bed." I was furious with him for his weakness, for abandoning me.

"I'll tell about that too." He had a collaborator's smugness. I hated him. I hated his fat face and his pretty hair and the look and smell of his alien, boy's body, and I imagine he hated me too for his own, interlocking set of reasons. But we had no choice in each other. The twoness of us was fixed for all time.

I didn't plan what happened to Mrs. Wojo, except in the sense that I had imagined a hundred different scenes of escaping her, a kid's imaginings in which I became a cowboy or a soldier or something else powerful and victorious. In the end, it came about because she forgot to secure us in the back yard while she did the laundry.

Because she always did that, kicked us out of the house when she had chores to do in the basement. I expect she didn't trust us to be alone and unsupervised in the house. We might steal food, or break something, or use the telephone to call long distance. We stayed in the yard until she was ready to let us back in, the door latched against us, and that was that.

Except for this particular day. I was thirsty, and impatient, and when I pulled at the handle of the door to rattle it, it opened. Kerry wasn't paying attention. He was sitting at the edge of the gravel, sorting the rocks. I went inside. I wasn't especially quiet about it, but the laundry machines were rolling and sudsing in the basement, and I guess they covered my noise. I went into the kitchen and reached up to the sink to fill a glass and drink. Then I went back to the landing and without any thought at all, I shut the basement door and slipped the bolt in place.

Nothing happened. I went back outside. I watched Kerry play with the rocks. After a while he looked up, squinting at me. "What were you doing?"

"I got a drink."

"Well I want one too."

"Go ahead," I told him. He got up, watching me in a mistrustful way, and we both stood on the back stairs. "See?" I said, presenting him with the fact of the open door.

I went in first and Kerry followed. He took a glass from the dish drainer, ran the tap, and drank. "Where is she?"

I pointed to the basement door. "Down there." He didn't understand at first. I dragged a chair over to the cupboard where Mrs. Wojo kept the cookies, climbed up, and pulled them out. They weren't a good kind, some flavored wafer, dry as toast, but I took a handful and pushed the package at him. He didn't take any. I opened the refrigerator and poked around, but there was nothing I wanted, only a lot of little bowls hooded in plastic.

"What are you doing?" Kerry whispered, stricken. Understand, at that point I was only feeling clever about evading Mrs. Wojo for a little while. I just wanted to break some rules before she reappeared to punish me. It hadn't yet occurred to me that she couldn't get out.

But then she was at the top of the steps, pounding at the door and making it shudder. "UNDO THIS LOCK THIS IN- STANT! I MEAN IT, YOU LITTLE SHITS!"

The swearing shocked us as much as anything. We stood to- gether on the step above the landing while she worked the door- knob, uselessly, from the other side. "OPEN THIS DOOR! OR I WILL SKIN YOU ALIVE! YOU THINK I'M KIDDING?"

"We have to let her out," Kerry said, still whispering. I shook my head, no. I didn't want to be skinned alive. "We have to," he said again. "We can call the fire department, they'll let her out."

"Are you kidding?" I said. New and wonderful ideas were swooping through my head like birds, like my head was a room with wide-open windows.

"DO YOU KNOW HOW MUCH TROUBLE YOU'RE IN?

YOU ARE IN FOR A WORLD OF HURT! I WILL BEAT YOU DOWN! AND THEN YOU ARE GOING TO JAIL!"

Her big black pursey purse was on the kitchen table. I dumped it upside down. I wasn't even thinking of stealing from her. I just wanted to be bad. In the mess of old Kleenex and gum and powder, I saw her key ring. Kerry saw it too. He grabbed for it but I got it first.

"Give it to me!"

"No!"

The basement door was still shaking. I got up my nerve and hopped past it to the back door. "Come on," I said to Kerry, but he just stood there.

"Kerry, honey?" Mrs. Wojo stopped beating on the door. "Are you there? I know you didn't do anything. I know it's not your fault."

The giddiness went out of me and my stomach pitched. Mrs. Wojo went on. "I know you're a good boy. Why don't you open the door and I'll fix you some Kool-Aid, the purple kind you like."

"She's lying," I said, and I swear on my life I saw black specks fly out of the keyhole then, like a swarm of black bees, and the next instant they were gone, and when she spoke again there was more of an edge to it, like she couldn't concentrate on both things at once, hating me and coaxing him.

"If you let me out, we can go to a baseball game. I bet you've never seen one of those, have you? We can sit up front so you can catch the ball when it comes into the stands. You can have a hot dog. Two, if you want them."

"If you let her out," I said, "she'll give you polio, like she did Frank."

She roared, and the door shook in its frame, and Kerry ran after me out to the yard.

I needed his help to unlock the gate, because it was just out of my reach, and it took a long time to find the right key and get it to turn. But we managed it, and then we were on the other side of the fence. The alley, now that we could see it for ourselves, was a place of marvels, rutted tire tracks, plastic bags blown against a fence, a lane of blue sky overhead.

We started running. It didn't matter what direction, since we were completely lost, and when we came to a street we slowed down. Nobody was following us. We walked a long time, and we probably looked pretty draggled when we walked up to a parked taxi, since we knew that taxis took people places, and asked the driver if he'd take us home. "We live on North Halsted," I said. "We were with our dad, at the ball game, and we got lost in the crowd."

Kerry stood gaping at me. It was the first big lie I ever told, but not the last.

The driver considered us, then talked into his radio, and got out to usher us into the back seat. He kept up a kindly, one-sided conversation as he drove. We didn't understand a word of it because of his accent. We kept our faces close to the windows, looking for our building.

And here it was, heaving up out of the vast strangeness of the city, and the maroon Chevy right in front! And our father standing over the Chevy's open trunk!

We set up a holler and the cab pulled over to the curb. We got out and ran to him, shouting. This time he was the one who didn't know what to make of us. "What's this?" he said. "Kids, how did you get here?"

"We took a cab," Kerry said.

"We ran away," I added.

"Wait here," our father said, and he walked over to lean into the cab's window. He spent some time talking to the driver, shifting his weight from one foot to the other, and finally he straightened up and the cab drove away with a friendly tap of its horn. "All right, you monkeys," our father said. "Run along upstairs now."

We scrambled up and burst through the open door, and then we stopped dead. The place was empty, except for the landlord's furniture, and some bulging plastic trash bags. Monica was sweeping the bare floor. She stopped when she saw us. "Wow." She looked at the broom, then once more at us. "Wow."

Our father came in after us. "Well isn't this a nice surprise. We were just on our way to see you."

We didn't say anything. He said, "Now don't get all upset. We knew you were in a real good place, that was the A-number-one most important thing."

"We aren't going back there," I said, and Kerry started to speak, but I crowded into him and he kept silent.

Our father said, "Then I guess you're coming along for the ride. Are you up for it? It's gonna be a little crowded, what with the car all loaded up. I don't want to hear a peep out of you, understood?"

We forgave them. What choice did we have? We got in the car and we drove a long ways to a different city, where we lived with different names. Everything up until then was left behind us. And in this new place, in ways that were both slow and sudden, we grew up.

I don't see Kerry very often these days, and we don't talk much, and never about Mrs. Wojo. I had my own bad dreams and I imagine he had his. Did she manage to break a window, call for help, get herself out? Was she even now out looking for us, picking up our trail? I worried about that for years and years. Or did she stay in that basement until somebody noticed her African violets all dead from neglect, her mail piling up, the bills unpaid? Sooner or later somebody would tap at the front windows, make calls, force the door. Sooner or later they'd find their way down to the basement and there she'd be, turned to leather and stench. Alive or dead, she was a vicious ghost.

Was it my fault for locking that door? For being bad and disobedient? For getting out of the car when we had been told to stay in? But why were we left in that car to begin with? Why was our father the way he was, or why was Monica? You might as well ask, why did Frank get polio and die? The world is made up of questions. Each of us has to live with our own answers.

INAMORATA

It was the best hangover Royboy ever had. It was possible he was still drunk. He was lightheaded and lazy-limbed, with a grin he couldn't get rid of and an unfounded sense of wonderfulness. Where had it come from, and what, if anything, had he done to deserve it? He couldn't say.

Most of the last twelve hours was a little iffy. A great deal of it, he just couldn't say. There had been an excursion to a bar—perhaps two or three bars—with his roommates, an impromptu celebration of Royboy's inheritance. That is, his access to the funds set aside for him by the successful, aggressively prose-cuted lawsuit in regards to a long-ago accident.

This accident had inflicted, on the ten-year-old Royboy, a grievous, expensive injury to his young brain. All that had since been patched up and made mostly right. Some residual stuff, sure, like these iffy moments. But each of his lost brain cells was like a tiny investment portfolio, paying off in a big, happy way.

He had turned twenty-two and that portion of the monies awarded for pain and suffering was now his.

"Pain and suffering!" Royboy and his friends drank to that, and drank again. The bartenders had been cheerful and obliging, and other customers looked on them fondly. There had been some girls. One of Royboy's friends saw a girl he knew, and that girl was there with her friends as well. The whole group had migrated from bar to bar and then back to the house of Royboy and associates. There had been music, and the kind of dancing that goes along with a lot of drinking, and at one point people had decided they were hungry, and started frying up eggs and bacon and potatoes. Everyone had been having such a good time. There had been some fun with a ketchup bottle.

Right about then, things had gone iffy.

Now it was morning, or at least, the sun was in the sky. Royboy sat in a recliner in the living room, in front of the big television screen. He appeared to be watching the television with great concentration, although the set was turned off. One of his roommates came in. He had just finished his shower, and he carried with him the perfumey smells of steam and shampoo and grooming products. His hair was slicked back in wet curls and he wore a T-shirt and athletic shorts. He watched Royboy watching the empty screen for a time. "Good show?" he offered.

"Hunh? No, it's that thing." Royboy flapped his hand in the direction of the television. "You know, the whasis."

"Shoe," said the roommate, whose name was Mikey. "Well it sure is a nice one. How did it get on top of the TV?"

"I put it there," Royboy said, but what he meant was, he put it there after he found it next to his bed.

"Why the shit-eating grin?"

"Because I'm happy."

"About what?"

"I don't know," Royboy confessed. Mikey nodded. They were all used to the spaces between things in Royboy's head.

"So this shoe . . ." Mikey began again.

"Yeah, I guess some girl was wearing it. I mean she was probably wearing another one just like it. You remember which girl?"

"I wasn't especially noticing footwear," Mikey said. "What's the big deal?"

Before Royboy had a chance to explain, another of his roommates came in, eating milk and cereal from a bowl in his hand. His name was Dave D. There had been another Dave, Dave M., and Dave M. had moved out, but Dave D. was still Dave D. "You guys look like roadkill," Dave D. said.

"Thanks. Hey, you recognize this shoe? The Boy wants to know."

"It would be kind of a fashion risk for you, Royboy."

"Screw you guys. I found it in my room this morning."

His roommates made an ooooh sound. Dave D. said, "You sure there wasn't a foot inside it? You know, the coyote date where you chew your foot off so you can get away clean?"

"Screw you upside down and sideways."

"Seriously, she was that good?"

"I don't exactly remember," Royboy admitted.

"Dude. You got it in your sleep?"

Royboy shrugged. Let them think that. Maybe he had, in fact, been asleep, or maybe he was awake and just didn't remember it, maybe it had been the greatest sex in his life, over and done with except for its blissful echo. Or maybe there had been nothing of the sort. Just this mysterious joy.

Dave D. picked up the shoe and examined it. "Pretty," he said. "What do you call this, Lucite?"

"Lucy Lucite. At least now we've got a name to go on."

"You guys. Give me that." Royboy hauled himself up from the recliner, a little wobbly in the knees, and snatched the shoe from Dave D. He liked the feel of the shoe in his hands, all smooth and cool. It was a dressy shoe with a high heel. It was made entirely of clear plastic except for the ankle strap, a line of silver beads. Just holding it reactivated the whole fizzy, grin-producing process.

The shoe was on the small side, though not tiny or elfin or anything like that. This was a relief. He didn't much care for little bitty women; they made him think of kittens and bunnies and other nonsexual things. Royboy tried to picture the foot that went inside the shoe, balancing on its icicle spike, and from there, the rest of the woman. He called up any existing girl-memories belonging to the night before, but these were only an agreeable, bright-colored femaleness, a kaleidoscope of bare legs and charm bracelets and pretty shoulders. He said, "So who was it knew them? The girls? How did they get here anyway?"

They thought it was probably due to another roommate, Lance, whose nickname was Lance the Pants. Lance was not available to answer questions. He had gone home with one of the girls, because that was just how he rolled. Mikey and Dave D. tried to remember if they had seen Royboy accompanying anyone in particular. They didn't think so.

"You were dancing by yourself with headphones on. I mean mostly by yourself. Every so often you sort of intersected with other people who were dancing, but it didn't seem like there was anything personal going on."

"So things must have got personal later. Did you tell her you're rich?"

"I'm not rich rich," Royboy said. "It's more like an income stream." Although the amount of money was large and whoopee-inducing. He should probably invest it or something. But investing was an anxious notion. It meant your money went somewhere else and had adventures on its own. And maybe that turned out fine but not always. The money was meant to last him the rest of his life, in case he was unable to achieve his full financial potential. That had been the language of the lawsuit. But that meant he ought to divide the number of years he expected to be alive into the total sum, and that too was an anxious thing.

Anyway, if he'd told the mystery girl about his money, she hadn't stayed around to try to get her hands on it. She was no gold digger. He liked her even better.

"So we'll ask around," Mikey said. "Do a little research. We can have another party and invite the same girls and see which one of them rings your bell. Okay?"

"I guess so." But what if the girl had run off half-barefoot because she was disgusted with him, and with herself for having anything to do with him? Well, if that was the case, he'd still want to talk with her and find out why. "Sure, let's have another party."

"We can fix the place up a little," Dave D. said. "Have a bunch of fancy drinks ready, fruit drinks, and cupcakes, and olives on toothpicks, shit like that. Call it a Ladies' Night." Dave D. had gone to school in marketing and thought in promotional terms.

"We'll take you shopping, Royboy. We'll dress you up fine."

"I don't think I want to get dressed up."

"No bow ties this time. Promise."

"I'm going back to bed for a while," Royboy said. His friends meant well, but they were making him nervous with all the things they had set in motion on his behalf.

He took the shoe back to his room and made a space for it among the piles of clothes that had never quite made it either into the dresser drawers or the laundry basket. He got into bed and rolled around in the sheets, sniffing at the pillows. No perceptible trace of girl. But he still felt a little of the shining, benevolent energy that had filled his head earlier.

It had either been a long time since he'd had a girlfriend, or else he had never had a girlfriend. It all depended on how you defined "girlfriend." Girls sometimes gravitated his way, but they tended to take themselves off pretty fast. (Although never before had one escaped before he could even form a memory of her. That was a first.) He wasn't very good at conversation. They got tired of waiting for him to say something interesting. Lance the Pants tried to give him pointers. "Just ask them a question they can run with, like, does she have any pets, or any brothers or sisters."

"Got it." Royboy nodded. "Piece a cake." The next time he and his buds were out for an evening, he spotted a likely girl at the end of the bar and ambled over to her. He said Hi. She said Hi. They smiled. Royboy asked her if she was having a good time tonight and she said pretty good so far. She seemed receptive. Her name was Sherry. She kept on smiling.

"So," Royboy said, summoning up his nerve, "do your brothers and sisters have any pets?"

Would anything ever change? Was he doomed to klutzy lonesomeness? He still had hopes that somewhere out in the wide world was an attractive female person who would see past his awkward surface and lack of vocabulary, down to the essential Royboy: a not-bad guy who wasn't inclined to cause problems, and who now had a little bit of money to spread around. She was out there somewhere, maybe even hobbling around on one shoe.

His roommates were as good as their word. They let it be known that there would be an actual, planned party, with food and drink and merriment. Royboy accompanied them to the liquor store and paid for the rum and mixers, the wine and beer, the bags of ice. At the grocery they bought a quantity of delicatessen items and bakery items, also supplies of hand soap and toilet paper. There was a debate about flowers versus no flowers and no flowers won, because they had never had such a thing as flowers in the house before and so didn't have vases. Vases were a bridge too far.

Mikey was put in charge of Royboy's hygiene and wardrobe. "Dress for success, dress to impress, dress not to be a mess," he intoned. "Let me see your fingernails. Not good. Do you have a nail clipper? Never mind, I'll get you one."

"Why can't I wear my normal clothes?" Royboy asked. He was wrapped in a bath towel and he felt unnaturally clean, like if somebody ran a finger down his arm, it would squeak.

"Because your normal clothes make you look like a farmer." Mikey rummaged through Royboy's top dresser drawer. "I need to introduce you to the concept of date underwear."

"I don't think I want to go to the party, Mikey."

Mikey sat down on the opposite side of the bed from Royboy. "You're nervous, right? That's okay. That's just adrenaline. Adrenaline is like a power surge. It helps you stand your ground in a fight or jump out of an airplane."

"I don't want to do either of those."

"Or ask a girl to dance. You want to be able to do that, right? The girl of your dreams?"

"If she's the girl of my dreams, she asks me."

"I'm gonna fix you a drink, kind of a pre-party thing. Chill you out. Then we'll go through everybody's closet and come up with your new, *GQ* look." Mikey reached over the stacks of laundry to the high-heeled shoe and gave it to Royboy. "She's waiting for you, buddy. But you have to step up to the plate."

The party blossomed. Girls, whole flocks of them, arrived and were provided with high-caliber alcohol in the form of rum and coconut, rum and pineapple, rum and orange juice, rum and rum. Dave D. was the bartender and he kept the drinks coming. Lance the Pants did his DJ routine. Mikey was the official host and greeter, steering the guests toward the bar and other hospitality venues. Royboy was installed on a sofa in the corner of the front room, and as each girl arrived, he sent a verdict to Mikey by way of head shakes or shrugs: *Nope. Nope. Maybe, no wait, I don't think so.*

He was dressed up in his borrowed party clothes, a V-neck sweater with a T-shirt underneath, and jeans so tight that he kept shifting around, as discreetly as he could, to rearrange himself. The party picked up steam. It ebbed and crested around him. Some of their guy friends had come too, and Royboy watched them maneuver—effortlessly, it seemed—among the fluttering girls. He didn't think the girl with the shoe was here, though he couldn't have said why. He just didn't feel it.

Finally a girl came up to him, sent by Mikey, he suspected, and leaned over him to be heard above the music. Her breasts were so well framed and presented, they reminded him of the items on display in the bakery case. "Want to dance?"

"Sure." He let her pull him off the couch and take him by the hand to where the dancing was going on. On those occasions when he danced with somebody rather than by himself, his strategy was to imitate whatever his partner was doing. This girl was moving up and down with a grinding shimmy, which just didn't work for him. He settled for doing what his roommates called his "monster dance," bending forward with his arms extended while he trod out the beat. The girl kept sending her encouraging smiles his way. Her cleavage smiled at him too. It was confusing. The sweater made his arms itch. In an effort to focus, he watched the girl's feet, though he didn't recognize anything familiar about them.

Then his brain must have taken one of its little vacations, because now he was dancing with a different girl, and he'd taken the itchy sweater off. Or maybe somebody else had. The party was banging. Everybody had loosened up. They were singing along with the music, or in some cases they were singing other things. This new girl was wearing more coverage on top than the last one, and on a point scale she wasn't as pretty, but she was dancing up close to him in a way that Royboy thought was friendly. She swayed against him. "How about we get some fresh air?"

"Sure," Royboy said. Always obliging. He followed the girl through the kitchen and out to the back porch. His roommates gave him encouraging nods. You the man, Royboy! At the far end of the room he thought he saw a different girl wearing the sweater he'd had on earlier. He had to wonder about that, but there was no time, because now here he was in this whole new situation.

The back porch was where they piled up beer cans for recycling. There was also a dried-out sponge mop, the sponge worn down to a husk, and the parts for a hot tub that Dave D. had acquired in a burst of entrepreneurial activity but had never managed to assemble. It was not a romantic place, but the girl declared herself enraptured by the stubby moon, which was rising, or perhaps setting, above the roof of the detached garage. She perched herself on the porch railing and let her bare legs swing. She was wearing one of those shorty skirts, which Roy-boy appreciated, though her shoes were on the disappointing, casual side. She said, "Tell me more about your accident."

Oh shit. Had he been going on about that? Sweat percolated up from a deep, anxious well. The girl took notice. "Hey, never mind, I can understand if it's a bad memory."

"No, see, I don't remember it. People had to tell me about it."

The girl nodded. She was one of those encouraging nodders. "Uh-huh." He was meant to keep talking.

"I was riding my bike and a car hit me." He didn't want to get into the rest of it because it was stupid and it made him sound stupid, like he couldn't get himself run over in some normal fashion. "How much did I tell you already?"

"You said the guy who hit you lost control of the car for some embarrassing reason but you wouldn't tell me what it was."

"Yeah, it's a little . . ."

"Yeah?" she echoed. More of the nodding. It was like her neck was coming loose.

"He was putting on deodorant."

Once she got it, the girl started laughing. Everybody did. "Sorry," she managed. She was trying to stop laughing by inhaling, but it only made her snort. "I mean, you couldn't exactly drive, I mean, how awful."

"Uh-huh." He didn't feel like telling her the rest of it, which was hospital hospital hospital, and having to wear a helmet to cover the soft places in his head, and how he'd been put back together like a meat robot. He'd had to learn fourth grade all over again. That wasn't so bad, because he liked fourth grade, where they'd played dodgeball and made a battery out of lemon juice, pennies, and zinc washers.

The girl got it together and stopped making nose noises. "Sorry. Sorry. Wow. But I guess you're okay now, right?"

"Pretty much." He disliked this part, because if he told people he was not entirely okay, it was like he was disappointing them. "I take medicine for these, ah, seizure events I have. Most of the time I don't even know they're happening. But it's a lot better than it used to be." He shrugged.

The girl looked at him, recalibrating. Royboy knew that look. It would be followed by either disengagement or a fresh wave of goopy sympathy. Instead, she hopped down from the porch rail, steadied herself by gripping his T-shirt in both hands, and started kissing him. Which was all right. He kissed back. He was trying to remember if he already knew her name, and if he didn't, if it would be necessary to know it.

The girl said, "Maybe we could, ah . . ."

"Oh yeah, sure," Royboy said, detaching himself, dragging his attention away from all the interesting, bodily things going on. They grinned at each other in the low-wattage moonlight, then made their way through the back door. The party opened around them like a mouth. Who were all these people? He hoped that nobody had made themselves at home in his bedroom for the purpose of having sex, as sometimes happened at parties. Behind him, the girl lifted his T-shirt and licked his spine, which he guessed meant she liked him.

Getting through the crowd was like surfing. You had to pick

a wave and ride it as far as you could, then wait for the next one. Royboy kept looking behind him at the girl. He smiled. She smiled. There didn't seem to be a lot to say, even if the noise had allowed for conversation. Facing front, he said, "Excuse me. Excuse me." Diving between arms, butting against butts. Somebody had turned the lights down and there were some special effects going on, whirling blues and pinks and silvers. His vision broke up into shards of colors.

Then he got smacked in the face. Smack! Royboy stopped moving and let the pain spread through him. "Hey," he said. And, "Ow!"

For a moment he thought it was one of the flailing dancers, then a girl with piled-up black hair stood in front of him, her arm cocked as if to take another shot at him. "Hey," he said again, wanting it to mean all kinds of things, like, What? and, Wait a minute!

The girl in front of him lowered her arm but gave him one of those laser beams of hatred looks, and vanished into the crowd. The girl behind him bumped into him. "Who was that?"

"I don't know," Royboy said. He did and he didn't know, and he didn't know how he did, except that sometimes his brain hotwired itself and presented him with a certainty: It was the shoe girl.

Meanwhile, here was this other girl. She was giving him a look that seemed to offer a choice between forward and reverse. "Ah," he said. "Mistaken identity."

It was a bad moment. Why couldn't he pick and choose when to go iffy? Why did he have to stand here all slack-jawed and paralyzed by idiocy? Shouldn't he find a microphone or something, "ATTENTION! WILL THE GIRL WHO JUST

SLAPPED ME PLEASE RETURN TO THE BAR!" She was nowhere to be seen. All the faces in the crowd looked pretty much
the same in the hectic colored lights, like the unnatural land-
scapes seen in photographic negatives.

"What's the deal?" The girl—the remaining girl, that is—
looked him up and down. "I don't want to get in the middle of
anything. Was that your girlfriend?"

"I don't know," Royboy said. Stupid but honest. "I mean, I
don't remember."

"So let me get this straight, there's times you forget things
right when they're happening?"

"That would be one way to put it, yes."

The girl looked around her as if seeking a witness to such
absurdity, then shook her head and walked away.

Royboy watched her disappear into the crowd of silvery
pink-blue dancers, then he made his way upstairs to his own
room. It was empty, and the bedside table drawer that Mikey
had stocked with condoms was undisturbed. It seemed that nobody, himself included, had been having naked fun here. He lay
down on the bed with the high-heeled shoe and balanced it
on his chest. It was weird, but the slap on the face had recharged
his happiness battery. He could feel little pulses of joy crawl-
ing beneath his skin. Who was this girl? He wanted to find her
and let her knock him around some more.

The next day, after everyone was up, and those ladies who
had been overnight guests were escorted home, Royboy told
the others what had happened, or at least, the parts he remembered, like getting clocked by the shoe girl. "It's like she has
superpowers."

"Or she's a magical being, like in Harry Potter."

"Pheromones. She's your perfect biological match. Something about your disability thing that keys in exactly to her chemical signature."

"Free what? Now you're making fun."

Dave D. said, "Sorry, man. But how hot was this girl, that you're all desperate in love? You need to take a deep breath, slow-walk it. Keep your cool, keep a little something in the tank."

"But maybe it's different for him," Mikey said. "Maybe the Boy imprinted on her. Like when birds hatch and think the first thing they see is their mother."

"She's not my mother! That's . . . I really really wish you had not said that."

"A poor choice of example. But I'm trying to come up with a theory, see, about how your specialness sets you up for a love-at-first-sight situation. Because it's not such a normal thing."

They considered this, the sun gilding the wreckage of the party and giving their hangovers a more kindly aspect. Lance the Pants said, "You know, love is kind of like brain damage. You're not in your right mind when you've got a bad case of girl fever. Think about it."

They thought about it. Mikey said, "Yeah, that's what I was getting at. You're all prepped for true love, Royboy, you're halfway there already. In a sense, you're gifted."

"No kidding?" Royboy was doubtful. He didn't think he'd been gifted even before he got run over.

"Sure," Dave D. said. "Like those, what do you call them, savants, who can calculate giant math problems. Like Dustin Hoffman in *Rain Man*. Congratulations, RB. Love has made you its bitch."

"Guys! I don't even know who this girl is, and even if I find her, she hates me!"

Lance the Pants said, "Yeah, but it's not like she doesn't care. If she didn't care, she wouldn't bother smacking you upside the head."

Royboy felt hopeful. Lance knew about these things. But they couldn't just keep having parties and hope the shoe girl would show up in a better mood.

A plan was devised. Tomorrow, Royboy and Lance the Pants, smoothest of the smooth, would embark on a mission. They would buy flowers, a shitload of flowers. ("Roses," Lance specified. "No substitutes. This is not a time for carnations.") They would seek out the female partygoers and present them with bouquets, sort of an after-party favor. The girls would be charmed. There would be opportunities for discreet perusal. Lance would do the heavy lifting, keeping the conversation going. All Royboy had to do was wait for his inner love alarm to go off.

He had such good friends! He was so grateful. But he wasn't as optimistic as they were. First they had to find the shoe girl, which would be tricky enough. Then he had to convince her not to hate him.

"That's called courtship," Lance the Pants told him. They had borrowed Dave D.'s van to transport the roses. "Courtship as in, paying court. Paying compliments. All those things you like about her. A compliment is gentlemanly, as in, 'I love your perfume.' Not, 'Nice ass.'"

"Maybe you should write this stuff down for me."

Lance was quiet, thinking, or maybe just driving. Lance looked like the good guy in a comic book. He had black shiny hair and a handsome, comic book face. Girls were always calling him up, inviting him to parties, barbecues, home-cooked meals. He danced so skillfully from one partner to the next, he let them down with such soft landings, that none of them seemed to have any hard feelings. He was a virtuoso. At the florist's, he convinced the girl who took their order to loan them five gallon buckets and fill them with water to keep the bouquets fresh. He selected a perfect red rose, presented it to her, and promised he'd bring the buckets back tomorrow—say, around five o'clock?

Now he said, "I don't think you should use any canned lines, RB. You need to go with your strengths."

"Okay," Royboy agreed. Then, "What are those?"

"Sincerity. Authenticity. Singleness of purpose. You know, I kind of envy you."

"Come on."

"Everybody wants to find true love. Me too. Sure. You think I don't get tired of chasing tail? It's like the guy said, an expense of spirit in a waste of shame." Lance had often found a working knowledge of the great poets useful. "But hey, this isn't a game for you, it's a quest for something life-changing. Transformative. The search for a soul mate. The yin to your yang. Here's our first stop. Let's get to work."

The door opened wide at the sight of Lance bearing roses. The girls exclaimed over him, and Royboy shuffled in behind. There were four or five and then six girls—they wouldn't keep still and it threw his count off—and they all had shiny hair and delicate wrists and ankles, they all smelled of meadow breezes. Royboy found them all very agreeable. He didn't think any of them was the shoe girl, but maybe that would be revealed more gradually. He took a seat in a corner and watched Lance the Pants do his thing.

"Lance, that was just the best party."

"That's because you were there, darlin'."

"Listen to you."

"I'm here to scatter rose petals at your feet."

"Hahaha."

"I love roses. I'm going to put mine in water."

"Sleep with one of them under your pillow, darlin', and dream of me."

"Oh Lance. Hahaha."

One of the girls detached herself from the group and sat down next to Royboy. "Hi, I'm Shawna."

"Oh, hi. Roy."

She was wearing pink pajamas, the satiny kind, with nothing underneath. She seemed to have forgotten this. Royboy tried not looking. He clamped his thighs together. Shawna said, "You're Lance's roommate, right? I thought I saw you before. So what do you do?"

"I help Mikey, uh, Mike, sometimes, at the Beverage Depot." He couldn't think of anything else to say about that. It didn't sound like enough. "Mike, he lives with us. Me and Lance. And Dave D."

Shawna's blue eyes opened a little wider to indicate that she found this interesting. Beneath the pink satin, her breasts shifted in slow motion. "So how long have you known Lance?"

Royboy began to explain. Mikey was his oldest friend, from way back in the fourth grade. He did not tell her the whole fourth-grade story because well because. He knew Dave D. from seventh grade and Lance from ninth. They had all stuck together somehow. Best buds.

"So . . ." All her questions began with a so. "Does Lance have a girlfriend? I mean a real girlfriend."

Could you have a fake girlfriend? Never mind. He allowed himself a glance at Shawna's nest-like crotch, visible beneath the layer of filmy fabric. He saw where this line of questioning was going. You didn't need an entire functioning brain for that. He said, "Lance is still out there looking for true love."

"Really?" The pinkness that was Shawna rolled and rippled beneath the pinkness of her pajamas. She sat with him awhile longer before she wandered away.

They visited a half dozen more girl-houses. It was pretty much the same story. The girls got the roses and Lance got the girls. It was a little depressing, even though Lance tried to cheer him up. "It's only the low-hanging fruit of flirtation. Shooting the breezy breeze. Chitchat love."

"Uh-huh." Lance was just being nice. There had been no sign of the shoe girl, but Royboy also seemed to have dodged the other girl who was mad at him. So he guessed he was breaking even, though it didn't feel like it.

"How we doing on roses?" Lance asked, and Royboy checked out the back of the van.

"Low," he reported. "Down to about an eighth of a tank."

"All right, let's say, one more stop. This hasn't been a total waste of time, now, has it? We're getting you out and about. Increasing your social visibility. Providing practice in the conversational arts."

"I don't have any conversational arts."

Lance didn't bother arguing with him. "So you're the nonverbal type. Strong and silent and solvent. That's not nothing. Grab that bucket, would you? We might as well do one big rose dump."

They parked the van in front of what looked like the girl equivalent of their own rented house. A little shabby and saggy, like their own, but with better curtains and no old newspapers on the porch. Lance rang the bell and ran through a list of names under his breath: "Alexa, Alissa, Amber, Andrea . . ." The door opened and a girl with a round face looked out. "Angela! How's the party girl?"

Lance stepped through the open door and held the roses out. Angela didn't take them. She sniffed, a long, soggy sound. "Are those because of Mr. Whipple?"

"Beg pardon?"

"Mr. Whipple died. Our cat." She regarded the roses bleakly. "He wasn't even sick or anything." She sniffed again, her nose turning pink.

"Aw honey, I'm so sorry. I didn't know."

"We took him to the emergency vet and they gave him some fluids and shots and all, but his kidneys shut down. We had him since he was a little, little kitten."

"That is so sad. Poor kitty." Lance, recalibrating, all sympathy. Royboy tried to look sad as well.

"We still have all his toys. His catnip mouse. His furry bunny."

Lance offered the roses again. "Why don't you take these to cheer you up. Is anybody else home?"

"Yeah." She called up the stairs. "Lance and some guy are here." She blinked moistly at the roses. "These are pretty. We could make a little wreath or something for him."

"You could," Lance said, giving Royboy a look that meant they wouldn't be staying long.

Two more girls came down the staircase, both of them looking subdued, bleakly mourning. Royboy gave Lance a discreet shake of the head. Nope. Nope. "Hey Lance," one of them said. "The cat died. It sucks."

"I know. But I bet there's some other little kitty out there right now who's waiting for you to bring him home and love him. Or her."

"That's a nice thought, I guess." Both the girls plopped down on the couch next to each other and stared at them. "Did you want a beer or something?"

"I think we're out of beer," the second girl said.

"We don't really need anything," Lance said. "I can see you aren't up for company right now."

Angela came back in then, with the roses crowded into a too-small jar. "This was all I could find."

One of the girls on the couch said, "Did you bring these? What's the occasion?"

Lance said, "Oh, it's just something Roy and I thought—"

The girls interrupted, galvanized. "Roy? He's Roy?"

"*The* Roy?"

All three of them were looking at him in a not-friendly way, like he was the one who killed their cat. Royboy shook his head at Lance: No clue. "I don't think I'm *The* Roy," he said.

"Buddy, you better hope you're not."

Lance said, "Maybe we could back this up a little. What's my bud here been up to? He's sort of cloudy on the details." Royboy nodded, trying to look humble and at the same time injured at being unjustly accused of whatever it was he did.

The girls weren't having any of it. "He has some nerve, showing up here. What's he trying to do to her, pretend it was all some big joke? It's not like she gets out much."

"Through no fault of her own," another girl said, loyally. "Men just don't make the effort with her."

"Her who? What? Guys! I mean, you're not actually guys, sorry." Royboy tried laughing this off. Ha ha. "Who?" he asked again.

"Laura. Don't tell me you don't even remember her name. Laura, your fiancée? Of course the getting married part was a little over-the-top."

"I am going to marry her. I just don't remember that much about her."

"So not funny," remarked one girl, shaking her head.

"Did she hit me the other night? I mean, I'm sure I deserved it."

"That happen to you a lot? Getting punched out? Yes, she hit you."

Royboy was relieved. He was at least in the right house. "I remember her hitting me. The other stuff, not so much."

"The old 'I was way drunk' excuse," sneered another girl. "Not very original."

"I don't remember if I was way drunk."

Lance said, "See, Roy has some brain issues."

"Now that is original."

"Seriously. It's like amnesia, but in small doses."

"Uh-huh."

"The result of getting smashed up by a car when he was a kid."

The girls looked at one another, wondering if they were getting scammed, or were required instead to feel bad on his behalf. One of them said, "Should he be out walking around loose? Allowed to reproduce?"

Royboy said, "That's a little harsh."

Lance tried again. "See, he's looking for the girl of his dreams. He found her but he lost her because he had one of his memory lapses."

"Well she sure remembers him."

Who? Who? Royboy was about to say, when the front door opened and all three girls began making furious motions with their hands, pinching and cutting at the air. What the? A girl with her dark hair in pigtails stood in the entry. It was her! The shoe girl! Waves of rainbow-colored love pulsed from Royboy's inner core.

The shoe girl scowled at Roy. "Hey," he said. "Nice to see you again." He thought she looked pretty, even if her expression was not so friendly. She looked like a little brown bird would look if you turned it into a girl.

"She can't hear you," Angela said, scooping and swooping with her arms and hands. The shoe girl did the same, looking agitated. "She says, 'Did he have sex with the,' I think she called her, the witch. Or maybe it was the other thing."

"No! But did we, I mean, her and me . . ."

"This is such an unusual situation," Lance remarked.

Angela said, "She wants her shoe back. You were sleeping on top of it and she couldn't wake you up."

"Oh, sure." Royboy nodded. "Not a problem. But why did she run off?"

Angela relayed this. The shoe girl spoke. She had a deaf voice, a little rusty. "I was afraid." Then she reverted back to sign language, which Angela translated as, "Embarrassed."

"Overwhelmed, maybe," Lance suggested, "by Roy's powerful love vibe, and his proposal of marriage, which was heartfelt but perhaps premature."

Once this was translated, the girl nodded. Roy said, "Ask her if she wants to get married."

"Baby steps, Roy. Baby steps."

Laura! The name rang like a doorbell, and from somewhere in a back hallway, Royboy's memory roused itself to answer. "We talked about stuff! I know we did, how did we do that? Hey, Laura!" He stooped to peer into her face. She looked wary. Confused. Well, so was he.

Royboy straightened again. Stepped up to the plate. "Lance, help me out here."

"What Roy means is, she made him breathe a new air. He's a changed man. He's smitten. Something like that?"

"Yeah," Royboy said. "Go on." Angela was translating as fast as she could, whipping the fingers of both hands into lines, circles, shapes.

"How can we understand these things? Two separate souls, circulating around each other like electrons around the nucleus of an atom."

"Not electrons," Royboy objected.

"Two incomplete halves made whole. Finding each other against all odds. Is it destiny? Enchantment? Scientists fail to find explanations. Poets keep trying. Our boy here, he might suffer from a small, hardly noticeable intellectual deficiency. But his heart is an off-the-charts genius. Did we mention he has a little money?"

Royboy turned to Angela. "Teach me some of the whaddya-callit. Signs. How do you say 'Hello'?"

"It's like a salute," Angela said. "Hand up to the forehead. That's it."

Royboy saluted. He watched Laura's hand waver, then slowly, slowly come up to return his greeting. Hello. Hello. Destiny? Enchantment? Magic? Mistake? Shall we dance?

CANDY

Her mother liked to stand at the bottom of the stairs and shout up at her. Her mother had knee problems from being totally gross and fat and she didn't climb stairs unless she had to. "Jan-ice! Jan-*ice!*"

Janice let her mother go on for a while, then she opened the bedroom door and looked out. "What?"

"Don't what me. Turn that noise off, nobody wants to hear it. I need you to take Nana's supper to her. You are not wearing that. I don't care. You turn right around and put on a real shirt."

Janice took her time. When she got downstairs, her mother gave her one of her looks. "What?" Janice said again.

"What do you do up there all day anyway?"

"Nothing."

"Well, you can do nothing downstairs."

Janice didn't bother answering. Her mother didn't really want her hanging around downstairs where they'd have to put up with each other. She was just being her usual hag self. Janice went into the kitchen and sniffed at the plastic container on the counter. Dark beads of moisture bubbled up under the plastic lid. "What's this?"

"Chicken and noodles."

"It looks like dead worms."

"Nice. It's your supper too."

"I don't want any, I'm on a diet."

"You don't need to be on any diet, you need to not eat chips and soda and all that greasy crap. Go ahead, don't believe me, someday you'll wake up with three or four extra inches on your hips and wonder how they got there. Now heat this up on the top of the stove with a little water, put it in a bowl for her, and make sure she's eating. Then come straight home."

Only her mother would make chicken and noodles when it was a hundred degrees outside. Her mother was the last one to be talking about what to eat. Her butt was as big as a garbage truck.

Her mother tied a plastic bag tight around the plastic container, then put it in another plastic bag. You could have shot the thing out of a cannon and still been able to eat it. She flapped her mouth some more as Janice was leaving, about how Janice wasn't as smart as she thought she was and it was all going to catch up with her someday and Janice said, "Yeah, sure." Her mother made it sound like she'd be glad if something really horrible happened, just so she could say she was right.

Janice opened the kitchen door and went down the back outside stairs. Their tenant in the basement apartment, Mr. Grotius, had his air conditioner blasting. He was probably sitting right in front of it in his old-man underwear. It was the hottest part of the day. Nana always ate her dinner way too early. The sky was flat and gray with heat, like another sidewalk reflected overhead. It was only June and already Janice was bored with summer.

Once she'd reached the alley and turned the corner, Janice took off her cotton shirt and tied it around her waist. Her mother wouldn't let her wear tank tops outside the house, which was so ignorant. Janice texted Marilee to meet her at the A&W and Marilee texted back OK. It wasn't like there was some big hurry to get to Nana's. Nana didn't think about eating until you put the food right in front of her.

Janice got to the A&W first and stood in line to get a root beer float. She sat down with it at a table in the front so she could see Marilee coming. The cool inside air made her bare arms prickle. The vinyl seat was cold too and she hiked up the legs of her shorts so the skin of her thighs was right up against the cold surface. She shifted her weight from one side to another, experimentally.

"What are you doing?"

Marilee had come in without her noticing. "Nothing," Janice said, getting busy with her root beer float.

"Well it looked extra queer. I don't know what I want. Split some fries?"

Janice said maybe she'd have a few, and Marilee got up to order. There was nobody interesting in the place. Like anybody interesting lived in the whole stupid town.

Marilee came back with the fries on a tray. She'd already squirted ketchup all over them.

"I don't want ketchup," Janice said.

"Then get your own."

"You could of just put the ketchup on the side."

"Big honking frigging deal," Marilee said, picking up a fry

and wagging it. They were best friends, but they were the kind of friends who had a lot of fights over stupid things when really it was all about who was hotter, Janice or Marilee. Marilee had prettier hair, straight and blond, but Janice was further along in the boobs department.

They might have gone on fighting, just because they were bored, but right then Richie Cruz and two of his buddies came in. Janice and Marilee agreed that Richie was hot. But really he was cool and smooth, like ice cream, like you could lick him all over. He had a curvy mouth and green eyes and beautiful black hair and all that was just from the neck up.

Janice's mother said that under no circumstances was Janice to have anything to do with Puerto Rican boys, who were even worse than any other kind. She said they acted like they owned every woman on the street, those Ricans, them and their wolf whistles. Which Janice thought was completely stupid; who ever heard of a wolf whistling?

"What are you doing? Don't look at him," Marilee ordered.

"Like he would care what I'm looking at." Richie was sixteen and they were just little punks that he ignored.

"You're looking right at his ass."

"Then he can't see me unless he turns around."

Marilee hissed at her to be quiet. One of Richie's friends was staring straight at them. He laughed and said something to Richie. Janice felt her face going red. Her ears buzzed with shame. "Real suave," Marilee remarked.

Janice ducked her chin. "What's he doing now?"

"Richie? Nothing. Anyway, I am not looking at him!"

Maybe Richie had girls checking out his ass all the time and was used to it. She felt so majorly stupid, she wanted to get up and run out of there, but that would be even worse. She stared at her knees and hoped the boys weren't going to sit down, and then she hoped they would, and Richie would check her out, his amazing green eyes finally turning her way, and she would speak up and say, "See anything you like?"

Marilee kicked her under the table. Janice looked up to see the boys headed for the door with their food. Richie was already past them, his beautiful head silhouetted against the glass, but his friend, the one who had laughed, turned around and grinned and did something dirty with his tongue, wiggling the tip of it between his teeth. Marilee and Janice both said, "Ugh!"

"That was nasty," Janice said.

"Totally."

"What do you think he said to Richie?" She had a sick feeling about that.

"Oh, probably, 'There's a little slut over there who wants to give you a blow job.'"

"Shut up."

"Well you do. You would."

"Oh sure, like you wouldn't, if he wanted you to."

"I would not," Marilee said, and it was her turn to go red in the face, a blotchy red because she had such pale skin. One of their arguments that circled around and around had to do with Janice being a slut and Marilee being a stuck-up prude. There was a lot of stuff she didn't tell Marilee anymore.

Janice ate another french fry, even though it was cold and covered in ketchup. What was the point of arguing about Richie? Neither of them was ever going to say two words to him.

"I have to get to my grandma's and back home before my mom wets her pants."

"Your brother's outside," Marilee said, pointing.

"Oh, perfect." Her brother Jason was two years younger, and

a complete brat. They got up to go and Marilee asked what she was doing tonight and Janice said nothing, maybe they could hang out, text me, and Marilee said she would. They weren't really mad at each other but Janice thought that someday they might be.

Jason and two of his little punk friends were riding their bikes down the stairs of the post office, trying to smash their brains in. "Hi freak," he greeted her.

"Bye freak."

"You're supposed to be at Nana's. I'm telling Mom."

"Go ahead, asshole."

"I'm telling Mom you said asshole."

"I am so, so scared."

"I'll tell her you took your shirt off."

Janice gave him the finger and walked on. The chicken and noodles were heavy and it was hard to keep the plastic bag from knocking into her bare leg. It was still hotter than sin outside, the kind of aggravating heat that made you want to scratch all your itchy parts into a rash. She looked up and down the street for Richie and his friends, but of course they'd gone. Still it was something to have seen him, like getting close to somebody famous, and if he came into the A&W once, maybe he'd come in again.

She had a hundred daydreams about how Richie and her would end up together. Sometimes there was a fire or a car crash and he saved her. Sometimes she saved him. There were other versions in which they got to know each other in unexpected and dramatic ways. But sometimes she didn't bother with any of these, and let Richie put his hands all over her and peel her like an orange, and why couldn't it be easy like that?

Instead of all the stupid teasing and hooting and things you weren't supposed to do except everybody did.

Nana lived in an apartment above a used-furniture store. Everything about her neighborhood was weird and depressing: the bakery with the cardboard wedding cake in the window and the dusty bride and groom on top, the lawyer's office with his name spelled out in English and in Hebrew, the barbershop that was never open, probably because nobody around here had hair anymore. Nana wouldn't move, even though Janice's mother kept after her to. She was afraid of ending up in the nursing home. When people got old like Nana, Janice's mother said, they got very excited about the idea of dying in their own beds.

Janice rang Nana's doorbell, then let herself in with her key. "Hi Nana, I brought your dinner," she called, in case Nana had forgotten she was coming over and thought somebody had broken in, or maybe was having an embarrassing bathroom episode. "Yoo-hoo, Nana?"

Nana was in her usual chair where she could see the television and look out the window, depending on which way she turned. She was as fat as Janice's mother, but shorter, like a car or something heavy had landed on her head and squashed her down. She wore one of her dresses that didn't quite button up over her shelf of bosom, so you saw the big white cotton bra underneath. It didn't really matter what Nana looked like since she never went anywhere. The television was on loud, some kind of talk show. "Hi Nana, are you hungry? Mom made you chicken and noodles."

Nana shifted around in her chair to see Janice better. "Put on some clothes."

She'd forgotten. "All right, Nana, it's just really hot outside.

It's hot in here too, is your air conditioner working?" Janice untied the shirt from around her waist and put her arms through the sleeves. Why couldn't anybody ever give her a break? "How are you today?"

"I have bad blood, maybe cancer."

"Well I bet you'll feel better once you have your dinner. Do you want to eat there? Or sit at the table?"

Nana pushed her way up from her chair and stumped over to the kitchen table. Janice was quick to turn the television down. She helped Nana get herself settled. Nana wore an old-fashioned hairnet, the kind you could use to catch fish, and her white scalp showed through her hair. Nana wasn't even all that old, seventy-two or -three, but she might as well have been a hundred. It was the same with Janice's mother, who was only forty, but she'd decided to give up on her looks and be somebody who never shaved her legs.

Janice dumped the chicken and noodles and some tap water into a pot on the stove. It was a solid, stuck-together mess and she prodded at it with a wooden spoon. Nana said, "Tell your mother, I need soap. Pink soap."

"All right."

"And rubber bands. It was on the television, about that girl."

"What girl?" Janice said, though she pretty much knew already.

"The one who run off and they couldn't find. They found her. All cut up."

"I don't want to hear about it, Nana."

"All cut up and thrown out like the trash. You know what they do to her first?"

"No, and don't tell me. That's—" There was a word for her grandmother always telling her the worst, most horrible stories, about girls getting raped and murdered and ending up in land-fills or somebody's freezer, a really good word, but she couldn't think of it. "—sick."

"She was a bad girl."

"How do you know that, Nana? Whoever hurt her, he's the bad one."

"She run off."

"Well maybe she had a good reason for it."

"No good reason. That thing between your legs? You can't see it but anybody else in the world can if they want to. Remember."

"That's sick," Janice said again. Sick was the clump of gluey food in the saucepan. It was the hot apartment and the shivery burning that rose up in her. Nana reached out and touched the back of Janice's bare leg with her fat soft finger, and Janice let out a little shriek. "Don't touch me!"

"That's right. You keep on saying that."

Janice walked home fast. It was a long way from being dark, but the sky had lowered another notch and the heat was glassy and she still felt a little sick, throw-up sick. Nobody was out on the streets in Nana's neighborhood, they never were, but what if somebody was watching her. Was it better to walk slow or fast? She kept her phone up to her ear so that anybody seeing her would think she was talking. She tried to think about Richie Cruz and how he could be the one watching her, following her, but that was no good because then his face blurred into some-thing unrecognizable and mean.

When she got to the post office, Jason was still there. He'd given up on running his bike on the stairs and was sitting on the bottom step, picking at his mosquito bites. "You have to come home with me," Janice said.

"I do not."

"It's dinnertime."

"Says who?"

"Just do it, okay?"

He gave her a squinting look, then hoisted his bike and walked it along behind her.

When they got home Janice said she wasn't hungry, she didn't feel good, she was going to bed. Her mother said, "What's the matter with you, are you constipated?"

"No, leave me alone."

"If you don't eat, you can't poop. Do you have a fever? Let me feel your forehead."

"Leave me alone!" She ran upstairs and locked her door even though she wasn't supposed to and texted Marilee to say she couldn't hang out. She turned the fan beside her bed up high so she couldn't hear anything, put the pillow over her head and fell asleep.

Her eyes opened up to darkness. She could tell it was late. She went to her bedroom door and looked out. The faintest light came from downstairs, the light over the stove that her mother left on all night. The television was off. Jason's door was closed and dark.

Janice used the bathroom down the hall and examined herself in the mirror. She brushed her hair and made her bangs poufier. She used the lipstick and black eyeliner she kept under the stack of towels, turning this way and that to see how she looked from different angles.

Back in her bedroom she locked the door again. She turned on the computer and the pink-shaded lamp next to her bed. The computer screen blinked and brightened. She typed in the address, then sat back to read. After a minute she typed in:

Hi, what are you doing?

He wrote back a minute later: *Nothing much. Waiting on u. Turn on yur camera.*

OK.

It was always sort of a shock when his face came swimming up under her fingers, so close. He grinned at her. *Hi beautiful.*

She shook her head like she didn't believe it. *Hi yourself.*

How iz my Candy girl?

Bored. Today just sucked.

Aww. How about I find me some candy to suck on?

She giggled. Candy was the name she used with him, not Janice, which was a stupid name that she imagined had a smell to it, like the inside of her house, which always smelled like cooked carrots. He said that Candy was perfect for her because she was so sweet. He said his name was Geronimo, like the famous Apache war chief. He was kind of bullshit but also kind of cool. *An thats what people yell when they jump out of airplanes, Geronimo!*

Why?

I dont know y they just do. Like here I come mofos ahmo mess you up! He was a little crazy, she liked that.

Geronimo bent over his keyboard. She had told him they had to type everything so nobody at her house would hear. *Tell me what was so bad today.*

Just stuff like my mom. Shes always on my case.

I bet she iz jealous. She iz not a pretty young thing like u. PYT!

Geronimo said he was twenty-five, but he was probably older, just like Janice said she was fifteen but she was really younger. He was sort of fat in the face and he combed his hair up into a little blond tuft. If she had met him for real, she might not have thought he was anything special, but this was different. She typed:

Ha ha ! My mom is so not pretty! I don't look like my dad either.

Maybe they adopted u?

LOL! That makes sense. They just went out and got a kid so they had somebody to boss around. She didn't really think that. There were pictures of her and her mom in the hospital when she was just a little lump in a blanket, then other pictures of her baby self gradually turning into her now self. But she liked the idea of it. It made a better story.

Geronimo was somebody new she'd met. There had been these other guys who she didn't like as much because they weren't online as much or they were just creepy. Geronimo was always there. He said he had a job with computers, he fixed different people's computers, he knew how everything worked. Then, for fun, he hung out on the computer! The camera showed part of the room behind him. It looked like an office, with shelves and messy piles of paper. He kept one of those giant-sized soft drink cups on his desk and drank from it through a straw.

Now he was typing something long. It came up a line at a time:

Don't let them. Boss u around. You need to live yur own life. Not be told everything u. Do is wrong. Because they want u under there thumb. Be strong.

Thanks. I will try to be.

Do or not do. There is no try!

Oh please, that is so lame! It was from *Star Wars*, but he'd had to tell her that. *Star Wars* was for old people.

So u have a boyfriend yet, PYT?

Maybe. She didn't want to admit to not having one.

Who iz this maybe boy?

His name is Richie.

U like him?

Of course I do, hes my boyfriend.

Why isnt he there?

My mom won't let him up here. In my room. That was true, sort of. Her mother would chase a boy away with a broom before she would let the two of them be anywhere with a bed.

Geronimo took a long drink through the straw and wiggled his eyebrows to show that what he was saying was meant to be funny: *How about I be yur boyfriend in yur room.*

Oh ha ha.

You hurtin my feelings. He made a hurt-feelings face, puffing out his cheeks so that his face was even fatter.

Get over it, she typed, because the idea was, he had to beg her, *Oh Candy pleez pleez,* because she was so beautiful.

Girl u killin me.

Tough.

Have some mercy.

She didn't type anything back, but she fiddled with her hair, then, like it was a casual thing, nothing she really thought about, pulled her top down so her boobs were out.

Candy girl u are wicked hot.

She leaned into the screen and made a kiss mouth. She squeezed her arms underneath her boobs so they looked really big.

Put yur hands on u.

Pretend it really was Richie Cruz, right there with her. She'd do this for him. Whatever he wanted. This and this and this. Her eyes were closed, seeing him. Then she opened them and it was Geronimo, his big white face filling the screen and his mouth loose and so close she could see the wet pink inside of it and she typed *I have to go,* and hit the kill button.

———

The next day Marilee asked what she did the night before and Janice said nothing, just fell asleep early.

I'm like a little freaked out, I'm not really old enough to be Talking to me? Geronimo offered, since she didn't want to say everything straight out.

Yeah.

But u want to, dont u?

I guess so.

Then sounds to me like ur old enough. I mean its natural. Natural is the way the real world iz, not some pretend story they tell you in church.

Not that anybody in her family went to church, but she knew what he meant.

Lie down on yur bed OK?

Why?

Becoz I been thinking of you on a bed. Pleez, Miss Sweet Candy, I got this craving for u, u are so beautiful booty full.

Ha ha.

Pleez.

Like this?

Oh yeah yeah! Now scoot back an wiggle some.

Janice and Marilee hung out at the food court in the mall, eating pizza slices. The mall was old and the stores kept closing down. After a while a different store would open in the same place, something disappointing like golf equipment or baby clothes. It was the totally boring headquarters of the totally boring summer. Some guys from their school were there but they were jerks, chasing around and throwing drinks on each other.

Richie Cruz had a girlfriend now. It was horrible but true. The two of them came into the mall a couple times a week, the girlfriend probably dragging him there so he could buy her stuff. They didn't know the girlfriend's name but she was Puerto Rican like Richie. Which was so unfair, since no matter how hard Janice tried, she was not ever going to be Puerto Rican!

Here they were again. Janice and Marilee watched them walk through the squares of glittering light from the glass walls, super slow, like they were a parade, the two of them waving from a float, see how we're all the way up here and you're down there. Richie! Easy on his feet, yawning like he just woke up, his green eyes half-slit. His black T-shirt stuck to his shoulder blades, it was so hot outside. Janice wanted to peel that damp shirt off him like the petals of a silk rose, send her cool breath across the muscles of his back.

The girlfriend said something that had the look of complaining: Why wasn't Richie paying her more attention, admiring her giant boobs or her ten pounds of makeup?

"She is so hoochie," Janice said. It was the most awful wrong thing, seeing this girl with him, the two of them together. She wanted to jump up and scream and rub the sight of them away.

"Look at that, she has her hands in his back pockets," Marilee said. "I mean, honestly."

"She seriously should not be doing that."

"I bet they have all kinds of sex."

"Well of course they do, duh!"

"You don't have to bite my head off," Marilee said. She was painting her fingernails yellow and holding each one up to admire it.

How could Richie not notice her, not know one thing about her, when she was so crazy with feeling, she was afraid of flying through the air at him like iron to a magnet?

Janice watched the girlfriend and pretended not to. She wished she had some secret superpower, like making people burst into flames. The girlfriend was extra extra hoochie. She wore a lot of gold jewelry, earrings and bracelets and some dangly stuff around her neck. She was busting out of her clothes in a horrible cheap way.

Marilee said that guys got bored with girls like that, once they got what they wanted off them. Janice didn't bother answering back. Marilee was boring herself. Richie Cruz's girlfriend made a pouty face and said something to him, then crossed the black-and-white tiles of the food court on her way to the bathroom. Her shoes had high heels and she took little bitty steps.

Janice said, "You know what she looks like? One of those foo-foo dogs on a leash, the kind with bows in its hair."

"Those little dogs are actually sort of cute," Marilee said.

"You know what I mean."

"Yeah, you want to be Richie's pet bitch."

"Oh screw you." Janice stood up. "I'll be back in a minute."

"What are you doing?" Marilee asked, but Janice ignored her. *Go for it! Geronimo!*

Richie Cruz was leaning against a wall, waiting, like he was used to it. His girlfriend probably spent a lot of time in the bathroom, putting on makeup and yanking underwear out of her butt. He yawned, a big gorgeous yawn that showed all his teeth.

Janice walked black square white square, black square white square, right past Richie. She couldn't look at him straight on, any more than you could look straight at the sun. But even with her eyes down she saw the creases in his jeans where they fit so good, she saw his hands with the thumbs hooked into the pockets. And he was watching her! He was!

She reached the Karmelkorn place and stood in front of it like she had some serious decision to make. Caramel caramel caramel, like Richie's skin. She bought a bag of popcorn and walked past him again, slower this time, putting pieces in her mouth and licking her fingers.

"I do not believe you," Marilee said, once Janice sat back down.

"Want some?" She shook the bag at Marilee.

"What were you doing?"

"Showing off my goodies." She was giddy. Her heart beat crazy. She watched the hoochie girlfriend make her way back from the restroom, feeling almost even with her now.

Marilee twisted the top shut on the nail polish with an extra hard tug. "That was so trashy."

"Yeah, well your fingernails look like they rotted and fell off."

"What does that have to do with anything?"

"Forget about it." Janice watched Richie and the girlfriend slow-walking out of the food court. The giddy feeling ebbed out of her. It hadn't been anything, she was so stupid, and now she'd messed up and it wasn't how the story was supposed to go.

Richie wants to go all the way, she told Geronimo. Even this late, it never really cooled off upstairs. She had the fan going but the heat hunkered down in the walls and didn't budge.

Well of course he duz. He is a man and u r a beautiful young lady.

I just don't know.

Geronimo was growing a beard, one of those soul patch things. It was like the tuft of hair he combed straight up, like he kept thinking of weird things to do to his face. He had all the lights in his room off so there was only the computer screen and its blurry glow.

Whats there to know? Just do what comes natural.

Hey where do you live anyway?

In a galaxy far far away ha ha.

Because I would just you know die if you showed up at my school or something.

Candy baby u got nothing to worry. I know how to keep a secret. Anyway I never leave the house hardly. ROTFL!

I mean who are you really? Because isn't it kind of pervy to be talking about this stuff.

She was pretty sure he talked to other girls. He hadn't meant to say so but he sort of did once.

Geronimo bent over the screen, typing. He was wearing a T-shirt that said "I Support Re-Cycling. I Wore This Yesterday." The sleeves made his arms look fat. *Well who are YOU really, come on Candy gurl.*

I have to go now.

Aw hey Im sorry. Im on yur side like nobody else is cuz I. Dont think u r bad just a beyootiful gurl. Doin what comes natural an that Richie is one lucky man. Pull yur pants down.

No way!

Just a little. Come on its practice. For when Richie asks u.

She had the worst underwear on, plain white cotton like a little kid's. She shook her head at the screen, no.

Y not?

Its pervy.

OK so dont. Just put yur fingers where it feels good.

No!

Y not?

She shook her head.

Candy gurl dont be fraid. Of beautiful sexy u. Feel the power of the Force! LOL! Becoz u got so much power u know it an u can let it loose. Jus a lil touch.

So it was pervy. She didn't care or she didn't care right now because it felt good so maybe she was a perv too. She kept her eyes shut, *Richie Richie Richie*, but at the worst possible moment she remembered their tenant in the basement, Mr. Grotius, who was maybe sixty years old and had a face like cigarette ash, all crumbly and gray, and long gray shaky hands.

She slammed the computer lid closed. She unplugged everything and turned off the light and covered herself up in the sheets, her sweat turning cold.

She finally got an iPod! Her mother said it was a waste of good money and if Janice was serious about music she could have kept up her piano lessons, but that was the kind of thing her mother could be expected to say. Janice saved up her birthday money and her babysitting money and went to Target and bought a pink iPod and all the things that went with it. Now at night, instead of getting on the computer, she listened to her music and made lists of the different songs she wanted to buy.

She didn't go online with Geronimo anymore. It was just one of those things you did for a while and then you were done with it.

Ordinarily she would have shown the iPod to Marilee but

Marilee was being a giant bitch these days. It was like they were through being friends. They hadn't had a fight or anything, they just quit talking. Marilee's Facebook page said she was going on vacation with her family to Colorado, and Janice started to write Thanks for telling me, loser, but decided not to. It would just make her feel crummier.

Then out of nowhere her mother said, "What is it you've been doing on that computer all this time?"

"Nothing!"

"Don't give me that. You're supposed to use it for homework. Not listen to dirty music."

Her heart, which had clenched up, began beating again. Her mother didn't know anything. "Define dirty."

"Dirty is dirty! You know it when you see it! Don't roll your eyes at me, you think you can do whatever you want well you can't, you want people talking about you, you want to be the kind of girl everybody points to when they see you coming? You act like it's no big deal to go around looking cheap, talking cheap, like everything in the world has changed but some things don't change. Men don't!"

And then her mother got a weird, pitiful look on her face and she said, "Baby girl, you have so much to learn," and made as if she was going to touch her and Janice jumped back and her mother's expression went back to its normal suspicion and contempt. "Fine. You keep on going down that same road, see where it takes you."

Her mother was unhappy for life because Janice's father hadn't wanted to stick around, who could blame him, and so she looked at everything like it was about her.

Maybe she was all over the Internet now being a famous slut. She'd made him swear never to do that but what if he got mad at her and did and her mother found out. Her stomach crawled into her throat every time she thought about it. Then another day would go by when none of that happened, and maybe nothing would ever change in her whole boring stupid life. Even her iPod got stuck playing the same song, one she kept trying to get rid of, a girl singer going on and on about a chance chance chance for romance mance mance, shut up shut up shut up.

Janice went to the mall by herself. There wasn't anybody else to go with now that Marilee had her head up her behind. She missed Geronimo, not for the pervy stuff, not exactly, but because he had been sort of a friend. She moped around trying on sunglasses and leather jackets and then she bought a Coke and sat in the food court listening to her music, which was the great thing about an iPod, you could always look like you were doing something.

She'd pretty much given up pretending Richie Cruz was ever going to notice her. It was all dumb and hopeless. She hadn't seen Richie or his trashy girlfriend and anyway who cared about them? They could do whatever they wanted. The summer had gone on forever. Every day she woke up with the same heat headache. Every day there was nothing for her to do except take up space and watch the world like it was a clock.

Then Richie Cruz walked into the mall, or no he was already inside but she hadn't seen him, and for a moment or two it tripped up her brain, she couldn't make sense of his being there. The idiot song buzzed in her ears, take a chance let's dance make romance mance mance, and here was Richie coming straight toward her with his sleepy, slow-footed walk, his thumbs hooked in his pants pockets, pointing down, lookee here! and he was smiling! Smiling at her!

Janice froze up. Dance dance dance. Richie and his green

eyes closed in on her. She thought she was going to be sick. He stood next to her chair. She couldn't even look at him. She smelled his dusky musky aftershave. She could have buried her nose in his pants pants pants. For a second she was afraid she had actually done so. He said, "Hey, can I see that?"

He meant the iPod. Janice unhooked the earbuds, still making their tiny noise, and handed it over.

Then he was walking away again. Not in any big hurry. He fiddled with the iPod, probably trying to change the song.

She just sat there. She would sit there the rest of her life.

But then it got even worse. From the same direction Richie had appeared, Marilee and another girl, another blond girl just like Marilee so the two of them looked like doll twins, came toward her with their heads together, whispering. They stopped at Janice's table, grinning and rocking back and forth on their heels, they were so excited about making fun of her. Marilee said, "We told Richie you were in love with him and you want to have his baby."

Marilee waited for Janice to say something and when she didn't, she said, "So anyway, now he knows you have the hots for him. That's what you wanted, right?" The two of them walked away, laughing and shaking their heads so their blond hair swished like horse tails.

After a while Janice got up and went home and when her mother asked her what she'd done with that music thing she was so excited about, Janice said she lost it.

Nana was sick. She went into the hospital and then she came home and then she went into the hospital again. All sorts of things were wrong with her, all her inside parts leaking and going flat. One of these days she would be dead but not right away. They had all gone to see her in the hospital this last time. The hospital was the kind of place that made you wonder if anybody got out alive. Nurses stalked the halls with carts full of blood and pee. The walls were tile and echoing. There was a smell of steam and fish sticks. Janice's mother pushed Janice and her brother forward. "Mom, I brought the kids to see you."

Nana was bundled up like laundry on the bed. She opened her eyes and groaned. "They cut me all up," she said. "Then they threw me away."

Now Nana was home from the hospital again. A nurse stayed with her nights, and Janice's mother went over before and after work to take care of her. Her mother was too busy to pay much attention to Janice, and she could have done anything she wanted except there was nothing she wanted to do. Mostly she hung around the house and watched whatever was on television. Nobody called her and she didn't call anyone.

It was like her life was already set out for her. She was never one of the popular girls and now she had a reputation as a slut without even doing anything, at least nothing that ought to count. She guessed she was a slut, there was something wrong with her. Once school started she would have to try and be invisible, get through it all until she was old enough to find some kind of job. Then after a while she would be old and fat like her mother and then even older like Nana and then she would be dead.

Janice's mother called her from work. "I need you to take Nana one of the beef pot pies, the rest of the bakery bread, and the strawberry jam that's on the counter. Don't tell me you don't have time because you do. Yes, cook the pot pie at home, what did you think, let it defrost and get ruined? I have to go to the bank and the drugstore, then I'll worry about your supper. No, your brother can't do it, I'm asking you. Now get a move on."

Her brother never had to do anything. If you were a boy you could run wild and people thought it was only natural. The pot pie was another one of her mother's bad menu ideas. It cooked up with burned spots on the crust, probably from being in the freezer too long.

Janice put all the food into a backpack, which was less embarrassing than plastic bags, and set off. There was a hot spot between her shoulder blades where the pot pie rested. The sky was dark in one corner and a wind pushed grit along the streets. It hadn't rained for so long that you didn't even think to worry about it anymore. The sky opened its mouth and thunder rolled out. Maybe she'd get hit by lightning and that would serve everybody right.

The streetlights had come on in the early dark. Nobody was out walking but once in a while a car whisked along. The first rain tapped against the fabric of the backpack, then she felt it on her skin. Perfect. Great. She was still a long ways away, and either she'd get there with a lot of wet food, or she'd be late, and either way it would all be her fault.

She ran across an intersection just ahead of the first sheeting rain. There wasn't such a thing as a store open around here, so she ducked under the overhang of an apartment building's parking garage. Wind blew the rain across the streets in a little surf. Her feet were wet. She thought about calling her mother but it would serve her right to worry a little. Anyway, you could kind of like being all alone and tragic in the storm, like somebody in a song.

A car pulled up on the street next to her, an old beater with a dent in the fender. The passenger door opened and the driver shouted something she couldn't hear. She bent down to get a better look and for one crazy moment she thought it was Richie Cruz, but it wasn't, it was his friend who had grinned at her and Marilee that time in the A&W, and he was waiting for her to get in.

She didn't right away. She hung back and shook her head and he motioned, come on, come on, and then he did a comical thing where he turned up his collar and put his hands palms up, like it was raining on him inside the car, and that's when she put the backpack over her head and sprinted to the curb.

"Hey, close the door," he said, once she was inside with the backpack at her feet and the windshield wipers struggling to push the rain back. "You want to flood us?"

She closed the door and the rain was all around them. She hugged herself because where she'd gotten wet was now turning cold. The boy said, "What are you doing out here, huh? You lost?"

She was trying to look at him without being obvious. She was trying to decide if he was cute or not. He wasn't really, but he wasn't too bad. She rubbed her arms along her legs until they warmed up, then she rubbed them some more because he was watching. She said, "I'm going to my grandma's place. She's sick, I'm taking her some food."

"Yeah?" He made an exaggerated sniffing noise at the backpack. "She gonna be a lot sicker once she eats what's in there."

On the dashboard, its wires and earbuds trailing out behind it, was a pink iPod. "Hey, is that mine?"

"I dunno. Could be. So you want a ride?"

"Give me my iPod back."

He put the car in gear and it nudged forward in the watery street. "What's it worth to you?"

He said it like he was trying to be tough but it came out nervous. He probably had to practice it. And right then and there, she lit up with knowing. It was all so simple. She was balanced between two different lives, two different stories, and the whole world waiting for her to choose.

He said, "Hey, what's your name, huh?" Nervous again. He took a quick look at himself in the rearview mirror.

"Candy," she said, and she smiled a candy smile. She was going to gobble him up alive.

FAITH

Et invenerunt lapidem revolutum a monumento.
And they found the stone rolled back from the sepulchre.

The parchment was so very old, it had a near-mortal smell of decay, like a pile of black, wet leaves. The pages were thickly lettered and difficult to decipher. The priest used one finger to track each word and sound it out. He tried to spend the best light of the day in reading, so as to spare his eyes. If he stared at the letters for too long, they whirled and pulsed and he had to bind the covers shut and put the book to one side, as he did now. He stood and went to the open window to clear his head. The sky was a blurred gold in this hour before sunset, and the air sweet with midsummer.

And who would not want to live forever on such a day, or on any ordinary day? *Whosoever believeth in me shall not perish, but shall have life everlasting.* It was the central mystery and promise of his religion. As old as the book he had held in his hands was, the events it spoke of were older still, unimaginably distant in time, and had taken place in another language on the far side of the world. That the account had survived at all was surely evidence of the divine, beyond the reckoning of human understanding.

And had every scribe and every translation and every argument over doctrine been part of the Lord's plan, sorting and shaking out the truth? Or had errors and frailty and bad faith corrupted it? If God's word was conveyed through fallible men, could it ever be free of their taint?

Mary Magdalene had not recognized the risen Christ at first, had mistaken him for the gardener. Thomas needed to feel Christ's wounds with his own hands before he was assured. Their confusion, and then their conviction, offered up as proof. Of course they had disbelieved at first, as anyone in any age would. The apostles at the empty tomb had not suspected a resurrection but a grave robbery. As anyone would.

The priest sighed and turned away from the window, because doubting thoughts came from the Devil. It was a dangerous habit, his fondness for argument and subtlety, a prideful pleasure in his own intellect. Anyway, he ought to be busying himself with the remainder of the day's work, for there was much to do.

Tomorrow was Saint John and Saint Paul's Day, with a special mass to be said. And right after, the blessing of all those going forth as part of the land agent's new enterprise, with so many hopes and fears riding on their journey.

There was also a guest for the evening meal, the land agent himself, and that too counted as work. The priest did not care for the man, though he had not known him long enough to back up his dislike with proven history. The land agent had managed to get himself invited for dinner in some fashion that the priest could not entirely recall. He had the unpleasant feeling of having been outmaneuvered.

What complaint, exactly, could he lay against the agent? A certain glibness, a facile and overagreeable quality that spoke of calculation. Hardly surprising, since it was the agent's business to coax, entice, promise, and whatever else he had to do in order to fill his quota of settlers. And he was good at his trade, that much was clear, although that did not mean one was required to admire him for it.

Now the priest chastised himself for being uncharitable, judgmental, as he inevitably was. How difficult, how exhausting, to be so constantly on guard against one's own nature! And then to fall into the trap of selfishness and self-involvement, diminishing his usefulness to others and to the flock he was meant to lead and serve.

He made his usual rounds of the church, securing it for the night. Before the altar, he prostrated himself on the stone floor and prayed to both Our Lord on his cross and to Saint Nicolai for humility, wisdom, guidance. He loved the quiet and beauty of the church at these times, just after the sacristan rang the evening bell. The last sunlight made its passage through the high windows in lozenges of ruby and amber. The smells of wax, wood, earth, linseed oil, and incense were as familiar to him as any from his childhood. Only in such solitude did his soul go still, and peace pass into him like a balm.

Then it was time to return to the everyday world and prepare himself for his guest. He waited in the small room where he took his meals until the housekeeper knocked and announced the land agent's arrival. "Our Lord's grace upon you," the priest said, in formal greeting.

"And upon you," the agent replied, bowing in an elaborate fashion, one hand held over his heart. "How are you this fine evening, Father?"

"Very well, thank you." The priest was relieved to see that the agent had put aside the outlandish clothes he wore when he gave his presentations, and was wearing a simple green coat. He held a cloth cap in his hands, and a leather bag was slung crossways around his body. "As I hope you are also."

"Well indeed. So kind, your invitation."

The priest murmured something meant to deflect such gratitude, and motioned to the agent to seat himself. The priest had arranged the chairs so that they did not face each other.

Out of distaste or squeamishness he preferred to keep the man at a little distance. An unworthy feeling but a genuine one. The agent had crimped, fox-colored hair, a mealy complexion, and a scant red beard that looked new grown, although he was past his first youth. His nose was sharp and his eyes an unreadable dark green, except for a kind of private amusement. Yes, better not to sit directly in the beam of those eyes.

The priest uncorked the wine bottle, spoke a word of blessing, and poured out two portions. They raised their cups. "Shall we drink to your enterprise?" the priest suggested, as he was meant to.

"May our Lord commend it," the agent said piously. He tasted the wine, considered it, then drank deeply. "This is excellent."

"It's made from the vineyard on the old monastery grounds," the priest said, by way of not taking credit for it himself. The agent's cup was now empty, and after a moment's hesitation, the priest refilled it.

"You will have fine weather tomorrow," the priest said, since he could invent no other conversation. "You should have a good road."

"Yes, I hope to make a strong start. Although the first day is often the most difficult, with complaints and wanting one or another thing that cannot be had. But they will come round soon enough."

"They are only children," the priest said, not liking the man's tone.

"And those already in the settlements will welcome them as if they were their very own."

The priest might have said more, but just then the housekeeper came in with the supper, and the agent's attention was drawn to this in a hopeful fashion.

The priest was amused to see the man's visible disappointment in the food, since he had not instructed his housekeeper to give them more than the usual plain fare. There was bread, and a wedge of yellow cheese, an onion, and a dish of ramps cooked with oil and eggs. In honor of the season, the housekeeper had thought to include a bowl of new strawberries, and at these the agent's doleful face brightened.

"These look very tasty," the agent declared, reaching out to take one but stopping short. He made as if to laugh at his own impatience. "Your pardon." He bowed his head, waiting for the priest's prayer.

"Our Father," the priest began, "and His son, our savior, by your grace and power do we receive these your gifts. We accept them now with thankful hearts." He could have gone on and made the agent sit longer before he started eating, but he told himself, sternly, not to put prayer to such a petty use. "In Jesus' name we pray, Amen."

"Amen," the agent echoed, and made a point of offering the bowl of strawberries to the priest, who indicated that the agent should go first. So much politeness, they were both likely to expire from hunger. The priest took his turn at the strawberries, then tore off bread from the loaf to dip into the ramps. The agent had a good appetite, the priest observed. One might call it greedy, the way in which he crowded so much onto his plate, then leaned over it, as if it needed defending. The agent's sharp nose even had a bit of a twitch to it, the priest fancied.

The priest had only a middling appetite, although he finished his wine and poured out another cup for them both. He got up to close the window against the night air, as it was growing chill. Immediately the room seemed to shrink in size, the candlelight drawing the walls in closer.

The agent made short work of his meal, then sat back and nodded in contentment. "My gratitude," he said. "For a man such as myself, with no real hearth or home of my own, hospitality like yours is much appreciated."

"I am more than pleased to share what I have with you," the priest replied, correctly. He hoped the man would take himself off before too long. Instead the agent gave every appearance of settling in and getting comfortable. He took another sip of wine and looked fondly at the bottle. One hand picked absently through his red beard for bits of stray food.

Just as the priest was ready to invent some excuse to shorten the evening, the agent said, "You're worried about the children."

"I have concerns. I can't deny that."

"Nor should you. Your feelings do you credit. In a sense, a pastoral sense of course, all of them are your children."

"I have been responsible for their spiritual upbringing," the priest said, knowing how stiff, even forbidding, he sounded. He would not have known what to do with children of his own.

"But it's such an excellent opportunity for them. A chance to make a life for themselves in a new place. Because surely, they have no such prospects here."

This was true enough. The children of poorer families, along with the younger sons of the more prosperous ones, were the ones going. If they stayed, they would be trodden under, with neither land nor goods to sustain them. It was no secret that many of those making the journey had been offered up by parents who could scarcely afford to feed them. These included children hardly older than babies who would be traveling by wagon, even though the land agent had promoted the enterprise for only those old enough to go on foot and do a strong day's work. The priest suspected that other corners might be cut as well. And this would be overlooked, since the expedition solved so many problems for so many people.

"But why only children?" the priest asked, out of some troublemaking instinct he allowed himself to give voice to. "Why not allow entire families? There must be those willing to go."

The agent began to explain once more, in a patient, instructive tone, that the settlement of new territories was a young people's task. That his master, the duke, was quite fixed on the notion of the settlers growing up as citizens of the new lands, without the sort of divided loyalties that those farther along in life must inevitably have. Of course, in time, once the work had progressed far enough, the children might indeed send for their other kin to join them. They would set their hands to labor and make of the place a garden, a marvel, a destination for pilgrims! There were echoes in this of the agent's presentations in the town square, his jingling jangling come-on, full of boast and wonderful visions.

"You will be able to work the children as you wish," the priest said. The wine was loosening his tongue. The room seemed close now, unpleasantly so.

For a moment the agent seemed caught off stride, but he recovered quickly enough. "I don't deny how much we need the labor. Would you believe me if I did? Life is difficult in the new lands. The forest is barely cleared, the fields only just planted. We need shelters built before cold weather comes. There are a thousand tasks! We need those who have no choice but to stay put, not strike out on their own. Are you accusing me of wanting the new settlements to be a success? Then I stand guilty. Do I shock you with my honesty? At least I hope it will help you to believe me."

The agent had leaned forward to speak, his chin nodding and a curl of his crimped, peculiar hair coming loose over his forehead. One hand fisted, striking the table. It was such a perfect picture of sincerity that the priest could not help, perversely, suspecting the man of putting on a performance. Before he could formulate any sort of response, the agent shifted in his chair, raised his hands in a brief, fluttering spiral, then let them drop again. He had a conjurer's quickness in his movements. "Your pardon," he said. "This work has become my very breath and bone. I think on it sunup to sundown, and the duke gives me no peace. Perhaps I'm too anxious on this eve of our departure. As for the children, they will be treated fairly. They will receive firmness and direction. For a child knows not what it needs, only what it wants."

He waited for the priest to duck his head in agreement, which he did, even though he had the nagging sense that the man had answered nothing. The agent passed his hands over his eyes, as if fighting off weariness. "It can be the most demanding and exasperating work, the repopulation effort. And you can't expect to see success—that is, the entirety of success—accomplished within one's lifetime. Rather like your own work, the salvation of souls. Only in the next world can your results be measured."

"I suppose so," the priest said, although he did not much like having his priestly duties likened to the agent's dubious enterprises. As if a priest would go capering around on a stage in the public square, tooting on a horn and clowning about!

"Now, Father, indulge me in one more matter, if you would be so kind."

"Certainly," the priest murmured, wishing that the agent would take himself off. He felt unwell. More than ever he disliked the man, more and more he found reasons for distrust and alarm. The agent was looking so fixedly at his empty wine cup that the priest poured the rest of the bottle into it.

"Why did you take holy orders? Did you feel a calling in yourself?"

The priest hesitated. The agent said, "Again, your pardon. An impertinence on my part."

"Not at all," the priest answered, though it was, if not an impertinence, at least a liberty. "I suppose I wanted . . . that is, I strove to perfect my faith. To become stronger in it."

"Ah." The agent nodded. "Only the saints are able to rise above all our human weaknesses. To trust without doubt, to accept without exerting one's own will!"

"Yes," said the priest, losing track of the man's words, agreeing foolishly to he knew not what. A headache had nailed itself to his forehead.

". . . in the matter of Jesus walking upon the water. A miracle? Or perhaps one of those occasions where the sun on the water tricks the eye and makes all distances suspect, so that a man walking on the shore appears to be in the middle of the sea. I have seen such things in my travels."

"But surely you have not seen the blind made to see, or the lame to walk, or the leper cleansed," the priest said, reproving him.

"Ah, Father, there can be such bold fakery among a certain class of beggars, it would break your heart to see it. No matter! If only I could turn water into wine, as our Lord did at Cana! Now that is a trick worth knowing!"

"It was not a trick," the priest said, but the agent was still pleased with his own joke.

"The one miracle I can perform? Turning the wine back into water! Ha!" The candlelight cast its long, drooping shadows over his face. One corner of his mouth turned up in laughter and the priest saw, as he had not before, that the agent was missing several teeth. "Such foolishness on my part," he said, recovering himself, reaching for the wine. "But our Lord gave us the gift of laughter, did he not? As well as our unsettled minds, a weakness we must guard against. Because who would think such blasphemous things, if they could keep from doing so?"

"The Gospel," the priest began heavily, but he could not finish his thought. It was as if the man had found some chink in him and was prying and picking at it. What if there were no miracles? No angels of the Lord in the empty tomb, one seated at the place where the head of the body had lain, and one at the feet? What if there was only the teller's desire to make his story better? "I'm sorry," he said. "Some passing weakness in me . . . a moment's faintness . . ."

The agent was out of his chair in an instant. "I've overtired you with my idle talk. I'll take my leave, with your permission, and pray for—"

The agent went silent, and turned his sharp nose to a dark corner of the room where a small scratching could now be heard. Noiselessly, he drew something out of his leather bag and took a few steps closer. Quicker than the priest's eye could follow, he darted after the rat that had emerged from its hole. He cast a long, stiff noose round the rat's neck and tightened it with a flick of his wrist. The rat squealed and flailed and then lay still.

"Nasty creature. Difficult to believe that it too is part of God's creation. Don't worry, Father, I will dispose of it for you."

He bowed and left, the rat curled up and dragging on the end of the noose.

The priest remained in his chair. When the housekeeper entered to clear away the meal, she might have been surprised to see him still there. But like all women who attended the priests, she had been selected for her advanced age, undoubted piety, and absolute lack of curiosity. The priest roused himself to drink a cup of water, then watched without energy as the housekeeper went about her chore. When she was turning to leave, he asked her, "Do you think it is a good plan, the children leaving for the new settlements?"

If the woman was surprised at having her opinion solicited, as had never happened before, she gave no sign of it. "If it pleases our Lord, he will favor it." And then she swept the table clean of crumbs and departed.

The next morning the church was filled in honor of the saints' day, the two martyrs. The priest looked out over the upturned faces of his congregation, each of them waiting (with differing degrees of attentiveness) for him to instruct, inspire, bless, absolve them. The sun shone in glory through the high windows. A fresh-scrubbed day, full of solemn promise. The priest spoke of the saints' humility and resolve, their willingness to sacrifice their lives as testament to their faith. "Can you even for one moment imagine yourself kneeling, waiting for the sword to cleave your head from your body? And can you then imagine yourself filled, not with fear, but with the greatest joy?"

They could not. A few of them rubbed at their own necks, as if feeling the cold bite of the sword. The priest continued. "Their faith was so pure and strong, they knew they were about to ascend straight into heaven! Heaven! We can't see it from here, it's always one hill farther than the last one we can climb! That place where there is no hunger or want or lack of any sort! Nor cruelty nor fear nor heartsickness!"

The priest paused to draw breath. In the far back corner of the church he caught a glimpse of the land agent, dressed once again in his gaudy, ridiculous clothes. As if this was a proper way to appear in church, or even to undertake a long journey. What was he doing here anyway, skulking around behind the pillars, distracting him? Why not come on time and sit in a pew if he came at all?

"Now the blessed saints sit in great glory alongside the Father and the Son, in eternal peace and grace," the priest continued, but the passion had drained out of him, and he only wished to reach the end.

The congregation shuffled its feet as he raised the host to consecrate it, then each of them took their turn to advance and kneel and accept the body and blood of Christ. Each one, that is, except for the land agent, who had vanished. The priest allowed himself relief at this, although he wondered why the man did not take communion.

Finally all was done and the last prayers said, and the people hurrying out the church doors and calling to each other, for those who were part of the expedition would be leaving right away. The priest followed more slowly, crossing the threshold into the welcoming sunshine. Why was his heart so heavy?

And here was the land agent, standing in the bed of a wagon, trading jokes with the crowd. There were two wagons, each hitched to a shaggy horse, and each with a tough-looking drover holding the reins. Where had these men come from? The priest had not seen them before. They were shabby, sour-faced, as if the prospect of exerting themselves put them in a foul mood. But the land agent capered and danced, playing a tune on a little pipe he drew out of his bag.

The youngest children were lifted into the wagons beside the sacks and barrels of provisions. The older girls, who would tend to them on the way, climbed up beside them. But the main body of the children would go on foot, and these milled around behind the wagons, excited at the prospect of their adventure. Even the poorest of them had been provided with whatever could be spared: new aprons or jackets, pouches filled with seed, tools for working the ground or for carpentry, awls, chisels, whetstones, thimbles, combs, cooking pots, anything that could be carried by hand or slung over a pole. Because only the youngest among them were unused to work. So many were underfed, near-starvelings. The priest's heart hurt, looking at them, and he felt shamed. Some had parents and some had none, and some of the parents wept but most were dry-eyed and resigned. It was for the best, and it had already been decided.

Now the land agent leapt from the wagon and, before the priest could anticipate or object, mounted the church steps until he stood on a level with the priest. "Good people!" he cried, loudly enough to still the crowd's noise. "What bright fortune! What splendid prospects! Children! Have you prepared yourselves? Will you come with me to the new lands, to work and earn your bread? No, not bread, tell me what you like better." He leaned down and cupped his ear to the crowd below.

"Pancakes!" a child called out.

"Pancakes with honey!" another added.

"Apples and nuts!"

At each new suggestion, the agent stepped back in mock astonishment, making his comical faces. "So it's pancakes you want? Pancakes with honey and apples and nuts?"

A cheer rose from the crowd of children. "Well then, we'd best get started. Because, as the good Father has said, we have many hills to climb!"

Here the agent bowed to the priest, and the priest, irritated at being made into an actor in the agent's show, had no choice but to call for prayer. The people below him lowered their heads, and he asked God to bless those going forth, to protect and cherish them and bring them success and happiness in their new lives, Amen.

"Amen," the crowd echoed, and the drovers whipped up their horses and the children called out their final goodbyes. First, though, before they got under way, the agent reached into one of the wagons and lifted out a little boy who was so frail and sickly, it was likely that his parents had only given him up so as to be spared the expense of his burial. The agent held him up on his shoulder until a woman came to claim him, and as he passed the child over, the agent also reached into his leather bag and gave her a coin as charity.

That should have helped to ease the priest's mind, but dread still weighed on him. Yet it seemed as if he was the only one in all the crowd who was not cheering the agent on, delighted at the town's good fortune. People cleared out of the path as the wagons nudged forward. At the very head of the column, the agent piped a merry tune. Goodbye, goodbye!

The crowd re-formed around the last of the children and followed them a ways beyond the city's gates, then stood watching

as the road lengthened behind them and the piping music faded
and went silent.

The priest turned and went back into the church and climbed
up to the bell tower, whose windows faced in all directions. To
the north, the road the children had taken, he could see a portion of the blue river curving away, with knots of pale trees lin-
ing its bank. At the very edge of sight, a smudge that indicated
the foothills of the great mountains. If he strained his eyes he
could make out a handful of moving dust that must have been
the expedition. Already they were much farther along than he
would have guessed. The priest watched until he no longer
knew what he saw, the trail of dust or just his wish to see it.

Within two weeks of the departure, the fine weather turned to
a thin, blowy rain that fell in wind-driven sheets. People wondered if the children had reached their destination by now. The
distances the land agent had described were vague. The new settlements were said to be at the edge of the northern sea, or perhaps farther east, beyond a great forest. No one knew for certain,
and people debated uselessly over the different things they'd
heard.

A gray melancholy settled over the town along with the rain.
In the first days after the children's departure, there had been a
lot of nervous, excited talk (and of course, some tears among
the mothers), then bouts of bad temper, as if people had misgiv-
ings about the children leaving and were casting about for someone to blame. But the rain softened the sounds of the world and
wore away at the heart the same way it can, over time, hollow
out stone. Rain dripped and dripped from the eaves, footsteps

puddled, and no one looked out an open door or window for fear of getting drenched. It was so much quieter without the children. Of course not every single child in the town had been taken, but enough had gone away so that if a child was glimpsed in the street, being hurried along by a parent, or playing some solitary game, people often stopped to stare.

The priest sent his prayers up into the clouds, and they came down as rain. Consigning the children to prayer was a substitute for thinking about them, and in any case, nothing could be done for them now. There was enough in his daily round of study and ministry to keep him occupied, if not untroubled.

Then one night, just as he was preparing for bed, he heard, or imagined he heard, a knock at the small side door that led to his own quarters. He listened again. In the midst of the voices of water he heard a human voice, thin and beseeching. He took a lantern and hurried to unbolt the door.

A boy sat in the mud beside the door, drawn up as close as he could to the shelter of the roof. The priest recognized him as one of those who had left with the land agent, an orphan who had lived off others' meager leavings and so had been eager to join the agent's expedition. He was worn and wet and one leg was stretched out in front of him. The leg was dark with blood. The rain washed a thin line of it and sent it whirling away into the muddy street.

Greatly alarmed, the priest helped the boy to stand and come inside. He dried him off, built up the fire, and set him to warm in front of it. The housekeeper had already retired, and she was half deaf at the best of times, so the priest himself went searching for food and drink. Then he coaxed the boy into letting him examine the injured leg, which was ulcerated and matted with all manner of dirt and bark and even small stones.

"You must allow me to clean this," the priest said. He heated water in a kettle and set to work with a cloth and a basin of the hot water. The child was exhausted and fearful but he only flinched once while the priest tended to him, washing the leg and stanching the blood and binding the wound with a bran poultice. He did not begin crying until the priest asked, "And where are all the rest?"

"Lost," the boy said, breaking down. He sobbed and shook. The priest went cold inside. When the boy had calmed himself, the priest asked what had happened.

"We walked a long way. We passed beyond the last farms and fields and into places where no men lived. It was hot and the dust got into our mouths. At night we slept on the ground. The way grew steeper as we came to the mountains and the little ones were footsore. Still they urged us to go faster. On the sixth day I caught my leg between the tongue of the wagon and the harness. I was cut and bruised and I lagged behind until the others were nearly out of sight."

The boy touched his bandaged leg, as if to remind himself. He was no older than twelve, and small for his age, and the miseries of his life had stooped his shoulders and made his head seem too large for his body. The priest gave him a mouthful of wine to restore him, and he started in again.

"It was night by the time I reached them. The road ran along in a narrow way between two high cliffs. It was dark on the ground but when I looked up, I saw the sky and stars in a gulf between the cliffs. The stars were like a pale river running through the sky." The boy shook his head and looked away. "I believe it is the last thing I will ever call beautiful.

"I was close enough to hear and smell the horses, and to see the last light of the fire, and I hurried on because I was so glad I had found them, and so hungry. And just as I approached, there was a horrible noise from all around, because men had come down from the hills and were shouting in a language I did not know, striding through the camp and making the children scream. The smallest ones they had no use for, and these they clubbed down or killed with their long knives. There were those boys who tried to fight back and they too were overcome. The girls . . ."

"Tell me."

"They made of them brides," the child said, shyly. After a moment he went on.

"I hid myself behind a rock and no one saw me. Finally they were done. The men piled the wagons with everything of value and they tied those still alive together with a rope and made the long line of them follow behind the wagons. The men were pleased with their night's work and they were laughing and calling to one another as they passed farther into the mountains."

"Where was the land agent? What happened to him?"

"He spoke to the men in their strange language. He drove one of the wagons away."

The priest stayed silent. The boy touched his knee. "Father? I did a terrible thing. Once the men had gone and it was all quiet, I walked among the dead, looking for food. I took food from their pockets. I moved their bodies aside so I could find something to eat. I dug in the ashes of the fire for the leavings. I could have, perhaps I could have . . ."

"Father?"

The priest roused himself and put both hands hard on the boy's shoulders. "Listen to me. You will tell no one what happened. No one! Do you understand? When you came to the pass in the mountains, it was daylight, and you saw the children in a beautiful valley, filled with fruit trees and shining waters and singing birds and flower scent. And as you went to join them, the cliff face crumbled and the entrance was blocked. You found your way home as best you could. That is what you will say. Do you hear me?"

The boy looked frightened, unconvinced. "You will not say what you saw! When you think of them you are to think of them in heaven, because that is where they are. Say it for me."

"They are in heaven."

The priest released the breath he had been holding and took his hands away. "Lay yourself down and sleep. No harm will come to you. The church will provide for you from now on."

The boy allowed himself one brief, upturned glance, then lowered his eyes once more. He seemed to understand what would be required of him in his new life. "Let us pray for them," the priest said. He folded his hands and searched for words as he might have sent a bucket into a deep well to haul up water. "Let us . . ." he began again, but nothing else came to him.

THREE

The first Ryan brother was three years older than the next, and the second brother three years older than the last. Three by three. Everybody had gone to school with one of them, or just ahead or behind this or that one. Everybody knew them or knew of them: Richard, athletic, smart, and capable. Gabe, who was artistic and charming. And Tim, the youngest, who had yet to demonstrate any notable talents and was most often described as "quiet." Their father, in many ways a difficult man, used his youngest son to keep the edge of his anger sharp. "I guess you think the world owes you a living, well, think again. You want to be a big fat loser? Fine, but you better pay your own way. I'm talking sooner rather than later, buddy."

Tim let the angry complaints roll off him. He was used to hearing them, and anyway, his father was probably right. He was a year out of high school and he still lived at home, in the basement. He worked construction and took courses, fitfully, at the junior college. His older brothers had laid down such clear trails of their own that he had no inclination to follow either of them and risk being some paler version. If failure was the only unused avenue left to him, he guessed he would be a failure. He spent his time in the basement smoking pot and lifting, and sometimes he went out with his loser friends. His father wasn't really serious about making him leave, because he was useful at repairing things around the house, and besides, he was already paying rent.

The boys' mother had moved out a few years ago, on account of the father being difficult, and lived in a faraway city. She sent them postcards of the beautiful views there, the ocean, harbors, bridges, and beaches. *My dearest boy*—this was how she addressed each of them—*I never stop thinking of you day or night, please don't forget me. Love, Mom.*

Richard, the oldest brother, was made impatient by these cards. Their mother had chosen to leave, fine. She should stick with it, not keep circling back around, apologizing. *Don't forget me,* what did that mean? You weren't going to forget a mother, but you didn't necessarily have warm thoughts about one who ran off. It was true that his father wasn't the easiest guy in the world, but she'd known what she was signing up for, hadn't she? Why couldn't she have kept her part of the bargain, remained the same as she'd always been: weary, anxious, soothing, ineffectual?

Richard did not put his feelings into such exact words. It was not his habit. When his mother came to mind it was as something unpleasant, distressing, and then he pushed it aside. He had other things to worry about. He was working on a graduate degree in business, and it was killing him. It wasn't that the course material itself was so difficult, only that for the first time in his life, the people around him were every bit as smart and competitive as he was. Test scores were one thing, but there was another, more subtle evaluation going on at all times. Who could cut it, who was marked for success, and who would fall behind. You were expected to carry yourself a certain way, project a layer of ease and confidence over the necessary killer instincts. Some of this came effortlessly to him. He'd played basketball and tennis. He had a jock's practiced nonchalance with his own body, and a stubborn focus on winning. He was a careful and deliberate speaker, funny at unexpected moments, winning people over. People liked him, approved of him, spoke of his leadership qualities.

But what if, in a moment of weakness or carelessness, the bright face he showed to the world slipped? He would be found out, revealed as he was to himself in his times of self-doubting: gnawed and anxious and timid. A secret fraud.

It did not occur to Richard that everyone else might also have their own secret and fraudulent self.

He had a serious girlfriend and things had gone on for long enough that a marriage seemed likely. They hadn't really talked about it, but they'd talked around the edges. Richard would finish his degree and find a placement in a good firm, and then he would be ready to establish himself as a married man. In the meantime, his girlfriend worked at the kind of job that could be set aside if the two of them moved to another city, or had children. She took note of how other people arranged their bridesmaids and invitations. Everything seemed to be on track, except for those times when one of them had some unaccountable spell of petulance or bad temper, or when the whole notion of being *on track* seemed a kind of joke that nobody ever got.

They were driving home from a dinner with another couple, an old school friend of Richard's and his newish wife. They had attended the wedding the season before. "They seem really happy," the girlfriend offered.

"Uh-huh."

"What, you don't think they are?"

One of her habits that Richard disliked was this kind of eagerness to interpret, or overinterpret, the barest things he said. "I didn't say that."

"Well you didn't sound very convinced."

"I suppose I meant"—he cast about for something that might get him off the hook—"they seemed like they were trying too hard."

"Really?" She shifted in her seat, getting comfortable for a session of exhausting analysis. "I guess they were kind of gung-ho. Finishing each other's sentences, all those cracks about him starting fires when he barbecues."

"Like they were in some kind of sitcom," Richard said, surprising himself at having arrived, almost by accident, at what he really felt. His friend's display of marital happiness made him want to grind his teeth. It was as if he'd never known his friend, as if they had not passed through all their wild-ass years together, as if getting married made you a stranger to yourself and everybody else.

"A hilarious sitcom about young married life," she agreed. Once more stretching herself out in her seat, dangling her legs in a way she no doubt intended to be kittenish, provocative. "But how do you tell the difference? I mean, if people are really happy, or just trying to sell you on the idea? What do they do to convince you?"

"Nothing. You don't have to *act* genuine if you *are* genuine."

"Goodness, why are you in such a bad mood?"

"I'm not," Richard said heavily, because once again she was

too eager to ascribe meaning and motive, cause and effect, to everything. But of course, he was now actually in a bad mood, and he disliked having to answer questions.

"Could have fooled me." She turned to look out her window in pointed silence. Thank God, a stop to the rattling noise of conversation.

He focused on his driving, powering past the slower traffic with the sudden acceleration that he knew alarmed her. She braced herself against the dashboard and recrossed her legs. Her skirt was short and it rode up farther on her thighs when she sat. She was wearing stockings that gave her legs a glossy, impermeable look. As if she wore them to taunt and frustrate him, along with all the other obstacles between right now and any hope of ending up in bed together naked. Because he was going to have to climb out of his surly temper (which she had in part provoked!), say the right solicitous things, humble himself, cater to her, make harmless, cooing noises. And this was what he had chosen for himself, everything that awaited, married life, a blind road leading over a cliff.

"Rich! Jesus!"

He had almost ridden up the bumper of a slower car. He braked, cut into the next lane, downshifted to reduce his speed. Someone behind them laid on their horn, then the sound flattened, left behind in their wake. Richard looked over at her. "Sorry."

"What are you doing, are you drunk?"

"I spaced out. I said I'm sorry."

"God!" She had been scared and now she was angry, and she wasn't going to let it go. "You get in a pissy mood for no reason, and you act out with reckless driving? What are you, a teenager?"

He didn't answer, didn't rise to it, and she sighed and tried coming at him from another direction. "I thought you liked Ed and Charmaine. I thought you were looking forward to seeing them."

He did. He had been. He could not account for his irritation, anger, and beyond that, the wave of desolation crashing over him. How did anyone ever know the first thing about themselves? What they wanted, what they ought to want. How to go about inhabiting any place of calm or satisfaction, so that at the end of your life you could look back and say, yes, well done. Or maybe the whole idea of worthy goals was chafing at him, the notion that all of life was a duty, a test, a series of chores to be undertaken with discipline and fortitude. What if, at the last possible moment, a clamoring voice rose up in you and asked, Why didn't you seek out joy?

His girlfriend reached over and touched his arm and it made him jump, although he was careful to keep the steering wheel steady. She said, "I'm not your mother. I'm not going anywhere. I won't abandon you."

No, she would not. He would have to find some other way of getting rid of her.

Gabe, the second brother, understood his mother's absence from the family in terms of freedom, and freedom was a good thing, sure. His dad was probably a big part of her leaving, since his dad could be a real bastard when he put his back into it. But maybe there had been more to it, things his mother hadn't been able to do because she'd been tied down by the whole house-wife deal. Plenty of his friends' mothers seemed to feel that way. Now that their kids were grown they had begun taking pottery classes and yoga classes and Italian classes. Why couldn't his mother have stayed here and done the same? How far away from them did she have to go?

None of them knew what her life was like in her new city. Gabe tried to imagine her walking on a beach and picking up shells. But that didn't work, unless he changed other things about her, let her hair turn messy, the wind lifting and tangling it. She'd be wearing different clothes from her usual knit pants and sweaters, some kind of loose, flapping cotton. Was she a hippie now, hanging out with a bunch of other old, comical hippies? Did she burn homemade candles, live in a commune? That was the kind of thing somebody his mother's age might do if they were trying to be cool. Did his mother have any notion of coolness? Something completely unsuspected? Had she gotten tired of being just another mom-lady, had they, okay had he, not paid her enough attention, had she told herself nobody would even notice she was gone? The whole effort of thinking about her made him sad, because he didn't want to believe that he had never bothered to know her at all.

Gabe shared a downtown apartment with two friends, and with their occasional girlfriends. The three of them and a couple of other guys were in a band called the Fractions. They played at parties and clubs and were working on their first CD. Gabe was the lead singer and he wrote all of their songs. He stood at the front of the stage, the amplified instruments thundering around him, the lights bleared and blinding, and sang:

"Babe, I got nowhere to go
No more cards to show
If you put that big old hurt on me
If you say it's not to be
Oh you bring me down down down so low"

He was good-looking, in a blond, reedy fashion, and his voice could hit notes that were nearly liquid with yearning, and at every set there were girls who knew they would treat him a whole lot better than the girl in the song, if only they were given the chance.

Of course all the band members had other jobs, real jobs. There weren't any big paydays in music unless or until you got to some higher level. Meanwhile, they worked as bartenders and couriers, waiters and temp clerks, killing time until their big break. Maybe there would be a big break, or maybe there would just be the next band. The Fractions was only the latest in the series of bands Gabe had been a part of since high school, because musicians came and went, came and went.

Gabe waited tables at a Greek restaurant, where his good humor and attentiveness made him a favorite. A restaurant was also like a band in that people came and went, customers and employees too, all except for Nikos, the owner, and his chief cook, the ancient and blasphemous Sam. These two had spent the last thirty years, and most of their waking hours, working together and arguing and sending the same plates out full of food and taking them back again empty. Nikos ran the front of the house while Sam presided over the tiny, smelly kitchen, the repertoire of souvlaki and pastitsio and moussaka, cooking up lamb and fried cheese and swordfish with fennel and tomatoes. It was a neighborhood place that was losing its neighborhood. Nor was the restaurant hip enough or good enough to be a favorite of the young, adventurous dining crowd. It had settled into a slow, comfortable decline that seemed likely to last for a while.

Then Sam started losing it. He mixed up orders, or he let them burn while he went out into the alley for a smoke. Gabe apologized to customers and lost more and more tips. Nikos shouted at Sam in Greek and Sam swore back and that at least had not changed. Sam grew more and more confused, more and more furious. He stood and puzzled over raw chickens while the soup pots boiled over. He charged into the restaurant with a push broom, telling people eating to move their god-damn feet. Nikos had the prep cook fill in, until an enraged Sam went after the man with a ten-pound brick of frozen cuttlefish.

The prep cook quit, as did the dishwasher. The waitresses turned indolent and stole drinks from the bar. Nikos took over more and more of the kitchen work himself, a towel wrapped around his waist for an apron, mopping at the sweat on his fore-head so it wouldn't land in the food. "Why don't you let the guy go? Get a new cook?" Gabe ventured to ask, but Nikos shook his head.

"The poor bastard got noplace else. Nobody else. He stay here where we can keep an eye on him." He nodded at Sam, who was guarding the walk-in cooler with a corkscrew.

Clearly it was time for Gabe to move on. He was neglecting his music while he stayed here, working more and more hours for less and less money. He was an artist, after all, even if he was a fitful and struggling one, with ambitions that went beyond the daily, grubby toil of putting one coin next to another and then another. Everything in the restaurant spoke of age and defeat: the row of booths whose seats and backs showed patches of sil-ver tape, the red-lit, shrine-like bar, the cartoonish mural of a Greek fishing village with its foreshortened boats and houses and twin blue smears of sea and sky.

Gabe cashed in his tips, took off his clip-on tie and brocade vest and laid them on the cashier's stand. He was free to go. And he was glad for that, although he was coming to believe that in freedom there was also a good portion of selfishness, a refusal to be bound up in another's life.

"Psst! Buddy!" And here was Sam, cowering next to the coatrack, reaching out to Gabe with clawlike, scrabbling hands. "Buddy! You got to get me out of here!"

Tim missed his mother. She had been a good mother, calm and constant, nursing them through illness and injury, refereeing their tantrums, dispensing justice. She sang them nursery songs and read to them from the big storybook with the gilt-edged pages, stories about talking trees and magic lanterns and journeys to far places, stories with happy endings. She had been the sweet to the father's sour, interceding during his worst spells, talking him down from whatever high ledge he proclaimed himself ready to jump from. When you thought about it, the only surprise was that she'd put up with things as long as she had. But then, they could not bear to really think about it.

Tim was the baby of the family, he'd grown up constantly hearing it, and had absorbed all the teasing and humiliations involved. Being the baby implied that there was something favored about his position, that allowances were made for him, special treatment given, but also that he was weak and unworthy. So maybe it was a weakness to miss her, and he didn't say anything to the others.

Tim was the only one to see her the night she left. He'd been asleep, he was the kid who had slept through the tree falling on the roof—another one of the family jokes—but on this night, something woke him.

He opened his eyes to darkness. He still slept upstairs then, and from the kitchen he heard small, snicking sounds, as of someone trying to be careful about opening and closing drawers.

Tim got up and went to the head of the stairs. A dim fluorescent light was turned on, the light over the kitchen sink. The furtive sounds continued. It would not have alarmed him if there had been more light, more noise, one of his brothers or his father pawing through the refrigerator, as they did often enough.

He eased himself down, stair by stair, his heart beating fast, the roof of his mouth dry, wondering if he should have grabbed a bat or golf club or something, wondering if he'd really be able to do that, take a swing at somebody. At the bottom of the stairs he angled himself to get a better view of the room, then stepped inside. "Mom? What are you doing?"

His mother turned and gave him a weird, almost hostile look, then she tried to rearrange her face into its usual Mom-like exasperation. "Nothing. Go back to bed."

"What are you doing?" Tim repeated. The clock over the stove read two a.m. She was dressed to go out, including shoes and her puffy jacket. "Are you going somewhere?"

"I can't find . . ." She kept her voice at a whisper. "There used to be a flashlight here someplace."

"Why do you need a flashlight?"

"Shhh. I just thought it would be . . . a good thing to have." She opened a drawer, closed it, then gave up and stood in the center of the room, waiting for Tim to either go away, or— what? What was he supposed to do?

"Should I go get Dad?" he asked, but his mother raised both hands, shaking her head, and in one hand were her car keys, and next to the garage door he saw the suitcase, which had been there all along. "Mom, what the hell?"

"Oh, sweetie." She came toward him, hugged him. The puffy coat enveloped him and, somewhere beneath it he felt her small, unquiet arms. "I am so sorry. I didn't want to have to tell any of you, I know that's cowardly, but it was the only way I could do it. I'm sorry."

"Do what?" he said, although by now it was beginning to form, even as he did not yet believe it. "Where are you going?"

She stepped back from him, sagged and shrank into herself. "I don't know. I haven't thought that much about it."

They were still whispering. "Did you and Dad . . ." He didn't believe he was asking these things. ". . . have a fight or something?"

"Not really. He didn't do anything, I mean, anything different." His mother looked down at her suitcase, as if waiting for it to take part in the conversation.

"So . . ." It was all too confounding. "When are you coming back?"

She didn't answer. She did not mean to come back. His heart hardened.

She said, "You could come with me. Sure you could. I'll wait for you to get dressed, go get dressed and pack some clean clothes. I'd feel so much better if you came too. I thought I wanted to be alone but I don't, really. I just don't want to be here in the middle of everything. Everybody. Please come."

"Mom, this is so crazy."

"Maybe it is." She tried laughing, but bit off the end of it. "We can go wherever you want. We'll get maps. See the big wide world. We'll live like pirates, you always liked those pirate movies, didn't you?"

He didn't like the way she was talking, rushed and fake. She didn't sound like herself. "No, Mom."

"You could drive. I'll show you how."

He was only fourteen. The idea of going somewhere, any-where, was nothing he was prepared for. What was she asking of him? He could not do it. He was too young and unready. Fear made him harsh. "Yeah, and if I hadn't shown up you would have left. Or if somebody else came downstairs you'd say the same to them."

"No."

"Sure you would. It's all bullshit."

"No, baby. It's really, really hard."

"Because you don't care about any of us. You're mad at Dad so you decide to take off, the hell with anybody else. Did you even leave him a note, huh?"

He was talking louder now, he watched her register this, watched her visibly droop and despair, knowing he could keep her here if he chose, either by raising the alarm or by simple guilt. Instead, from some confusion of hurt and spite and sym-pathy, he picked up her suitcase and opened the garage door. "Come on."

His mother followed without objecting, and that was how Tim knew she truly wanted to leave. He put the suitcase in the trunk and opened the driver's door for her. He let her hug him again, giving nothing back, and watched her face through the car windshield as she mouthed Goodbye, Sorry, Love You. Then she looked over her shoulder to back the car out, and when she was clear of the garage he put the door down again.

Once it was established that she was gone, they didn't much talk about her among themselves. The father's official attitude was, If that's what she wants, screw her, and it was difficult to tell if that was the extent of his feelings. In time, Richard and Gabe moved out and only came around when they needed to retrieve some of the things they'd stored in the garage or the attic. Every so often, the father assembled them in restaurants to mark occasions like birthdays and the unavoidable holidays. The wifeless house resisted celebrations.

For Tim's graduation from high school last spring, they ate Mexican food at a chain restaurant and his brothers passed him a number of slurpy strawberry margaritas. He drank them down and let them do their thing. He wasn't accustomed to being the center of anyone's attention, and he was glad when the reason for the gathering seemed to recede from view. The father held the menu close up, then at arm's length, as if trying to decipher a secret message. "What the hell are flautas?"

"Just get nachos, Dad, you'll be happier," Richard said. He wasn't drinking anything but water. He'd put on some weight since his days of playing team sports and he was trying to work it off.

"They're these fried tortilla things with stuff inside them," Gabe said. "I know, they sound like they have something to do with farts." He liked to keep the jokes going when he was around the rest of them.

Tim sniggered. "Fartas, huh."

"I'd like mine with beans, please."

The two of them laughed like fools. "Another intellectual evening," Richard remarked. He was glad he hadn't brought his girlfriend along, although everyone might have behaved better if she'd come.

The father put his menu down. "What I really want is a steak, they have steak here? Whose idea was it to come to this place anyway?"

"Mine," Tim said. "I bet they have steak, Dad. We can ask the waitress. Or you could get steak fajitas."

"Ah, never mind. I can get steak some other time." The father was making an effort. He ordered the combo platter and looked around at the walls, which were decorated with sombreros and paper flowers and some gloomy, icon-like pieces of painted tin. "This is nice. A little atmosphere. I don't guess it's authentic or anything."

"It's authentic Mexican restaurant," Gabe offered. Tim thought this was funny too. He was buzzed. He was hoping nobody asked him, for the hundredth time, what he was going to do after graduation, and so far they hadn't. He was relieved to be done with school. He'd only promised to sign up for the community college courses to get everybody off his back. They weren't anything you had to keep doing.

The father's attention stirred then, and landed on Tim, probably because he'd been trying so hard to avoid it. "So," the father said. "The graduate."

"Yup."

"With your whole life before you," the father intoned, making it sound funereal.

"Yup."

"Is that all you know how to say? That's brilliant. Your education has served you well. For something. At least try not to join the goddamn army. There's a shooting war going on, they need cannon fodder."

"Who said he was joining the army?" Richard asked. "Why even bother worrying about it? You weren't going to run off and enlist, were you, Timmy?"

Tim shrugged. "Maybe I'd be good at it." He had a moment's vision of how it would be, the hard parts of running and drilling and the people whose job it was to make you miserable, and how he would suck it up, take everything they dished out.

"Good at getting shot?" The father ha ha-ed.

"At being a soldier. It's something you can be good at."

"Seriously?" Gabe said. "You'd want to do that? Serve your country?"

"I didn't say I wanted to. Just, I could if I had to."

The father said, "Well you don't have to now, it's all volunteer. Volunteer, that's one word for it. These days it's kids signing up for the bonus money. The dead-enders who don't have anything else going for them."

The sons were suddenly occupied with eating, giving it their total attention. The father wished he had not said that last, since it was a pretty good description of his youngest son. His wife had always said he was too hard on him, and Tim wasn't someone who responded to bullying, her name for it. Of course she had always shielded him, taken Tim's side. Her baby boy. It made him angry at his wife all over again, but of course she wasn't here, and so he was obliged to be angry at Tim instead.

The sons didn't look at one another, but all of them recognized the familiar destination of their family outings. The father always worked himself into one or another variety of bad mood. Look at him jabbing and stabbing at his food, as if it wasn't quite dead enough on the plate. They were used to him, his outsized and demanding presence in their lives. Of course they were resolved never to be like him. As if it would be hard to avoid falling into such an obvious, gaping hole, such an abyss! And yet each of them was afraid of finding in themselves some part of him: his arrogance, his anger, his loneliness.

Tim always wondered if it was his fault that his mother had not come back. Maybe if he had gone with her he might have talked her into returning, sooner or later. He would have known what to say and his mother would have admitted that things weren't all that bad, she had just needed to get away for a little while. A happy ending, which meant everything going back to the way things were.

Instead there was this waiting and waiting, while the thing you were waiting for kept not happening, as his life itself was not yet really happening.

That Thanksgiving, the father surprised them by announcing that they were all invited—that is, expected—home. The father said that he and "a friend" would be preparing the holiday meal. What friend? the sons asked, and the father said she was just a lady he knew.

Tim got phone calls from Richard and from Gabe, asking him what was going on. Was the father dating somebody? *Dating*, meaning, having sex. Richard said, "That would be just weird. I mean, he and Mom are still married."

"Actually, it's weird that they're still married," Tim said.

"Yeah, okay. Who is this 'friend'?"

"No clue."

"Has he been going out at night, bringing women back to the house?"

"Not that I've noticed."

"Noticed? You do live there, don't you?"

Tim didn't answer. There were days when he and his father only saw each other in passing, or not at all. Neither of them did any real cooking either, which made the prospect of a Thanksgiving dinner that much more difficult to imagine.

Richard broke the silence on his end. "I guess I'll be there. It's not like I have to be anywhere else." He had recently called things off with his longtime girlfriend.

Another silence drooped between them. Tim said, "It'll be all right. It's just a dinner."

"Why is it so hard for people to . . ." Richard trailed off.

"To what?"

"I don't know. Stick with the plan. All right, see you Thursday."

Gabe called next. "Hey bro, what in the world? The old man's stepping out?"

"Looks like."

"Damn. Should we be happy about it?"

"I guess it depends on the lady." Tim tried to match his brother's jaunty tone. He had no idea, really, what sort of woman would take up with his father. It was even harder to think of his father engaged in courtship, making the kind of effort required to charm and attract. Maybe it had been one of those online things.

Gabe said he hoped she could cook, whoever she was, and Tim said that would be a plus. Their mother had a repertoire of dishes that nobody else in the world made exactly as she did: chicken pie, short ribs, sausage and macaroni, lemon cake. Was it childish and stupid to miss her for her cooking?

"Anyway," Gabe said, "he's at least trying to go forward. Mom made her move, he's finally making his."

"Do you think he ever talked to Mom after she left? Tried to change her mind?"

"Doesn't sound like something he'd do. Even if he did, he wouldn't tell us."

"Not if it didn't work."

"Huh." Gabe considered this. "He wouldn't in the first place."

"Maybe he should."

"Dude, that train has left the station."

"Mom's not a train," Tim said, irritated at how easily his brother seemed to be dismissing her.

"Well, duh. But honestly, guy, you ought to be more worried about Dad's new girlfriend moving in and wanting to paint the bathroom pink."

"You know, not everything is some hilarious moron joke."

"Whoa, where did that come from? This little wounded-sensitivity thing?"

"Forget it," Tim said, retreating.

"You think you're the only one who has to deal? Huh?"

"No."

"I do the best I can. You don't have to like it. In fact, I don't give a rusty fuck if you do or not. See you Thursday. I'll have to leave early, we have a band practice."

The father prepared for Thanksgiving by consulting a grocery list and bringing home a turkey and all the things that went along with turkey, the bags and jars and cans. There was an effort at cleaning. Tim swept the front porch and used the leaf blower on the driveway because the father fretted about the house making a good impression, which told Tim that she hadn't been there before.

"What's her name?" he asked, the night before Thanksgiving, when the father was digging around in the good china, trying to find things like gravy boats and pickle dishes.

The father looked like he was wondering if this was a trick question. "Francine."

"That's pretty."

The father gave him a look of deep suspicion. "Where do you guys know each other?" Tim asked, pushing his luck.

"Through some friends."

"Yeah?" His father didn't have any friends. Tim thought it was what you said when you met somebody in a bar. "Well it's really nice of her to come over and help with Thanksgiving."

"Yes, it's very nice of her, and I don't want any attitude from anybody."

Tim retreated to the basement for the rest of the evening. He woke up late the next morning to industrious sounds coming from the kitchen overhead. Cupboards slammed, pots and dishes collided, water ran in the sink. High-heeled shoes trotted across the floor, then his father's more lumbering tread, the woman laughing, saying something with a teasing lilt to it. More of the collisions and thumps. It sounded like a herd of cattle, flirting.

He took his time showering and getting dressed. Good smells were percolating through the house: onions, sage, roasting bird. When he climbed the stairs to the landing just off the kitchen, his father said, "Come on in here, don't just skulk around. Francine, this is my youngest, Tim."

The father was wearing a sporty plaid shirt that Tim had not seen before. The father caught him staring at it and Tim looked away.

Francine said, "Why, you two could be twins. Hi Tim, I'm so pleased to meet you." She held out her hand and they shook, though there was a moment when he thought she might be preparing to hug him, and he braced himself. She was short, curvy, thick-bottomed, perfumed, with curly dark hair and a made-up face. She wasn't going to quit smiling. She was doing her damnedest.

Tim said he was pleased to meet her also. He and his father avoided each other's eye. Neither of them believed they could be mistaken for twins, or wanted to believe it. "Wow, look at this food," Tim said, safely diverting the conversation. "Did you do all this?"

"I made the pies last night," Francine said. "Everything else, your dad helped. Oh of course you did. You got that big old heavy turkey in the oven for me." Francine made as if to squeeze the father's arm, then thought better of it and veered away. The father looked glum.

"Can I help with anything?" Tim asked.

"You can find the good wineglasses and set them out," his father said. "Try not to break them."

"I brought some Chianti," said Francine, wagging a bottle. "It goes with anything. Can I pour you some? Oh, but you haven't had breakfast yet. Are you hungry, hon? Can I fix you anything?"

The food smells were making the sides of his empty stomach rub together, but it was just too weird, seeing Francine wearing one of his mother's aprons, addressing him with her same anxious concern, and while Tim didn't necessarily dislike Francine, he was pretty sure he disliked her being here. He said he'd grab something to eat later, thanks.

Richard arrived at the appointed time, and then Gabe, and both were presented to Francine. "I just can't decide which of you is handsomer," she declared, seeming to involve all four of them in the competition. She gave the father a mirthful look. "Now you know I'm just kidding."

"Ha ha," said the father, gamely.

"He's kind of a sexy daddy, isn't he?"

Nobody said anything. The brothers all wondered just how far things had gone. There was a hectic, unconsummated quality to such talk.

"So Francine," Gabe said, rescuing them, "do you always

cook a big Thanksgiving dinner? I mean, this is huge." He indicated the kitchen, where ranks of serving dishes were deployed, waiting to receive all the different foods that were baking, stewing, browning.

"Oh, not always. Not when it's just me. But I'm Italian, see, and we always did food in a big way. I miss that. You know?"

They said they knew, yes. About missing things.

"So when your dad said he didn't have any plans, I thought, why not? Why not make the effort. Food, it's such a universal whaddyacallit. Language. My grandma? Nonna? She didn't speak a word of English, but everything she cooked spoke of love."

"That's nice," Richard said. He had adopted a stoic, ironic manner that the father liked to call "wiseass."

Francine said, "She passed away two years ago from this horrible cancer. It got into her brain and made her spit at the people who were taking care of her. Spit, spit, spit." She put her wineglass down, picked it up again.

It was then that the rest of them realized she was rather drunk, in a voluble way.

"I'm sorry to say, once she died, a lot of family things just fell apart. There has been some very negative behavior. From my supposed nearest and dearest."

They all nodded. Sure. Unfortunate.

"But listen to me, such a bringdown, and anyway I'm not going to waste any more breath on the son of a bitch. Well, back to work." She headed into the kitchen, walking with care on her high heels.

There was a football game on, and the three brothers sat in the den to watch while they waited for dinner. The father stalked in and out, keeping track of the score. It was hard to tell if he was happy or embarrassed or what. From time to time, Francine came in, holding herself erect, humming under her breath, carrying plates of cheese and crackers, or olive spread, or little sausages baked in biscuit wraps. "Now, don't spoil your appetite!"

They were all drinking beers by now, slamming them back just to cope with the strangeness of everything. Increasingly, it felt as if they had been assembled under false pretenses. They watched the football players collide and get up and do it all over again, and though they didn't talk among themselves, little cartoon thought bubbles were almost visible over their heads. This was a bad idea, and, Who is this gal anyway?

Scraping noises came from the kitchen, then they heard Francine say, "Phooey." The dropped lid of a pot rang on the floor. "Ouch!"

"Need any help in there?" the father called.

"No, no, it's really easier if everybody stays right where they are!"

The brothers looked at the father, who shrugged. "She's used to running her own kitchen," he said, but he got up and went in to see what he could do.

Eventually the dinner was ready. Some portion of the food had not made it to the table, and some of it was missing components, but there was enough variety and volume to smooth it over. "That damned turkey," Francine said cheerfully. "The little thermometer thing popped out too early, the drumsticks were all red and bloody."

"There's plenty of white meat," the father said as a warning, and the brothers all murmured that white meat was really their favorite.

Francine filled her plate but wasn't eating. "Come on," the father said, noticing. "Don't tell me you spent all day cooking and you aren't going to have any."

"I promise I'll get around to food," Francine said. She dipped a finger in her wineglass and put the finger in her mouth. "Right now I need a little vacation from it. How's that stuffing, Ray?"

She meant Rich, but they let that go. "Real good," he said. "Tip-top."

"I apologize for the gravy. Gravy's not one of my strong suits."

"It's fine, Francine," the father said. "You're not going to hear anybody complaining."

"They are wonderful young men. You're wonderful too. In your own way. But I can see how you all might take up so much room, you'd make a woman sick at heart."

They all ate quietly for a time, then Tim asked to be excused. He took his plate to the kitchen, then went downstairs and fired up his pipe, blowing the smoke into the bathroom exhaust fan.

A little later, he heard Francine's high heels on the stairs. "Hi," she said. "You mind? I'm making what they call a strategic retreat in good order."

She was already descending. "Sure," Tim said. "Be my guest."

"You are so busted! I don't suppose I could have some of that pot."

He waited for Francine to get comfortable on the other end of the couch, then passed the pipe to her. Her lipstick had rubbed off and it made her look shifty and blurred, like an out-of-focus photograph. She drew in the smoke and coughed, but managed to hold it in. "Thanks," she said. "I can feel a definite mellowing. My Nonna? Every year before the holidays she'd go down to the hospital, and I'd go with her and help her take out her hairpins and her earrings and take off her rings, and she'd get a good old-fashioned electric shock treatment, and then she'd be fine to come home and cook cook cook for everybody."

"Whatever it takes, I guess."

"I shouldn't have said that, about your mom. I mean, what do I know?"

Tim kept silent. She said, "That doesn't necessarily mean it was wrong."

"Families are messed up," Tim offered, not sure if he was saying something wise, or just being a jerk. His brain felt sludgy.

They passed the pipe back and forth a few times. Francine said, "I made apple and pumpkin pies. I forgot to ask what kinds you guys like."

"Those are both great, really."

Francine squinted at him through the pillowy smoke. "You're a nice kid. You're tired of being the baby, aren't you. Who could blame you." She stood, steadied herself on the couch back, then bent over Tim and kissed him on the top of his head. "Bye now."

"Bye," Tim said, but by then she had already climbed the stairs and was gone.

He waited awhile longer, though he could not have said how long, until everything was quiet upstairs. The kitchen was empty except for the wreckage of pots and pans and plates strewn about. In the dining room, his brothers sat on each side of the cleared table. "Where's Dad?"

"He'll be back. Sit down," Rich said.

"Where's—" Tim began, but Gabe made a gesture with his thumb and closed fist, the sign of an umpire signaling, "You're out." Tim sat.

The father came back in and put a piece of notebook paper on the center of the table.

"That's her address. I couldn't find a phone."

Tim almost asked, Who? But there was no need. The father said, "You have to talk to her. Get her to come home."

The brothers kept silent. The thought bubbles above their heads were blank. Finally Richard said, "Dad, we can try and talk to her, but you're the one she ought to hear from."

"She won't believe a word I say."

They considered the truth of this. Gabe said, "So why now? I mean, it's been a pretty long—"

"How many more nights like this you think I can stand?"

At first they were embarrassed, then, one at a time, they began to snigger and giggle, half-choking on the laughs they tried to keep down.

"She was a handful."

"A pistol."

"A work of art."

"I hope you didn't give her a house key, Dad."

The father lowered his head into his folded arms on the tabletop, and only gradually did they realize that he was sobbing rather than laughing.

Should they comfort him, or pretend it wasn't happening? There was no history for this, no guide for the pure awfulness of it. Finally Richard reached for the piece of paper like a man picking up the check in a restaurant. "It's okay, Dad. I'll help you. We'll think of something."

Richard and the father wrote a letter—that is, Richard wrote it and the father read it over and said, after much scowling and gritting of teeth, that it was all right. The letter spoke of the father's regrets that he had so often lost his temper over so many unimportant things. He understood now that he had been hard to live with, that he had too often ignored her or taken her for granted. He respected the choice that she had made, he hoped that she was happy in her present situation ("Situation!" the father said, rolling his eyes), since happiness was more important than anything else. ("No it isn't," the father said, but Richard insisted on leaving it in.) And he hoped that with his new, changed attitude, they could resume their life together, make a fresh start. The father enclosed a generous check, emphasizing that there were no strings attached and she should spend the money in any way she wished.

They mailed it off and waited. The next week, the check was returned, with *So kind. But I don't need money* written on the memo line.

Next Gabe said he'd take a turn. He thought about what he wanted to tell her, how he thought he understood her, or at least wanted to understand. Then he holed up in his apartment with his guitar, and after a number of false starts and late nights, he produced a tape of himself singing:

> *"A heart that's free is a lonesome bird*
> *It flies so high, no one can follow*
> *Is it an eagle or a swallow?*
> *Sometimes it hears a distant word*
> *Was it a yesterday or tomorrow?"*

There were two other verses, about the bird soaring over land and sea, and all the wonderful things it saw, and then turning in its flight and riding a strong wind home.

The mother sent a postcard, a picture of a seagull soaring over the ocean waves. *So beautiful. But I am not a bird.*

The father despaired. "I wonder if I could make things up with Francine," he said, meaning it mostly as a joke, but not entirely.

"I could try," Tim said. "I mean, try to talk to Mom."

"You?" The father was lying on the sofa with his arm over his face. He was shielding his eyes from the overhead light, which he always said was too bright, but the gesture gave him a tragic aspect. Now he sat up. "What could you do?"

Tim shrugged. "Maybe I could drive out and see her."

The father studied him. Tim said, "It's slow at work. They can't use me that much anyway."

"Boy, one of these days you'll have to find yourself a real job. I suppose you want to take my car."

But Tim said no, he'd just take his truck. So he loaded it up with some camping supplies in case he decided to camp, his clothes, and food that would be easy to eat, packages of crackers and lunch meat. Before he left, the father took out his wallet and extracted a quantity of bills. "Here. In case the battery craps out, anything like that."

Tim thanked him and they shook hands. Then he said, "What should I tell Mom if she asks me why anything would be different? If she came back."

The father thought about this. "Tell her, now I know she can leave if she wants to."

In the rearview mirror, Tim saw him standing in the driveway, looking helpless and irritated.

He drove all that first day and into the night. The land didn't change much, farm fields, mostly, and the highway straight as tape. He stopped and got a room at a truckers' motel, something he had never done on his own, and he half-expected somebody to tell him he was too young or in some other way prohibited from making such transactions, but no one did.

The next day was much like the first. He played his music and ate some of the food he'd brought, and watched the highway signs announce the different destinations. At sunset he pulled into a roadside campground with a shallow green lake, and pitched his tent at a campsite on its far end. It was still chilly at night and he bought firewood from a gas station out on the highway and got a fire going in the burn pit. He ate the hamburgers he'd bought and watched the play of the flames and the smooth dark water beyond.

Music from somebody's radio reached him from a campsite farther down the shore. He could see people dancing in the light, and shadows from a lantern hung on a tree branch. A girl walked out of the darkness and stood at the edge of the firelight. "That's a nice fire you got going," she said.

"Thanks."

"You mind if I sit here for a while? Some of the guys we came with are kind of jerks."

Tim said that would be fine. She sat down on one of the cement blocks that ringed the burn pit. She'd brought two beers with her and asked if he wanted one, and Tim said he did. She had long, pretty hair that picked up the colors of the fire, copper and red. "Are you from around here?" she asked.

"No. Just stopped off for the night."

"That's too bad," she said. "I could use a new friend."

"I'm just here for the night," Tim said again. A log burned through and collapsed in a flurry of sparks.

"Well, that doesn't have to be a big problem."

In the morning she kissed him and said she'd better be getting back before her friends finished sleeping it off. He watched her walk away down the trail, hopping from one stepping stone to another.

That day he came to the mountains. The truck's engine labored in the thinner air, and his head too slowed down. Tim drove up and up, around the mountains' curves, and got out at the observation post at twelve thousand feet. The peak was bare of trees, and snow frosted the scrub growth. The lack of oxygen made him clumsy. He didn't stand there long, in case he took a wrong step and fell all the way to the bottom of the world.

That night he camped in one of the park campgrounds, where the rangers handed out warnings about fires, hypothermia, animals. It was too cold to sleep in the tent, and so after a couple of hours he got up and tried to stretch out in the truck's front seat. He didn't sleep well, imagining he heard stealthy, blundering sounds around him, and once, when he raised his head to look, he saw a piece of the darkness detach itself and move unhurriedly away. He watched for long enough to be sure he wasn't making it up, and then he lay down and slept.

Once he left the mountains, he hurried through the brown country that lay beyond. He passed little desert towns spread out along the highway like spilled bones. The truck's air-conditioning petered out to a current of lukewarm air. He rigged some of his shirts over the windows for shade. The desert was so big and empty, it canceled out any memory of green or coolness. He had never been more alone in his life. He felt how being alone might be something to exult about.

Here was another range of mountains that he had not expected, but that was all right, since he was willing to be surprised by things. There was a snow squall at the top of the pass and the truck's tires kept skidding sideways, and it took almost an hour to get down to where it was only raining. Not until he reached that point did he allow himself to imagine how it might have felt, sliding off the road's edge in a cage of crumpling metal.

Then he came out of the mountains, and here was the very end of the highway, and the city where his mother lived, and the street and the house where she lived. Tim went straight there and rang the bell.

She opened it and they knew each other right away. She was a little thinner and grayer. She hugged him and stepped back to look at him and then hugged him again. "You've grown up," she said.

He told her all about his trip (except for the part about the girl): the long highway and the mountains and the campfires and the desert and driving through the snow on the pass, and she shook her head and said, "Some of that sounds a little dangerous."

"I guess."

Tim rested while the mother went out for groceries. She cooked a dinner of his favorite foods, and while they were eating, Tim said, "Dad wants you to come home."

"I know."

"You don't have to just because he wants you to."

"It's nice here," the mother said, folding her napkin into pleats. "But there are many things I miss. Including him. I don't expect you to understand."

Tim kept silent. "Hey," the mother said. "Don't look like that. It killed me to leave. I died and went to guilt heaven. But it would have killed me to stay too. You don't know what you really want until you end up doing it. Are you done eating? Let's go for a walk."

Fog was rolling and roiling in from the west, turning the sunset bleary. The mother said there was a place where they could see the ocean, and so they walked down a street of stucco buildings with red tile roofs, to a barricade at the end. Far below it was a wide beach and the crashing ocean waves. The air was chilly gray, and the mother took Tim's arm and leaned into him. "We have so much to catch up on. And when we get back, so much to set to rights."

"I won't be going home with you," Tim said, and the mother stepped away from him, searching him with her look.

"I'd like to try living somewhere else. Doing something else. I could learn how to do a lot of different jobs."

"Tim."

"I give him the excuse he needs to be angry. It's always been that way. It'll be better for you if I'm not there. Better for me too."

"Do you feel you have to do this for me, honey?" The fading light turned her face and hair silvery. "You don't. Your father can change his ways. Don't give me a brand-new sorrow."

Tim shrugged. "Sometimes you don't know what you really want until you end up doing it."

"I have never blamed you for anything that night. How could I? You were just a child."

"Well I'm not now, am I."

They watched the moving water for a while, until the pale sun vanished and drew the remaining day with it, and then they started back.

The eldest brother sent the princess a casket filled with gold, and the second brother sent her a bird that sang the sweetest songs. But the youngest brother said, "I have no gift to offer, only a tale to tell, and at the end of the tale, I will speak no more. I give you all my unsaid words from this day forth, the secret names of everything I love."

THE CURSE

The parents were not home—they were the kind of parents who went places at night—and so Massey kept watch, parked on a side street half a block away. It was cold enough for the car windows to steam over and he rubbed a section of glass every so often to clear it. The house was a single-story brick ranch, a design so ordinary and utilitarian that even if you had not been inside it, as Massey had not, you knew its components. Three bedrooms, two baths, kitchen with breakfast nook, the family room arranged for the worship of television. But at night it took on a dim and secret look, all the windows covered over with blinds and swaddling curtains.

Phoebe's car, the Civic they let her drive, was parked in front. It was almost ten o'clock and Massey had been watching for more than an hour, his attention diffuse, wandering. Now and then a car rolled down the street, but none of them pulled into the driveway behind Phoebe. Other houses showed lights, people watching the news, finishing up the dishes, collapsing into the end of their days. He had no particular curiosity about them. He was almost peaceful sitting here, or at least he would not be peaceful anywhere else.

Massey's phone buzzed. It was a text from Phoebe: *I see you*.

Massey started the car, putting the heat on high. He'd kept it off because a running car was more conspicuous. So much for that. He drove the mile back to his own house, the headlights sweeping across its frozen lawn. He waited for the garage door to roll up, slid into his space, parked, and went in through the kitchen.

"Me," he announced, in case anyone was paying attention. Lila was probably upstairs reading. His son was in the den, playing one of his computer games. Massey stood behind the screen and to one side of it until the boy was forced to acknowledge him. "Time to wrap it up, Kev."

"All right," his son said, still distant, absorbed.

Massey got a Coke from the refrigerator and sat at the kitchen table. Phoebe was going to take her time coming home just to demonstrate that she could ignore him, and her curfew. And probably to make a point about how pissed off she was. It would be better to have all that out in the kitchen.

He heard the garage door twenty minutes later. Phoebe came through the door ready for battle. She said, "I do not freaking believe you."

"You were supposed to be home at ten."

"Yeah, and you were supposed to be doing what?" She was blazing. The cold and the anger turned her cheeks red, a delicate flaring and fading of blood. "This is such shit."

"Watch your mouth."

"You know what we were gonna do? Order a pizza and have them deliver it out to the car. God, you are just incredible."

"That's about enough." From the sounds in the next room, Massey could tell that Kevin had registered the argument and was retreating upstairs.

"So did you observe any, you know, criminal activities? Was I cheating on my Spanish homework? Because that's what Maura and I were doing." Phoebe hesitated just long enough so that Massey knew she wasn't sure about what came next, how to best sustain her anger, and that gave him some advantage.

He said, "If you weren't doing anything wrong, then you've got nothing to worry about."

Phoebe gave him a look of tight-mouthed hatred, then walked to the base of the stairs. "Mom!"

They both waited. It wasn't a thorough fight until Lila got involved. Phoebe dumped her backpack. Massey glanced at an ad circular on the kitchen table. They heard Lila moving in the upstairs hallway, a grim, stalking tread. Phoebe came back into the kitchen. Massey counted the stairs as Lila came down: twelve, thirteen, fourteen. She was wearing her bathrobe and the fabric made small crinkling sounds.

"What's so important that I have to get out of bed?" Her disgusted look took in both of them. She already knew.

"He's been spying on me again."

"Not spying."

"Hanging around Maura's house like some pervert!"

"Her parents weren't there," Massey said, addressing Lila. "She neglected to mention that."

"They went out to a movie! God, now he wants to tell them what to do too."

"If there aren't going to be any adults in the house, we need to be aware of that."

"What, I need a babysitter? Why don't you just lock me in my room?"

Lila sat down at the kitchen table, opposite Massey. There was a jar of hand cream on the lazy susan; she opened it and rubbed some into her knuckles. "We've talked about this," she said. "Dave, we had an agreement."

"Honey," Massey said to Phoebe, "it's not you I don't trust. Or Maura. But say other kids stopped by, even kids you knew and thought were your friends. It's just so easy for things to get out of control."

"He means, have sex," Phoebe informed her mother. "Maybe I should, just so everybody can stop worrying about it."

"No," Massey said, meaning, Stop talking.

"Because then I'll be, you know, defiled. A lost cause."

Lila said, "If you mean that as a joke, it's not funny."

"No, see, it's hilarious. I can post it on Facebook: Finally lost it! I can—"

"Not one more word!" Massey shouted, so loud and thundering that it made them both flinch, jarred their expressions of hard contempt into something like fear. And he knew he could do this, roar and stamp and overwhelm them, just as he knew he would be made to regret doing so.

It didn't take them long to recover and to close ranks against him. His wife said, "Really, Dave. Yelling doesn't help anything."

His daughter said, "See? See how he acts?" She shook her head and her bright hair slipped across her shoulders. They looked so much alike. Two versions of the same fair-skinned, fine-boned woman. His wife softened and weary, his daughter all sharpness and quick anger. And now neither of them was on his side.

"What you need to understand, honey," he began, hoping to win them over with calmness and care, "is that nobody ever plans on terrible things happening—well, normal people don't. But sometimes they do happen. Given the opportunity. The circumstances. Say that there's alcohol involved. Other stuff. Don't roll your eyes, you want to tell me I'm wrong? Nobody ever brings anything to a party? I'm not saying the boys you know aren't good guys, most of them, I'm not saying they would ever set out to hurt you—"

"But they are, of course, easily inflamed hormonal dirtbags and you can't take your eye off them for a second. Nice. Kevin has so much to look forward to. Are we done? I still have to read a chapter for history."

Massey said nothing. Lila said, "Don't stay up too late." Phoebe sniffed and left the room and took her time on the stairs.

Lila said, "You can't keep doing this. It's unhealthy. For you and her both. And it doesn't work."

"All right."

"And this time you mean it."

Massey gave her a heavy, irritated look, but he'd left himself nothing to say.

Lila got up from the table and went to the sink, running water and making a racket with the plates. The bathrobe made her look bulky and insulated. "You think I don't worry about the same things you do? Like I haven't imagined every horrible situation? Of course I have. I'm her mother. But if you push her and push her like this, she'll end up doing something stupid out of spite."

"She doesn't need to be going out on a school night," Massey said, by way of not answering.

"I suppose she doesn't need to go away to college either."

"That's not for another year."

"And by that time we'll have provided her with sufficient guidance and progressive amounts of responsibility and independence so she can handle it."

"Didn't colleges used to have curfews, codes of behavior? No boys in the rooms, three feet on the floor in the lounges, that kind of thing?"

Lila actually laughed at him then. "I'm sorry, but you're just being ridiculous."

"I hope I am. I really do."

Later on, in bed, the lights off, the two of them rolled into the quilts and blankets, the furnace thrumming against the cold, Lila said, "She's a good girl and you shouldn't worry about her."

"She's not the one I'm worried about."

Lila's hand found its way through the blankets and rubbed the back of his neck. "I can't believe that when you were that age, you were really so bad."

Her breathing slowed and lengthened and she slept. Massey knew that was exactly why he worried. He had not been so bad, not at all.

The next morning Phoebe was still mad at him, making a point of ignoring him as she fixed her toast and ran up and down the stairs, assembling all the components of her day. Kevin ate his cereal in front of the television, watching some show that looked like one of his video games, muscle-bound robots warring with each other. Lila was getting ready for work in the half bath off the laundry room, the only place in the house, she said, that she could call her own. Massey stood at the kitchen counter making his lunch. Phoebe stalked back and forth often enough to make her point, and Massey accepted this as his punishment. When he was ready to leave the house, he waited for her to come downstairs again, hoping to cross paths with her one more time and say something that might make things good again between them. But she eluded him and he drove off without speaking.

Massey didn't buy the idea that kids were so different nowadays. Sure, they had their phones and everything that went along with the phones, and it was easier and quicker to do themselves harm with pictures and words. But there had always been a stream of private, subterranean talk, excluding parents, teachers, and those unlucky or uncool kids who existed as objects of pity and scorn. Just as there had always been needy, complicated friendships, alliances, feuds, outright wars. And the great confusion of sex gilding everything, its dramas played out in ways that were entirely private yet entirely public, and the best you could hope for, as a parent, was that the damage be survivable.

The summer that Phoebe was eleven, Massey was sent to pick her up from a day at the swimming pool. He parked the car and went out to the raised concrete walkway, looking down. It was late afternoon and a line of shadow moved almost perceptibly across the water.

Crowds of kids were still in the pool, or quick-walking along the concrete apron. Every so often one of the bored teenage lifeguards would rouse himself to yell "No running!" Or "No cannonballs!" In the single lane roped off for lap swim, a very old, pale man wearing a bathing cap swam up and down so slowly it looked as if he was drowning.

It took Massey a minute to spot Phoebe's bright green two-piece swimsuit. She was sitting on the edge of the pool with two other girls, their feet dangling in the water. A boy swam up to them and scooped handfuls of water their way, making them squeal. Then the boy propelled himself halfway out of the pool and made a grab for Phoebe's swimsuit straps, trying to pull them down. More of the squealing. The girls kicked water at him.

"Phoebe! Get over here now!"

She squinted up at him. They all did. The boy pushed away from the wall and dove smoothly underwater. Phoebe got up and came to stand directly beneath him. "Hi Dad."

"It's time to go. Get your things."

"Can we give Shelby a ride?"

"All right. Hurry up."

"We have to take showers first."

She'd wrapped herself in a beach towel. Her small, wet head protruded from the top, her bare feet from the bottom. The sun was fading fast and her teeth chattered.

"Make sure you dry your hair," Massey told her, and she headed off for the locker room. Massey found a spot at the pool's entrance and waited. He watched other people leaving, including some of the kids Phoebe's age, but he couldn't tell if the boy who had grabbed at her swimsuit was one of them.

Phoebe and her friend came out, dressed in shorts and T-shirts. Their hair was damp and combed and they carried their wet suits and towels in printed canvas backpacks that resembled toys. "That doesn't look like dry hair to me," Massey said.

"The dryers weren't working right. It's pretty dry." She spotted the car, and the two girls went on ahead of him. Phoebe was taller and her bare legs and backside were taking on the first signs of definition, though she still had a child's skinny, breakable-looking body.

When they reached the car, the girls got into the back seat and Massey told them to make sure they fastened their seat belts. He asked where Shelby lived and set off in that direction.

And though he knew better, he could not keep from asking, "Who was that boy, the boy who was into all that horseplay?"

"Horseplay," Phoebe said, trying out the word, and she and Shelby had to giggle at it, and pretend to be horses, nudging each other and neighing.

"Phoebe? You know the boy I mean? Who is he?"

"Oh, Billy Robillio." Shelby made another horse sound, cracking Phoebe up.

"Well you tell him to leave you alone. I don't like that kind of carrying on."

In the rearview mirror, Massey saw the two girls rolling their eyes and making comical faces at each other. "Phoebe? If I see him putting his hands on you again, or any of the other girls, I'm going to report him. There's no place for that kind of thing."

That turned them quiet. They rode along in silence for a few minutes, until Massey, attempting to lighten things, said, "Phoebe and Shelby. That practically rhymes. You're like, the BB twins." Nobody laughed.

They dropped Shelby off at her house. Massey said to Phoebe, "You want to come sit up front?"

She got out and opened the passenger door and settled herself next to him. Massey reached out and brushed a piece of her hair from her forehead. "Did you have fun today at the pool?"

"Yes."

He waited, but she didn't say anything more. He said, "I didn't mean to make it sound like you were doing anything wrong, honey. But you have to make sure that boys know the limits. That they respect you. Pretty soon you're going to be a grown-up young lady, and it's going to be important. Okay?"

"Okay," Phoebe said, but it was clear he'd missed by a mile, and when they arrived home she went upstairs to her room, and later, after dinner, Lila said to him, "What did you say to Phoebe to get her so upset?"

"She's upset? I did something?"

"She says you yelled at her about some boy at the pool."

"I didn't yell at her. The boy was trying to pull her swimsuit top down."

Lila considered this. "Well, that's not so good. But it happens. Swimming-pool stuff."

"She needs to know what is and isn't acceptable."

"She also needs not to feel guilty, or self-conscious about her body. You don't want to be one of those kinds of dads, do you?"

"I'm not sure what kind you mean," Massey said, but his wife was done talking.

Of course he knew what she meant. He was exactly that kind of dad. He always had been, and he saw no reason to apologize for it. His daughter was eleven, twelve, thirteen. Already there was reason for caution. Phoebe and her friends engaged in superheated yearning over each insipid, overpopular boy singer who came along. They mooned over the music, the videos, the online dribblings of other fans. Massey guessed these fantasy boys were less of a problem than real ones, but still. She was growing up pretty, giddy, gossipy. He worried that she would turn out superficial and empty-headed, too easily led into bad decisions, or rather, no decisions at all, only the giving way to impulse and vanity. He was stern with her about homework and about chores, and of course there were things like sleepovers and nights out that received extra vigilance. She might outgrow her flightiness in time, and part of a parent's job was to provide sober, rational, killjoy guidelines in the meantime.

His son? He was different, less worrisome. Kevin, two years younger than his sister, was smart, nerdy, wiseass. His friends

were the same way. They all spent too much time indoors playing their computer games, they had bad complexions and wore
sloppy T-shirts printed with cartoon characters. No girl would
have looked twice at any of them. Massey had not been that kind
of kid—he'd never been one to sit still for long—but he knew
that boys could more easily make up ground. Kevin wouldn't
cause anyone problems, and eventually he'd find himself some
well-paying, incomprehensible job, and everything else would
sort itself out.

Of course he loved his children. But that love was always balanced against dread.

He enrolled both kids in karate classes, hoping to toughen
them up some. The classes were advertised as "No Contact,
High Impact," and taught all the traditional poses and kicks and
blocks. There was emphasis on good citizenship, respect, self-
confidence. Massey watched the first session through the glass
window of the waiting room. Kevin and Phoebe were in different age groups at different ends of the gym. Both groups lined
up in their white, pajama-like uniforms, bowing to their instruc-
tors. Then there were drills, with the students encouraged to
plant their feet, lunge, shout war cries.

Kevin plodded through the exercises, dutiful but uninspired.
Phoebe barely went through the motions. She stood in the back
row and fiddled with her hair while the instructor spoke, looking around the room as if for escape. When she had to assume
poses, she slumped and drooped. The instructor came over to
her and positioned her arms and legs, which Phoebe allowed,
but in a passive, deadweight fashion.

After the class, Massey asked both of them how they liked it.
Kevin said it was "okay."

Phoebe said it was "totally stupid."

"What didn't you like about it?"

"All of it. I'm not going back."

"Phoebe."

"You know who's in that class? Caitlin Donovan. And she is gross!" Phoebe rolled her eyes to indicate grossness. She had the kind of mobile, sharp-featured face that did almost too good a job of showing disdain.

"What's so wrong about Caitlin?" Massey asked, honestly curious. "What do you mean, gross?"

"She just is. She has zits that look like hamburger."

This cracked Kevin up. He snorted and wheezed. "Hamburger," he managed.

"Well it's not like you're going to catch her zits," Massey said. "Besides, if Caitlin takes the class and you don't, she could learn how to kick your butt."

"Kick your butt," Kevin said, doubled over.

"You need to give it a chance, Phoeb. You don't want to be a quitter."

"Caitlin's going to tell everybody I was there! With her!"

The next week when it was time for karate class, Lila said Phoebe had cramps and didn't feel like going. "Oh for Christ's sake," Massey said, confronted and confounded by one more universal female trump card, the declaration of weakness. Kevin went to two more classes until he broke his big toe attempting a flick kick.

But wasn't he also glad that Phoebe was pretty and queenly? What if he had a daughter with zits like hamburger?

Phoebe was fourteen, fifteen, sixteen. She poked along in school, getting good enough grades, though never entirely good ones. She was passionate about clothes, makeup, hairstyles. So far there had been boys on the periphery, packs of boys who showed up at movies and football games, boys on the other end of a phone. But no actual boyfriends. Phoebe was not allowed to be in a car alone with a boy, or to give boys rides when she drove. Only through his wife's intervention had she been permitted, on this particular night, to travel in a vehicle with a boy-who-was-a-friend, along with another couple. Massey pointed out to Lila that groups of kids often enough did stupid, dangerous, even criminal things, the herd instinct. Lila told him he was being unfair and unrealistic.

It wasn't an argument he was going to win. "Stop right now," Lila said. "Stop making such a huge deal out of this." Phoebe's friends were due to pick her up soon, and the three of them were standing in the front hallway, where Massey was still making a huge deal out of it.

"Do you know the accident rates for teenage drivers? Would that be of any interest to you?"

"It would not," Lila said. "I have to finish the laundry. Do you know the divorce rates for couples where men don't help with housework? I thought not." She left and a moment later the heavy-duty noise of the dryer started.

Phoebe and her friends were headed to a cookout at someone's house. The parents would be in attendance. Massey had already spoken to them, further mortifying his daughter. The driver had been told to go straight to the party and then straight back, with no furtive detours. "I'm going to wait upstairs," Phoebe said. "Planning my elopement." She had her mother's gift for sarcasm.

"Funny," Massey said, but she was already on the upper landing, and a moment later her door slammed.

Left alone, Massey surveyed the hallway and the living room. A pair of tennis shoes had been left at the foot of the stairs. He kicked at them, and at a pile of newspapers in one corner, scattering pages, and then he picked up the shoes, hurling them against a wall.

"Dave?" Lila came back in then. "What in the world?"

"How can you have people over here when the place looks like this? Huh?"

"What is the matter with you?" Lila bent to retrieve the papers. "Seriously."

"It's a goddamn pigsty," Massey said, but his anger was draining away, replaced by shame.

"Then clean it up instead of having a stupid tantrum. And stay out of the way if you're going to be unpleasant."

So Massey went out to the garage and sorted through the drills and drivers on his workbench. A car pulled up in the driveway, the front doorbell rang, and he heard Lila greeting someone, the mumbling, moony boy whom Massey had met before and was forced to dislike mostly on principle. Then Phoebe came downstairs, and there was a brief bit of conversation, Lila cautioning, Phoebe saying sure, sure, obviously anxious to be gone, and then the front door closed again.

Massey stood to one side of the garage door's window, looking out. The boy's car idled in the driveway, its headlights two narrow beams. Phoebe crossed in and out of them, running down the front path. She leaned down to wave to somebody in the car's back seat, then opened the passenger door. Music, loud and hectic, escaped through it, then the door slammed shut. The car backed out onto the street, shifted gears, and headed off.

Massey took his car keys from the rack next to the workbench. He started his car and drove off after them. He saw their taillights far ahead and sped up. Then loitered at a stop sign so as not to get too close. The house with the party was on the other side of the freeway. He lost them once they reached the on-ramp, but once he got off again and reached the house itself, he saw the boy's car parked on the street behind a line of other cars, and he turned and drove home.

Once he got there Lila asked him where he went, and Massey said he'd needed sandpaper, and Lila said she hoped that meant he was finally going to finish one of his famous woodworking projects. And she would wait up for Phoebe, no, she didn't mind, she was going to read, and he should just go on to bed.

This was how he began the habit of following her, waiting for her, keeping watch. He ran through all manner of excuses, how he had to go out to buy one thing or another, how he just happened to be at the same gas station, just happened to be arriving home the same time she did. He guessed he should have felt some dread or particular worry on these nights, Phoebe loosed upon the world, but no. As long as he was nearby, no harm would come to her, and he could breathe easy.

Of course he got caught out, and then caught again, and there were scenes, and this most recent time, when he was pretty sure he had used up the last of his meager excuses.

Lila was waiting for him when he got home from work that night. "The kids are out," she told him. "They'll be back after dinner. That's all you need to know. Let's go sit in the den."

Massey followed her. Lila was still in her work clothes. She was the customer service manager for a loan company and she always dressed up, because, she said, it made people who came in to argue or beg about their payments behave better. Today she wore a gray tweed jacket and a slim gray skirt and heels. Her hair was pulled back and fastened with a clip. Massey wished she'd changed clothes. He felt like one of the bad customers, attempting to wheedle his way out of the late-payment charges, someone who had spent all his money in a tavern.

"So I'm in trouble, huh?" he said, trying for a jokiness that might make it all more bearable.

But Lila wasn't having any of it. She stared him down, her look equal parts sadness and distaste. "I want you to go see a counselor. The insurance covers it."

"Like, a shrink?" He hadn't expected this. He didn't want to let on how much it alarmed him.

"No, not a psychiatrist. A counselor. There's a difference. It's just talking."

"This seems a little extreme, don't you think?"

"The way we're living around here seems a little extreme." Lila drew a business card out of her jacket pocket. "Here, I made the appointment. It's written down for you."

Massey took it and looked it over. Sharon Glaser was the counselor's name, spelled out in a fancy, elongated typeface. A string of letters after her name, signifying degrees and certifications of some sort. He didn't like that she was a woman. He didn't like any of it. "So I go, or else? Is that it?"

"Don't make me get to or else."

"I go and talk to her, that's all I have to do?"

"No, you talk to her as a way of changing your behavior. I want peace in this house. I don't want to referee any more fights."

"And everything is all my fault, is that it?" He wasn't ready to give ground. He didn't want things dug out of him and held up for scrutiny and judgment.

"I can't think what else to do," Lila said, but wearily, as if even her anger had worn out, and she was going to sit there until someone made her get up.

The waiting room of Sharon Glaser, she of the many alphabet letters, was furnished with one of those fake-rock waterfalls that Massey guessed was meant to be soothing. He was not in a mood to be soothed. He was hoping to strike some bargain with the woman, where he would admit to being overprotective about his daughter, even foolishly so, and she would say that was understandable, and Massey would promise to do better. He could see it working out that way, him being cooperative, regretful.

And here was Sharon Glaser herself, calling his name and beckoning him back into her office, shaking hands with him as if to demonstrate that she'd been taught to do so in a brisk, manly fashion. He guessed he'd expected somebody more on the motherly side. Sharon Glaser was thin, fortyish, with glasses and a lot of curly, energetic dark hair. Her clothes were unfancy, khakis and a sweater, and there wasn't much in the way of makeup. She looked like somebody who coached high school sports.

At the same time he was sizing her up, Massey realized she must be doing the same to him, in some knowing, professional way. He wasn't young enough anymore to enjoy being looked over by any woman, for whatever purpose. He'd come straight from work and he wore his usual job site clothes, jeans and boots, and he guessed he was clean enough but he was afraid they might mark him as crude and jerk-like, the kind of man who would bluster and bully a daughter, or beat up her boyfriends, and he wasn't really, or he wouldn't be here in the first place, would he?

"Come on in, find a place to sit," Sharon Glaser said. There were four black leather chairs arranged around a low coffee table and Massey took the closest one. "How are you today?"

Massey said he was good, thanks. Let's get this show on the road. The coffee table had a box of Kleenex for the weepers, and one of those desktop metal sculptures, chrome spheres and blades, so people would have something to look at. As he was now doing. Sharon Glaser settled herself in a chair opposite and said, "Why don't you start by telling me why you're here."

This confused him. "You mean my wife didn't tell you? She made the appointment."

"She made it with my secretary. We haven't spoken."

He would be allowed to give his own side of things, then. That made him feel better. "Well, it was her idea. Not mine. Just so you know. We've been having some problems with our daughter—or I guess, my wife thinks I'm the problem." He was aware of blundering into defensiveness and blame. He shook his head, in a more-in-sorrow-than-in-anger fashion. "She's sixteen. My daughter, Phoebe. I worry about her. Not that she causes us any real trouble. Attitude, sure. Kids that age, you know?" Sharon Glaser's expression was perfectly neutral and receptive. Some of the alphabet letters were probably a degree in making the right kind of faces. "I just like to be careful about where she goes. Who she goes out with. My wife thinks I'm being unreasonable. Too strict."

"And does Phoebe think so too?"

"Oh yeah. Big-time."

"Do you have any other children?"

"Yeah, my son. He's fourteen." Massey shrugged. "He's not a

problem. Or he'll be a different problem. Boys. Don't you need to take notes or something? I mean, excuse me, I haven't done this before, but I thought you'd take notes."

"I've found that it makes people self-conscious," Sharon Glaser said, pleasantly. "It makes them wonder what they just said that made you snap to attention, and then they stop talking. I make mental notes, and when the sessions are done, I write them down." She smiled. She had an answer for everything, but she wasn't snotty about it. He thought she was probably okay. He wondered what she'd look like if she fixed herself up a little, and didn't settle for the female jock look.

"So you and your wife disagree about setting the rules for your daughter." Massey nodded. That's what it boiled down to. "Would you like to work on some negotiating strategies, ways you and your wife could come to an agreement about what's appropriate for Phoebe?"

"Sure." Massey nodded again. "That would be a good thing." He thought they were making progress. He could do this.

"All right." Sharon Glaser seemed pleased also, as if he was catching on, as if this was all it took to get things ironed out. Fine-tuning the communications. "But talk to me a little more about why the two of them, your wife and your daughter, are fighting you on this. Why you're on different sides."

She waited while he made a show of thinking about it. There was some difficulty he'd need to steer past, but he couldn't see its shape clearly. He spread his hands in a who-knows gesture, chuckled. "I was hoping you could explain women to me, doctor."

"I'm not a doctor," she corrected him, but in a nice way, not like she was offended or anything. "Do you think your wife is careless, or indifferent about what your daughter does? Is she a disengaged parent?"

"I wouldn't say that."

Sharon Glaser was waiting for what he would say. So was Massey. "Ah, they don't know the things that can happen when kids are running around without supervision, when being on their own is all brand-new to them. I mean, they know, they hear about all the depraved stuff—you know? Like that girl in Pennsylvania?—but it's like it doesn't sink in."

"Why are you more tuned in to the dangers, do you think?"

"I guess because I was a teenage boy myself." Massey shook his head, chuckled again, as if remembering, what was the word: "hijinks."

"You grow up around here?"

"No, out West. Tucson. Home of the Sun Devils."

"Oh, I went to a conference in Tucson once. Pretty place. All those mountains. You get back there much?"

"Not really."

"Any family still there?"

"My mom. And my brother, he's pretty much in charge of taking care of her. That's just the way it worked out." Massey would have liked to move on. Everything she said was a question, and what he had taken as ordinary curiosity, run-of-the-mill conversational filler, was instead intended to throw some sort of net over him, but he couldn't just leave things hanging, and so he said, "I guess I'm just not the high school reunion type." He wasn't. Never went to one.

Sharon Glaser appeared to be struck by a genuine spontaneous thought. "You know there was a movie about a high school reunion set in Tucson. *Romy and Michele's High School Reunion*. Do you know it?"

Massey shrugged, meaning he did not. Didn't want to.

"Try and see it sometime. It's pretty funny. Sometimes that's the best way to look back on high school, when you can see it as a comedy."

"I guess," Massey said, indicating he was not very interested. There weren't any clocks in the room and he didn't want to look at his watch, but he hoped they'd reached at least the halfway point. "So, these negotiation tips."

"Yes, we can talk about those. But first, what are the important things, the basic guidelines you want to set for Phoebe?"

"No alcohol. No drugs."

"Understandable."

"Not that you can ever be a hundred percent sure, hell, even fifty percent sure, that some wiseass won't show up with that kind of thing. I mean, why else do kids have parties?"

"Not too many ice cream socials around, huh."

"Yeah, a dying breed."

"Were you much of a party animal, back in the Tucson days?"

"I did my share of partying."

"Probably a little spicier than the comic movie version, I'm guessing."

Just as he was getting ready to tell Ms. Sharon Not-A-Doctor that it had been a real pleasure, and if she was so interested in Tucson, she could get a plane ticket, she threw it into reverse. Headed off in a different direction. "Could you tell me a little about how you and your wife decide other issues. Other conflicts. Just so I get a bigger picture here."

"Ah. Well, happy wife, happy life. I guess she pretty much rules the roost."

"You're okay with that?"

"What choice do I have? No, really, my wife is just more of a manager type than I am. She's smart about money, she keeps us on track." Massey hoped that came across the right way. "It's like any partnership, the two of you have different responsibilities. Mine are along the lines of follow-through. Implementation. Like, if we go on vacation, she packs the suitcases and I carry them around. Seems like most couples I know operate pretty much the same way."

"You mean, the wives make most of the decisions," Sharon Glaser said, making it not a question. How did she keep track of the time? Was there a clock he couldn't see?

"I guess they take the lead when it comes to, you know, family life," Massey offered. "Maybe that's why we're having this problem, she's so used to calling the shots."

"What I hear you saying is, women have all this power. But at the same time they need to be protected. Like you feel the need to protect your daughter. Have I got that right?"

"I guess. I don't know." He was going to just shut up now.

"Because maybe it's not a contradiction. Maybe it's women's sexuality that gives them their power, but it also makes them vulnerable. It's possible to have a complicated response to that. To resent that power, to imagine how it might be undone—"

"Whoa." Massey held up a hand. "Sorry, this is getting a little too wacky for me."

"I know it can be difficult. But what you seem to be most worried about where your daughter is concerned is sexual misbehavior, sexual victimization. You referred to the case in Pennsylvania, the kidnapping. Not something like a car accident."

"Of course I'm worried about car accidents. Is that something I have to spell out?"

"And you aren't expressing any particular worries about your son. He's not the reason for the conflict with your wife."

Massey stood up. "You're going to have to excuse me. I guess I'm not smart enough to see how this is supposed to help. Thank you for your time."

Sharon Glaser stood also and opened the office door for him. She didn't seem particularly upset. She was probably used to pissing people off with her nosy-ass questions. She held out her hand and Massey shook it, though he didn't want to. "Please think about making another appointment," she told him. "Therapeutic goals can take a while to achieve. This first session is only"— her face lit up, pleased with herself—"the ice cream social part."

Oh ha ha, Sharon. "I'm pretty sure you have us all figured out already," Massey said, meaning to be sarcastic. He wished he could have come up with something worse to say. He would have liked to tell her the fake waterfall was stupid.

"It doesn't matter what I figure out. It's what you figure out," Sharon Glaser said, with her aggravating, smartest-girl-in-the-class smile. "Very nice to meet you, Mr. Massey."

Yeah, you too, dear. He walked out to his car and started it but he didn't want to go home yet, so he drove for a time around the edges of a shopping mall, and then in another loop that took him out beyond the new, raw housing at the town's edge, and back again to his own neighborhood. He stopped at the liquor store and bought the expensive dark beer that he favored when he felt like spending money.

He already had things all figured out. That didn't mean you could do anything about them.

Nobody was there when he got home; a note said they were all out shopping. Massey fixed himself a sandwich and opened one of the beers and ate in front of the television, a History Channel show about World War II, all smudgy gray film footage.

Lila hadn't known him when he was young, before he'd made the move East. They met when he was already here, just starting out on somebody else's crew and happy enough to be pulling down a paycheck. Lila was the ambitious one. There was a series of steps he'd had to take to get to running his own business and the good living it brought, and each one of them had come about because she'd talked him through it, backed him up. He was grateful, and he thought she knew that, even if he didn't go around announcing it every five minutes.

No one from his family had come to their wedding, or done much more than send a couple of Christmas cards over the years. Massey had explained this to her as bad blood between him and the others, the usual sad shit: alcoholism, fights, divorce, first one, then the other parent heading off in different directions, Massey and his brothers and half sister and half brothers never living under one roof together, one of those families with an asterisk that required a lot of explaining. All that was true enough, but that didn't mean you could draw any straight line between the way he grew up and the trouble he'd made for himself. Nobody would have been very interested in his excuses anyway.

When Lila and the kids came home from their shopping trip, Massey was upstairs. He heard their voices and the familiar racket of doors opening and shutting, but he stayed where he was. Lila came in to find him lying on his back in bed. "Hey there. Did you get any supper?"

"Yeah. You buy out the place?" She was carrying two big paper shopping bags, which she set down on the end of the bed.

"Want to see?" She took out some packages wrapped in rustling tissue paper and undid them. Massey had been hoping they might be lingerie, or some kind of sleepwear that wasn't flannel, but she held up a sweater-and-slacks set, the kind of thing she might wear to work.

"Very nice."

"You don't like them."

"Did I say that? They're fine. You will look like one badass customer service rep. People will pay right up."

"Thanks. That's the look I was hoping for, badass. So how did it go?"

"Okay, I guess. She was okay."

Lila folded the clothes and put them on her dresser. She sat down on the bed next to him and looked him over, as if the appointment might have left a visible mark on him. "Did she come up with anything helpful?"

"We have to learn how to negotiate. Like, you're North Korea and I'm America."

"Uh-huh. What else?"

"Ah, guidelines. Decision-making tools. I'm still chewing on it."

"All right. Are you going back for another appointment?"

"Still chewing on that too."

Lila started to get up and he pulled her back down, one arm around her waist. "I'm trying," he said. "It's just a lot of new ideas, you know?"

"As long as you're trying."

"Do you ever feel like, even when everything's going all right, or especially when it's going all right, that there's some horror movie version of your life that's going to come sneaking up behind you?"

Lila raised herself up to look at him. "No. What are you talking about, that's creepy."

Massey said nothing. He was creepy, then.

"I'm sorry, I didn't mean to sound so . . . You just surprised me. I didn't know you felt that way. Want to talk about it?"

"It's not a big deal," Massey said. "More of a stray thought." He repositioned his arm, drew her in closer. He had reckoned that there would be sex involved as part of the deal, his willingness to keep the appointment, and he had been right about that.

He woke long after midnight, got up, used the bathroom, waited to see if Lila woke also, as she sometimes did. She slept undisturbed. Massey closed the bedroom door behind him, stood in the hallway, listening. His children's rooms were dark and silent. Moving as quietly as he could, he went down the stairs and stood in the living room, looking out the front windows.

The furnace muttered. Warm air came through the vents and stirred the sheer curtains. The world on the other side of the window—his lawn, the empty street, his neighbors' lawns and darkened houses—were locked in dead-of-winter cold, sealed by a thin layer of glazed ice. Nothing moved. No shadowed figure crept across the bare ground. No darkened car drove by too slowly on the street. No churning storm, no mighty robot creature from his son's video games, shaking the ground beneath his feet. The bare trees were petrified by the glittering ice, and even the wind had stilled. It was frozen and unearthly, but the view calmed him. Nothing would happen here. He could sleep for a few more hours and wake up to an ordinary day.

He wasn't going back to see Sharon Glaser, he knew that. He'd get through his troubles on his own, as he always had. He might have asked her, *Do you believe that some events, the impor-*

tant ones, set other events in motion, like all our choices get fed into, like, a funnel that gets narrower and narrower. Until whatever comes out the other end, it was all decided a long time ago. You ever believe that?

And Sharon Glaser would have done her best impersonation of thinking about something, with her head inclined to one side and her eyebrows doing a little dance, and who knows, maybe she really was thinking about it, and then she would have thrown the question back at him: *It's not important what I believe, Mr. Massey. It's what you believe. Therapeutic goals. Complicated responses. All the rest of the ideas I have to explain to you because you are as dumb as a rock.*

He tried again. *I guess I'm talking about fate, or doom? If that's the right word? Set in stone. Fixed outcomes.*

Well Mr. Massey, if I didn't think people could change, and change their lives, their outcomes, I wouldn't be in this business, would I?

He'd tried to find those guys on the Internet once. One was still in Tucson, it looked like he ran a janitorial service. One might have been in California, but there were a lot of different matches for the name. One he couldn't find. He tried to look up the girl but she was off the grid too, hadn't left any tracks. Maybe she got married and changed her name. He liked to think she'd managed to make that kind of a life for herself.

There was no need to dredge any of that up, for himself or for anyone else. The records were sealed. He hadn't cared about it at the time, too sunk in catastrophe to appreciate the difference between an adult and a juvenile, but he did so now, and for that at least he was grateful.

He stopped following Phoebe and her friends on their nights out. It was as if the appointment with the counselor had done some good in spite of his distaste for it. The weather took a halting step toward spring, or at least toward the end of winter. Phoebe was still wary of him, waiting for him to turn back into Asshole Dad, but he guessed he had that coming. There was something closer to peace in the house, at least as much as you could expect with the four of them always scrambling off in four different directions, work and work and school and school. Weren't families meant to do things together once in a while? All this time he'd measured them against the wreckage he'd grown up with, and thought himself lucky.

"We should go on a vacation this summer," he told Lila. "Before the kids get too old for it."

She was at the computer, going through a coupon website. "They're already too old."

"I'm not talking about Disneyland. More like a resort, a beach or a lake, maybe."

Lila turned around to look at him. "You can get away from work?" He could never get away from work.

"Sure. For a week, maybe. Where do you want to go?"

"Me? I'll go anywhere I can sit in the sun and get a margarita. You better talk to the kids before you get too carried away."

"Or you could talk to them."

"Dave."

"All right. Talk to offspring. On the to-do list."

"And Dave? It's so nice of you to try to do this. Even if we never end up going anywhere, it's nice that you want to."

Kevin said yes, without much prodding. He'd been spending time reading lately, the kind of paperbacks with pictures of vaguely Nordic, vaguely prehistoric warriors on their covers. He kept a thumb in the pages to mark his place while Massey made his pitch. "Could we go someplace where they have boats?" he asked, when Massey was done laying out the possibilities.

"Boats, what, rowboats? Cabin cruisers? Speedboats?"

"I don't know, maybe a sailboat."

Kevin didn't seem to want to elaborate. Massey studied him, unable to connect anything he saw with the request. Kevin wore his usual all-purpose T-shirt and athletic shorts. His legs were getting longer, and, Massey noted, hairier. "Sure, buddy. There's lots of places for that. We could head up the coast of Michigan, or out East. Find a place for sailing lessons, if that's the kind of thing you want."

"Cool." He was waiting to get back to his reading, and so Massey left him. Did his son have some kind of buccaneer fantasy, picked up from one of his lurid books? Or was it some unsuspected jockish impulse? He couldn't think of a way to ask.

Phoebe's door was closed. Massey knocked, announced himself, and a moment later Phoebe said, "Come in." The words dredged up out of a reservoir of vast reluctance.

Massey opened the door halfway. "Got a sec?"

"I have an environmental studies test tomorrow." Her notes were spread out on the desk around her. Her phone was there too. Did they never turn them off, stop talking and texting and tweeting?

He decided not to say anything about the phone. "This won't take long. I wanted to see how you'd feel about all of us taking a vacation this summer."

"It would activate my gag reflex."

"Someplace on the water. Ocean or lake, either one. Everybody else is up for it."

"Then everybody else can go. I'll stay at Maura's." Phoebe's chair had a swivel seat and she used her foot to push it from one end of its arc to the other. She was wearing black, stretchy tights and a T-shirt with its hem tied up in a knot, clothes that suggested yoga or dance classes, though he was pretty sure she didn't do either of these.

"I don't think so. Either we all go or nobody goes."

"Then I guess we stay home," Phoebe said, almost happily, maybe because he'd made that one so easy.

"Why don't you think about whether there's any body of water you might enjoy hanging out at for a week, anyplace you'd look forward to, anyplace that might impress your friends if you said you were going there."

"Tahiti."

The conversation had dead-ended in pretty much the way he had expected, but Massey wasn't quite ready to give up. "Think about it," he repeated. "Let the idea grow in you." He looked around Phoebe's room, which had gone from pink to militantly not-pink a few years ago. Now it was decorated in moody shades of black and gray, with some throw pillows in sunset colors: magenta, orange stripe, copper graphic. "Your room goes good with your hair," he said.

"What?" Phoebe wary, ready to take offense.

"Just, the colors. I guess that's why you picked them. It's like the room doesn't make that much sense until you're in it."

"Thanks, I guess." She was almost smiling, and Massey guessed he'd lucked into saying something endearingly stupid, as dads were meant to do. What did he know about fathers? His own hadn't been around that much, which was a good thing, given the way things went down when he was.

"You know how pretty you are, don't you? I guess I don't have to keep telling you."

His daughter locked the fingers of her hands together and stretched both arms over her head, stretching out the lovely curve of her back. "I guess you can tell me once in a while."

Just as, once in a while, he could tell her to be careful, careful, more than that, vigilant, wary, sober, mindful—

"Dad? I really do have to study."

You could luck out. Dodge the bullet meant for you. Who would have thought, given the crapped-out family he'd grown up in, that he'd end up with a woman like Lila and a couple of decent kids? All of them muddling along as best they could, the occasional rough patch, sure.

That was life. His, theirs. Not perfect, because no family ever was, but not the sad, distant, failed, hurt and hurtful people who'd raised him, or made their halfhearted efforts at doing so. Luck could save you even when you didn't deserve it.

And the rest of it? Sometimes it was a dream but not a dream. A memory but not entirely a memory. There were gaps. No memory of pleasure. At least not the part you'd expect. He'd been too drunk. He'd stopped after a while and let somebody else take their turn. The real enjoyment had been the invention of different, novel ways in which the girl could be positioned, posed, what different substances might be applied to her, what methods and items could be used for purposes of insertion, while the girl, who might have consented (although not in the legal sense) to some if not all of what had happened, at least at the beginning, mumbled and drowsed and moved her hands as if trying to swat away insects. How naked she was! So much unexpected, secret skin! He had never seen a real naked girl before, only pictures. None of them had. She was like something washed up on a beach or dropped out of the sky, an object of curiosity as much as cruelty. So that leaving her where and as they did at the edge of a parking lot, fouled, bruised, exposed, her hair matted with semen, indicated they had simply exhausted their curiosity and lost interest. They were tired, they were ready to go home and sleep, and that was what they had done.

It was a dream but not a dream. Massey woke up from it fast. Here was the real and present world, the darkened room, the coolness of the sheets, Lila asleep beside him, this life he could reach out and take hold of, his heart calming itself, his gratitude for all the things he did not deserve.

And then the telephone rang.

The doctor was very careful with his words and he was speaking slowly. He said, "I want to prepare you for what you're going to see. The side of her head and face which impacted the windshield are heavily bandaged. We have already sutured a portion of her scalp back into place. She's intubated, the machine is breathing for her. She is not conscious at this time. She is not in pain. There are orthopedic injuries, one shoulder and some cervical vertebrae. We don't know if we can save her eye. There's a lot we don't know yet. Please be certain that we are doing everything we can for her."

Massey and Lila held each other. Lila was not crying but her breath was short and rasping. Massey had turned to stone. The doctor said, "Do you have any questions now? I know you'll have them later."

"My son," Massey said. "He's out there with one of our neighbors. What do we tell him?"

"Nothing you'll have to take back later. Are you ready? Would you follow me please?"

The doctor led them through a set of double doors and along a hallway that turned and turned again. The boy who had been driving was dead. They didn't know him, or how Phoebe had ended up in his car when she was supposed to be somewhere else and with someone else. Was he drunk? High? Or just reckless? These were no longer important questions. The doctor slid open a glass door and stepped aside.

Lila screamed from a place deep inside of her and her legs went out. Massey caught her around the chest and took most of her weight so that she only sagged, not fell. An orderly came and stooped over her. "Let's get her . . ." the doctor said. And, to Massey, "I'll be right back."

The glass door slid closed again. The small room was dark except for a light over the bed and the banks of green and yellow lights belonging to machines, the one pushing air in and out, the others taped to her wrist, delivering medication, he guessed, and monitoring vitals.

He made himself look at the worst of it: everything that was swollen, bruised, displaced. Then he sat down on her good side, where a portion of Phoebe was still recognizable, still beautiful, and smoothed the hair away from her forehead. If she slept for a hundred years, he would stay here, keeping watch, waiting, as he was meant to be.

I thank the court for the opportunity to speak. I am grateful for the punishment handed out to these boys. But punishment is not always justice. They are going to pay their debt to society and then put it all behind them. You would hope they think about what they did to my daughter every day of their lives, but I know they won't. They're too low-down. Just look at them. Snotty little losers. I guess each of them has a mother who loved him. Maybe still does, though it's probably a lot harder for her now.

Well I'm a mother. And my beautiful child cries herself to sleep each night. She is precious to me. These boys have no feeling for that kind of thing. They are ignorant of every kind of feeling except sorry for their own stupid selves. So maybe they should go on in life and in time have their own daughters. And know that kind of sweetness and grow the heart for it. And then have that child taken from them and broken.

That is what I think would serve justice.

Again, I thank the court.

YOUR SECRET'S SAFE WITH ME

He was her first husband, but she was not his first wife. Of course Edie knew this, everyone knew this, since her husband was a public figure, a prominent, even famous man, at home in the wider world. He was exactly twice Edie's age, fifty-six to her twenty-eight. It was only to be expected that given his years and his stature, he had a history, had endured paroxysms of romance, tragedy, betrayal. Edie had a little old history herself, but it was pretty much like everybody else's.

Anyway, the first wife had died, all those years ago. Died! Struck down by a galloping cancer, leaving him with two small children. When Edie said how dreadful, sad, lonesome, it must have been, he turned his face away, the memory unmanning him. "It was a terrible time," he said. "I wasn't the parent I should have been."

"You were overwhelmed. Anyone would have been."

"I was not at my best. I have some regrets."

"Well," Edie said, when it was clear he was not going to say more, "You got through it. Your children got through it and they turned out fine. That's the important thing." She had not yet met his children, the two boys, who were by now grown-ups, a few years older than herself. She assumed they were fine, because he had not said otherwise.

He gave her a sideways look from beneath the hooded crescents of his eyelids. "You always believe the best of me. I love that about you."

"Thank you," Edie said, although there was a whiff of something insulting about his words, as if she was being praised for a charming stupidity.

"I have my share of rough edges. Rotten history. Sometimes I think I haven't been fair to you, gobbling you up so fast."

Edie murmured that he mustn't be silly.

"I was lost in the wilderness for such a long, long while. I had become a caricature of myself, an intellect on legs. Such a glittering surface! So much abominable cleverness! But when I groped around for my heart, there was only this hard, stunted kernel. I lashed out. I hurt people. I caused damage."

"I can't imagine," Edie said, meaning, she could not imagine he'd done anything all that terrible. He was fond of talking in grand terms.

"There are still some resentments circulating out there. Bad blood. Just so you're aware."

He waited until she nodded: Okay. "But everything's different now, thank God. Thank God for you." He buried his mouth in her soft and ticklish places, and Edie mewed and giggled.

Edie imagined he might have had a difficult relationship or two, or three, in his past, women who had tried to fill the awful void that made all his fame so hollow, only to fall victim to his bitterness and confusion. She understood how such things might have played out, though she wished he'd given her a few more specifics. They had only been married for a very few weeks, if you counted the actual civil ceremony and not the extended, honeymoon-like trip to Barbados that had gone before it, and they had not known each other all that long no matter how you counted.

Edie knew a fair amount about the second wife, the one who had preceded her. The Afro-Swedish beauty, even more famous in her own realm than her husband was in his. She of the long Masai limbs and cinnamon skin and unearthly clouds of pale hair. Edie thought she understood this chapter also. The woman was dazzling; he was bedazzled. They were both celebrities, it was a celebrity thing. It was not a marriage that anyone expected to last very long, and it had not. Her husband was not considered an attractive man. People had made certain jokes.

Edie remembered, before she actually met him, seeing him from time to time on television, catching glimpses of him as she clicked through the news channels and serious panel discussions. (She was so shallow. Her own viewing tastes ran to reality shows about wealthy people behaving badly, and crime dramas with wisecracking detectives.) And she had not paid him much mind. Honestly? Because he was not attractive. Yes, shallow, she had wallowed in shallowness, if that was possible. He had a funny name too, Milo. Milo Baranoff. Milo's forehead was bald and shiny. Two wings of dark hair crept down over his ears like horns. His nose bent slightly to one side. He commanded interest and attention because of his widely read pronouncements, the force of his personality, the droll and entertaining gloss he brought to important issues.

And once Edie did come to know him, she saw how this

could be so, how a person's magnetism, how their *soul*, could shine through, transcend the fleshly wrapper. She understood then how a particular fault—the pallid wart protruding through one of Milo Baranoff's eyebrows—might become something you could stare down, acknowledge, accept, dismiss, once you were well and truly in love, as she was.

They had met at one of his lectures, part of a Great Thinkers series sponsored by the midwestern university where Edie had matriculated, graduated, and then hung on grimly as an instructor in English composition. She had meant to make her big move by now. Her life embarrassed her. It was a February night. The darkness outside was sleety. The lecture hall was in an elderly building; the room swooned with radiator heat. Perhaps because of the bad weather, only a smallish audience had assembled, feeling self-conscious about their lack of numbers. Edie's roommate, another instructor, had talked her into going because the roommate wanted to seduce the professor in charge of the Great Thinkers series.

Edie squirmed inside her too-hot sweater. Her head felt clogged and she was pretty sure she was coming down with something. She wondered if she was even capable of a Great Thought. It seemed unlikely. All her thoughts were tiny and ignominious, a swarm of outdated coupons and missing socks.

The professor, the one her roommate had the thing for, took the podium and wrestled the squealing microphone into submission. He said it was a particular privilege to introduce tonight's speaker, who was known far and wide for his elegantly formulated commentaries on matters cultural and political, for his many well-received essays and books. He rolled out the list of Milo Baranoff's publications, accomplishments, awards. "He is a man who brings formidable gifts of intelligence, observation, and humor to bear on the issues and dilemmas of our troubled times. Please join me in welcoming him."

As he ceded the microphone, the professor singled out Edie's roommate with a smile. The roommate bridled and nudged Edie in the ribs. Milo Baranoff stood at the podium and made a show of riffling through his notes, which he hardly needed. He had given such talks so many times before, and besides, he was buoyed by his honorarium check and the excellent dinner at the college town's one good restaurant.

He began, "Ours is an age of near-constant scientific discoveries and hurtling technological innovation. Who can keep track of it all? At what a breathless pace we take on challenges both unimaginably vast and unimaginably small. We now know that in four billion years' time, our galaxy and the Andromeda galaxy will collide. We have a branch of physics called supersymmetric theory, which postulates as-yet-undiscovered subatomic particles. It is a time of wonders. We have computers that sing to us, and prosthetic hands controlled by impulses from the brain. A hundred years ago, who could have imagined such a thing as the Hubble Telescope? As a cell phone? Let us not forget to bow down to the humble television remote control!"

This was a laugh line, and Milo Baranoff allowed the laughter to run its course. "It's true that certain natural phenomena, certain diseases, and even mortality itself still elude our efforts at understanding. But here is what I offer up for you to ponder tonight: Is existence itself a solvable problem?"

Edie did not much care. She had a headache that felt as if a thick rope was being pulled from one ear to the other. By touch, she rummaged through her purse and came up with a Tylenol, which she dry-swallowed. She closed her eyes and Milo Baranoff's voice seemed to draw her through passageways and corridors, tunnels and labyrinths, always floating back at her from somewhere just beyond her comprehension. His voice coaxed and exhorted, demanded and wheedled. It was exhausting to try to keep up with it, and to fathom what it wanted from her. Acquiescence? Counterargument? Synthesis? She lacked a sense of larger purpose. Her existence was a problem waiting to be solved.

The sound of applause brought her out of it. She opened her eyes. They felt sticky. Her roommate said, "Come on, let's go be conspicuous."

"I think I have the plague," Edie said, but she followed her roommate up to the front of the room, where Milo Baranoff was receiving tributes.

The roommate made a beeline for the professor while Edie sagged into a chair. Nearby, Milo Baranoff was signing copies of his books for people, asking them how their names were spelled. It was oddly comforting to hear him speak from so close, as if she'd finally caught up with his voice and now could rest. Her roommate returned. "Come on, we're all going out for a drink."

"I can't."

"You have to. It looks weird if it's only me. Edie!"

So she went. She and Milo Baranoff trudged across the icy parking lot behind the other two, who were chatting and bumping against each other as they walked. Edie had muttered something to Milo when they were introduced, something about having a cold, sorry. Milo kept silent. Edie didn't look at him, only down at her own shuffling feet, which seemed much farther away than usual. When they reached the professor's car, Milo said that no, he was fine riding in back, and he opened the door for Edie. They went to a grown-up bar, a place serving pomegranate martinis and cognac. Edie and Milo sat on one side of the leather booth like a pair of elderly chaperones. Across from them, the professor and Edie's roommate made vivacious conversation and sniffed each other's hair.

When it came time to order the drinks, Edie said she didn't want anything. Her lips were chapped. She drained her water glass and bit down on the ice cubes. Milo spoke to the waiter. "Have the barman boil some water, steep a slice of lemon, then add two spoonfuls of honey and a shot of whiskey." The waiter gaped at him. "And I'll have a Scotch rocks." To Edie he said, "People often suffer through my speeches, just not literally."

Edie saw her roommate giving her a warning look: *Don't be a giant buzzkill.* "Ha ha," Edie said, and when her toddy arrived, she drank it. Stealthy heat invaded her bones and she felt recharged, almost jolly. The other three were talking about a frivolous movie that had just come out, a movie that none of them would ever see but which was easy to make fun of without seeing it. Edie joined in with a remark or two and laughed along with them and then toppled sideways off the slick leather seat and got herself tangled up in Milo Baranoff's knees.

She had not really passed out, but she pretended she had, since she was so mortified. She was revived with cold cloths and face patting and she let her eyelids flutter open weakly. Yes, she told them, she was all right, just a little woozy. She was not going to admit that the whiskey had ridden an express elevator to her brain and she had simply lost her balance.

"At least you didn't barf on him," Edie's roommate said, once they were back in their apartment and Edie was laid out in bed on her back, like a tomb effigy.

"Please don't say 'barf.'"

"Next time you don't want to go someplace, just say so."

"How did you leave it with him?" Edie asked, meaning the professor.

"He told me to have a good semester. Something about you falling into that guy's lap made everyone focus on their inappropriate behavior."

Three days later, a package arrived for Edie via express delivery. She opened it and found a volume of classic Japanese poetry, illustrated with beautiful ink drawings on rice paper. Enclosed was a note from Milo Baranoff, three lines typed on a folded sheet. *Dear Edith, I wanted you to have a keepsake that might serve as a better memory of your evening. I hope that you are feeling much better by now, and that this small gift will find favor with you. Best regards, M.B.*

Edie wrote back. *Dear Mr. Baranoff, you are too kind. Yes, I am on the mend from my illness. The poems are lovely both to look at and to read. I wish I could be as wise and graceful as they are. Please call me Edie, since the only Edith anybody's ever heard of is Edith Wharton, which is fine but a little misleading.*

She read the note over again and again before she dared send it, wondering if it was too smart-aleck or flirty. What she got back was a copy of *The Age of Innocence* bound in soft green leather, and a note: *Do you suppose you might bring yourself to call me Milo?* She felt a little bad because while she thought Edith Wharton was all right, she did not consider herself a huge fan.

They exchanged e-mail addresses and phone numbers. Edie sent him a CD of a band she liked who played '80s pop songs on a theremin. And a cartoon she clipped from a newspaper, showing a lady reclining on a fainting couch with her enervated wrist pressed to her forehead. He sent flowers, irises and peonies.

When they spoke on the phone, Edie had the same sensation

of his voice leading her on to some perplexing destination, teasing her with all the things she had yet to learn. They talked about this and that. His travels, books he suggested she read. He asked questions about her family and her growing-up, he encouraged her to talk about the small news of her day. He seemed charmed by whatever she said, as if he found glittering facets in her that no one else had previously suspected, including Edie herself. Edie told herself not to be foolish, and tried to keep her own conversation with Milo light and amusing.

He hardly knew her, or she him! But there was something intense and superheated about this long-distance intercourse, especially as it extended over the weeks, something private and conspiratorial, as if the selves they offered up to each other were better and truer than the rest of the world would recognize.

Often Milo called her in the late evening, after he had returned from some symposium or gala. He lived in New York City, of course, in an apartment he called "the castle," which he seemed to mean ironically, although Edie was not entirely sure of this. She imagined him coming in the door and emptying the contents of his pockets onto a silver tray that stood ready to receive them. He would loosen his tie, fix himself his Scotch, stand at a west-facing window thinking his complicated thoughts, his mind reaching out to her, then pick up the phone and dial her number. Edie did not know if he had a west window, but it made for a better story.

"I get so tired of all my opinions," he complained. "I seem to have staked out positions on nearly everything, and now I can't remember half of them. Someone is always reminding me that I've registered passionate advocacy or opposition about stem cell research or organic farming, and then I have to pretend I still care one way or the other."

"You could demur. Say you're trying to free yourself from all ego-driven conflicts."

Milo laughed his bark-like laugh. "You'd be the only one in on the joke. You're the only one who knows me that well."

"I like thinking I do," Edie said shyly. Milo seemed to believe that likewise he knew her better than anyone else did. Certainly he knew the self she was attempting to be for him, the one who was re-reading *The Age of Innocence* and taking notes.

A silence. Over the phone line, Edie heard the ice cubes in his drink making their small, celebratory noise. Then Milo said, "How would you feel about coming out here for a visit?"

"Oh . . ." She would feel confused. Panicked. "New York, I've never been there."

"Then it's about time you did so. Please understand me, I am not proposing anything untoward. There's a small hotel nearby where I'd make a reservation for you. Everything on the up-and-up. Of course I would cover all your travel expenses."

"Oh," Edie said again. She was having trouble with the concept, the notion of a man paying out real money for . . . what, exactly? "That's very generous of you to offer, but . . ."

"I would want you to feel entirely comfortable about the arrangements," Milo said, mistaking her total slack-jawed amazement for maidenly hesitation. "If you know anyone in the city, anyone who could accompany—that is—escort you, it would be perfectly fine."

"My sister lives in Philadelphia." Would she want to explain any of this to her sister? Did she want to take such a leap, alone or escorted, into Milo Baranoff's lair, and confront the real, actual man? But then, spring break was coming up. It wasn't like she had big plans of her own.

"It would be lovely to meet your sister. I mean, it would be

lovely to see you again. Give us a chance to catch up in person,"
Milo amended, as if aware he'd been sounding too brisk. There
was a note of uncertainty in his voice that made Edie like him
better. She said she would think it over and get back to him.

All his insistence on propriety naturally made her think
about sex, whether sex with Milo was within the realm of pos-
sibility. She walked right up to the edge of that notion and
stopped. None of her boyfriends had offered especially pro-
found experiences; sex was simply one of the things you did together if you were a couple, like cooking dinner. Edie had come
to believe she was lucky that way, not to be passion's plaything,
not to have to go through a lot of impulsiveness and contortions
because her loins were burning, her various parts throbbing,
etc. So that sex, with Milo or anyone else, was not a deal breaker.
Just one more item on the ledger, waiting to be revealed as a pro
or a con.

In the end she said yes, she would fly to New York for five
days of her vacation. She called her sister Anne in Philadelphia
and told her she was visiting a friend and that it would be great
to see her if Anne could get away. Her sister said, "What's this
really about, what kind of friend? How old is this guy anyway?"

"He's just a friend friend."

"So what is he, sixty? Seventy? Eighty?"

"Thanks," Edie said. "Yes, he's ancient, that's why he likes me.
He's too feeble to get anybody more attractive and desirable."

Anne sighed. She was married, a mother, she affected a certain dreary worldliness. "Well, they say it's better to be an old
man's darling than a young man's slave."

"I only met him the one time! You make it sound like we've
plighted our troth!"

"Don't get so upset. I'm just saying. I suppose he has money?"

In the end it was decided that Anne would come up at the beginning of Edie's visit and share her hotel room for a night or two. On her way back from New York, Edie would go to Philadelphia to see her young niece and nephew, whom everyone assumed she adored spending time with.

Ten days later, Edie flew to Chicago, then to LaGuardia, which alarmed her with its smallness and meanness, as if she'd deplaned into a bus station. Milo was unavoidably engaged that evening; he had said he would send a car for her. No one had ever done such a thing for Edie before, and it improved her mood a great deal to see the driver waiting with her actual name written on a piece of cardboard. It was just then turning dark and the city lighted itself for her as she rode. The hotel was small and choice, its lobby paneled with green-veined marble, like something under the sea. There was no problem with her reservation, as Edie had feared. She was installed in a peach-colored junior suite with a bathroom large enough to play cards in. She ordered dinner from the extravagant room service menu, as Milo had insisted she do. Her sister was not expected until the next morning. It was delightful to have everything, even, as it seemed, the entire city, all to herself.

Her sister, when she arrived, approved of the hotel and the suite. "Not bad."

"I imagine it's just the way he does everything," Edie said. "First-rate."

"Hm," Anne said. She stood next to Edie so that they were both reflected in the vast bathroom mirror. Both of them were long-necked and pale-skinned, with yellow hair and surprised-looking eyebrows. Anne had always been considered the prettier of the two, but her skin wasn't holding up well and she wore her hair in a short mom-cut that spoke of defeated vanity. Some balance of power seemed to shift as they stood there, having to do with these reflections, or perhaps with Edie's new and inexplicable status as the object of a noted figure's attention, and this might be why Anne plucked at the sleeve of Edie's cotton blouse and said, "You aren't wearing that to meet him, are you?"

Milo had called Edie's room late last night and they had had one of their usual conversations, made somewhat disorienting by the fact that there were only a dozen blocks between them instead of all those intervening states and a different time zone. "I can't wait to see you," Milo told her, and Edie said she couldn't wait herself, although neither statement was really accurate, since Milo had been able to wait an entire evening while he did whatever it was he had to do instead. And Edie was beyond nervous; she was doubting the whole premise of her association with Milo, which was that through a fluke, a happenstance, two such amazingly compatible people as themselves had chanced to meet. She was losing heart. She was an idiot.

Milo said, "I had a dream about you. I dreamt I was walking along a beach, and the ocean beyond was entirely calm, a beautiful pale green, and the winds blew you ashore in a seashell, like Botticelli's Venus."

"Don't be silly," Edie said. She was pretty sure that Venus was naked in that painting, and this was concerning. "That doesn't even sound like a real dream. I bet you made it up."

"I did," he admitted. "I wanted to have a dream about you, it seemed like a nice thing to do, but I've been taking these sleeping pills and they give me nine hours of a blank screen. Okay, you make up a dream about me."

"I dreamed you were the pilot of a plane I was on, and terrorists tried to hijack us, and you explained to the hijackers that exercising power was a transactional process and that no one on the plane had agreed to any contingent rewards or punishments. That confused them and they left us alone." She had picked up a lot of the lingo by now.

"What, I bored the hijackers into submission? That does sound like me."

"You were heroic," Edie said. He liked it when she was pert and impudent. They both laughed, and Edie felt better about everything.

Milo had told them to take a cab from the hotel the next morning. Anne sniffed that he could have come there himself to meet them, and Edie thought the same, although she did not say so. She was wearing one of Anne's dresses, drapey and cream-colored, "so he won't send you back right away," Anne said. "I hope you're going to have time for some shopping." They took in the Upper East Side neighborhood, which was all about living well, with its townhouses and pleasant sidewalks and the lacy shade of the spring trees. A few people were walking fretful dogs, or dawdling expensively over coffee, but there was a sense of hidden life behind every window. Who were they, those who inhabited such a place? No one Edie could imagine knowing.

Milo's apartment building was less imposing than most of its neighbors, which both relieved and disappointed Edie. They rang his bell and were buzzed in, to a lobby with a black-and-white checkerboard tile floor and a great many mirrors in gilt frames. "Good quality, a little old-fashioned," Anne pronounced. "I imagine he's used to it. Set in his ways." Edie wondered if the stylish ex-wife had lived here, if she'd fretted at the lack of designer oomph.

They took a rasping elevator up to the fourteenth floor and started down the silent corridor. The carpeting was thick and gray and blotted out their footsteps. At the very end of the hall a door opened, and Milo himself stepped out. "Venus approaches! Come here and let me gaze on you!"

Edie did not dare look at Anne. She didn't want to have to explain about Botticelli. Blushing, she allowed herself to be enveloped by Milo's hug, her forehead grazed by his bearded kiss. She introduced Anne, who seemed to have retreated into some zone of private amusement. Then Milo ushered them inside. "Enter the castle!"

Edie's first impression was of dark wood paneling lit by mellow sunlight, dust whirling in the shafts. There were a great many things to look at: paintings in heavy frames, high bookshelves turning the walls into canyons, tiny, stained-glass lamps, lit red or golden, African tribal baskets, dolls' heads, an old-fashioned clock cased in china. Milo led them around a corner and the apartment opened up into an expansive room with pale-blue-figured carpet underfoot, more and more bookshelves, scrolled and carved furniture, and high, narrow windows that allowed for slices of the sky. East, west? She was too turned-around to say.

"Let me show you the place," Milo said, after they had finished admiring things and were at risk of having to talk to each other. They followed him through a dining room with a fireplace and some baronial chairs, past a small, cluttered study—Milo apologizing unseriously for his disorganized habits—down a back hallway, where a kitchen was indicated, though they did not enter it. Then around another corner—the place was huge; it was actually two of the original, 1930s apartments combined, Milo said—to what seemed to be an entirely separate living room. This one was furnished with sleek modern couches and chairs and glass tables, hunkered together like a herd of prey animals amidst all the Old World excess of the rest of the apartment. More evidence of the glamorous wife?

Edie was paying great attention to the rooms so as not to have to look much at Milo himself. In her mind's eye, whenever she'd thought of him in all this time, he was dressed in the dark suit and tie he'd worn the night they'd met, or some variation of it. Those were the clothes in which he appeared on television or on book jackets. Now, confusingly, he was wearing a canvas shirt and suspenders, like a suburban dad in a catalogue. He seemed overanimated, nervous, which Edie put down to the peculiarity of the situation, the not-quite-in-focus quality the two of them had for each other after so much elevated, long-distance carrying-on.

"Those are the bedrooms," Milo said, stopping so abruptly that Edie and Anne nearly collided with him. He made a shooing motion. "Not fit for inspection. At least, not by ladies. Ladies such as yourselves, who ought only to be surrounded by . . . beautiful things."

She and Anne looked at each other behind Milo's back. Anne widened her eyes and lifted her shoulders, indicating puzzlement, wonder, mockery. *Is this guy for real?* Edie tried to tell her, silently, to behave herself.

Milo led them through a different set of passages and hallways so that they were once more in the big room they had first entered. A rolling cart set with plates, silver, teacups, and covered dishes had appeared in their absence. There must be a servant in the place, although they had seen no sign of one. "A bite to eat?" Milo offered, and settled the sisters into chairs around a low table. "Will you have tea? Riesling? Some strawberries, or a macaroon? It's a little early for lunch, but I believe we have a very nice smoked salmon here. Oh, and blini, please try some. They're really only good while they're hot."

From different recesses of the cart, Milo produced a great number of foods, all of them unexpected, choice, novel, presented on frills of watercress or beds of rock salt, dishes made from oysters or eggs or almonds or apples, nothing Edie had thought she wanted, but which, once tasted, seemed to satisfy cravings she had not known she possessed.

Anne seemed happy enough filling her plate with the different offerings. And Milo, Edie was relieved to see, turned relaxed and host-like, fixing the beam of his attention on Anne, asking her about her children, her exercise program, the difficulties of parsing the real estate market in her area, the engaged and serious solicitousness Edie recognized from their many talks.

From time to time he smiled at Edie, as if to say, you see how good I am at this sort of thing, how I can turn it on at will, but you and I have moved beyond this, we have no need to make mere conversation. Edie's hand lay idle in her lap; Milo reached over to take it in his own.

"Isn't it funny," Anne said, "that you and Edie should share so many interests. I mean, honestly, aren't you what they call a public intellectual?" Anne had not missed the hand-holding.

"Oh, but she's a private intellectual," Milo said, and brought his other hand on top of Edie's to entirely envelop hers. She loved it that he refused to retreat or be ashamed, that he had the confidence of his age and station. She was so used to moody boys who spent more time sidling away than reaching out. Right then, her inner gyroscope began to tilt in Milo's direction.

They were still eating when, from a distant room, the sound of a telephone started up like a drill. Milo excused himself and left to answer it. When he came back a few minutes later, he had changed into a dress shirt and tweed jacket. He was rather out of breath. "I hope you'll forgive me, but I have to go attend to some business, some business with my publisher. I won't be gone as much as an hour. Would you like to wait here for me? I want to take you both around the corner to a gallery . . . A friend of mine owns it . . . Amusing items he gets in from time to time. I thought you might enjoy . . . A thousand pardons. With your permission . . . "

"Of course," Edie said, since there was no way to respond otherwise. "We don't mind waiting."

"Make yourself comfortable, do," Milo said, and hurried off.

Anne and Edie looked at each other. "Maybe there was some kind of deadline," Edie said.

"Maybe he's just a hinky guy."

"This food is killer."

"He knows how to order a meal," Anne admitted. "Who cooked it all, elves?"

After a minute or two they stood and began to wander the room, examining the pictures and the furniture. There was quite a lot of everything: tapestries, silver-plated candlesticks, fringed curtains, small items in mother-of-pearl or quartz or jade, a pair of glazed blue ginger jars, bookends in the shape of horses' heads. "Clutter," Anne pronounced.

"It's a particular aesthetic," Edie said. She wondered why she was defending him. She owed him nothing. She was free to dislike his decorating taste if she chose. But she didn't want to dislike it. And even Anne allowed that it was all impressive and museum-like, and that being a public intellectual must pay pretty well.

For a moment they loitered at the door to the next room, then, giving in, set about exploring. The dining room looked as if no one ever ate a meal there. A hall bathroom was utilitarian and disappointing. They peered into the kitchen, which was clean and empty and not particularly new. It was just like a man, Edie thought, not to care about a kitchen. They turned away and paused at the closed door of the study. Anne tried it but it was locked.

"Huh." They looked at each other, considering. "I guess he figured we'd be snooping."

"Let's go on back," Edie said, not liking the idea of getting caught wandering the house. And for all they knew, the maid or butler or whoever had produced the food was somewhere on the premises.

When Milo returned, they were sitting where he'd left them, attempting to read some of the highbrow magazines available for browsing. ("No television," Anne had pointed out.) Milo apologized again and said that publishers were so often this way, leaving everything until the last minute. He seemed more relaxed now that he'd attended to this chore. Edie imagined that there were all manner of high-stakes negotiations that went along with a book deal.

Milo took them to the gallery he'd promised, and a couple of antique stores that looked a great deal like his own living room. He purchased gifts for each of them—he insisted!—a set of painted wooden blocks for Anne's children, a garnet necklace for Edie. They stopped for coffee at a delicatessen where Milo was well known, where little tables were squeezed up against the window, and they selected pastries from a glass case filled with spun sugar and cakes glazed in bitter chocolate and whipped cream swirled into architectural forms. Edie thought that she liked New York, at least this part of it, Milo's part.

He took them by cab back to their hotel. "So that you can

rest up before dinner. I hope you'll be in the mood for some-thing rather special." Edie watched the cab drive away, Milo's arm flung expansively across the back seat. She was going to have to make up her mind about a number of things.

"I'm not going to dinner," Anne announced, once they were back in the room. "Tell him I have the vapors. Tell him I broke a tooth. I'd just be in the way."

"Come on. He probably made reservations, the whole deal."

"Well then you can have both the orchid corsages. The two of you broke the ice. You'll be fine by yourselves."

Maybe they would, but Edie was anxious all over again. She put on her best outfit, a black dress, and a bra Anne loaned her. She fastened Milo's garnet necklace around her throat. "I just don't know," she said, examining the mirror.

"You have to get used to the boobage. Trust me, it's a good look on you."

"I guess." She wasn't too sure about her new, aggressive chest. The garnets felt cold against her skin. They looked like a line of blood around her neck. But she was just being silly. For all her anticipation, she hadn't thought anything through. She didn't know whether she wanted to fall in love with Milo, or just have a dandy time in New York, or something in between. Well, she didn't have to decide yet. She only had to go to dinner.

Milo met her in the hotel lobby, and if he was particularly attentive to her cleavage, wasn't that the intention? Suddenly she imagined a time far into the future, when she and Milo would tell and retell the story of this day, how nervous she had been, how he would admit to being nervous also and doing his best to cover it up. And as if this had already come to pass, as if they already had the ease of long intimacy, Edie smiled and al-lowed herself to be admired, appraised, valued, like one of the beautiful objects in Milo's apartment. For once she could set aside all the degrading effort of wanting to be liked, all her hopeful offerings-up of intelligence, sociability, willingness to be a good sport, all the things, in short, that made it difficult for anyone to ever really like you. She would simply shine.

She saw at once how right Anne had been not to come. Edie made Anne's regrets, Milo expressed his disappointment and solicitude, and then they could move on. Milo had a car waiting. He put his hand beneath her elbow as she stepped off the curb. The evening sky was the color of sherbet, a tender orange. They settled themselves in the back seat and Milo murmured, "This is exactly how I imagined it. Seeing you again, the pure tonic of you. You make me feel as if I've rediscovered spring."

After that, who cared what they ate? Edie hardly paid attention, it might have been ostrich or hamburger. She and Milo sat next to each other in a banquette, much as they had weeks ago, but this time she was aware of the agreeable mass and heat of him, a man who, no matter what his age, might be said to still be in his prime. The maître d' and the chef both made a point of coming by their table. Different bottles of wine were served to them, each one more fragrant, heady, and rare than the last. Edie allowed them to fill her up, and then to spill over. "I am being seduced," she thought airily. She could not recall anyone else ever bothering to do so.

In the car back to the hotel they kissed, enthusiastically if without much accuracy, and when Milo escorted her into the lobby and took his leave, he bent and kissed her hand. Edie felt like a film star or legendary trollop, a woman who might walk around naked beneath a fur coat.

Anne decided to go back to Philadelphia the following day. "Could I just point out, you really don't know the guy? I mean, know know. It doesn't matter how much your souls sing to each other."

"I don't know why you have to turn everything into a cheap joke," Edie said. She was shaky from last night's wine and excess of feeling.

"He's not a normal person. And I don't mean that in a good way."

"Because of course you know him so much better than I do," Edie said nastily. But they made up before Anne left, and agreed that Edie would call when she was ready to make plans for Philadelphia.

She felt better once Milo called, and they spoke in a way that was both shyer and more conspiratorial. It was as if something had already been decided between them. Edie took a cab to Milo's apartment. He met her at the door and they kissed, this time with more expertise. "I can't stop thinking about you," Milo murmured. It was one more new experience for Edie, hearing such a thing from a man. The pale wart in his eyebrow winked at her, but she ignored it.

As before, there was a meal waiting for them: wine, tiny quail stuffed with orzo and capers, and clouds of meringue. Everything delicate and frankly aphrodisiac. Not a normal person? She thought she could get used to not normal. They picked the little birds apart bone by bone, drank their fill. Milo said, "How right it feels to have you here. It's as if we've already done this a thousand times."

"Yes, it is." By now it was not surprising to her when Milo said things she had already told herself. They were that in sync. Had she already told him that she loved cherries? Or had he simply intuited it? Nothing was not fated.

"I feel so absurdly, perfectly contented. I'm afraid someone will come and steal it all away."

"No one's going to steal me from you," Edie said, surprising herself with this declaration. It was as if Milo's grand speaking style was rubbing off on her.

"How can you be so sure? You're young, how can you possibly know your own heart? Let alone want anything to do with such a leaky old, battle-scarred creature as myself. How can I ever make you happy?" In sudden, alarming fashion, he pitched himself forward until his head rested in Edie's lap.

Edie did not believe that two years away from thirty was exactly young. She could have told Milo that none of her previous age-appropriate boyfriends had made her happy for more than fleeting moments, nor had they considered her happiness as something for which they took responsibility. Hadn't she done all the things that were recommended for a blissful, partnered life? The dating, the putting herself out there. The cultivation of hobbies, talents, opinions that were meant to make her interesting and enticing. None of this had produced any splendid results. Why shouldn't she take this other, unexpected path? Give herself over to forces greater than herself, to mystery, to magic, to love! Milo's shiny head in her lap might have been a crystal ball. She raised one hand to stroke it . . .

. . . And just then, in a mirror on the far side of the room, she caught a glimpse of something. She gave a little yelp.

Milo raised himself up. "What? What's the matter?"

"I saw, I don't know what it was. This *face*." In fact she was unsure if she had seen the front or the back of a head, it was that disturbing. She had an impression of something that looked like the inside of a baseball after the cover has been torn off.

"Oh, that's just Amparo. The maid. Perfectly discreet. Please, pay her no mind."

"There's someone else here?" Edie struggled with the thought. But Milo's warm breath was in her ear, his hands making their discreet explorations. This was no time for balkiness.

On this occasion, she did get to see the bedroom.

She did not go to Philadelphia. She only returned to the midwestern college town to pack up her belongings and arrange for a substitute to teach the last weeks of her classes. Her roommate said, "I don't understand. You're running away with Milo Baranoff? Is this, like, a performance piece or something?"

Her sister Anne was more somber. "What kind of life do you think you'll have with him? What do you expect you'll do all day?"

"I can help him with his work. Read things, take notes. Schedule his appearances. Oh come on. You think that's worse than grading freshman comp papers? Anyway, I can always get some kind of a job." As Edie spoke, this future job took on form and shape in her mind. It would be somewhere smart and fast-paced and she would share an office with interesting, oddball people. She would come home and tell Milo about them.

"Don't feel you have to marry him. In fact you probably shouldn't."

That made Edie sore. Her married sister had made Edie's state of single blessedness a matter of solicitous concern. "We haven't discussed it," Edie said, although they had.

"And how did the one wife die?"

"She had cancer! He never talks about her, it's too painful."

"You know in all the piles of stuff in those rooms, I never saw one photograph. Not the wives, the kids, nothing."

"I expect he keeps them in albums. Is that the worst thing you can say about him, he doesn't display family photos?"

"Okay, look, I'm not that far away. Call if you need anything."

"I'll come visit sometime soon," Edie promised, full of good intentions. She was relieved to have gotten off this easily.

It didn't matter what anybody else thought. Milo made reservations for their Barbados trip, a villa with its own private white sand beach. "Unless you would rather go to Switzerland," Milo offered. "I mean, Barbados is a little out of season." But Edie said no, they could save Switzerland for some other time. Back on campus, she would have been arguing with her lying students who would swear they really had turned in their final papers and she must have lost them.

Milo arranged for her to charge clothing at various stores. It was unclear to her just how he did this, since, once she thought about it, she had never actually seen him handling money. Barbados was balmy and easeful. They ate flying fish, and pigeon peas with rice, and pumpkin fritters and drank a great many fancy rum cocktails, because with Milo, there was always considerable attention paid to the pleasures of the table. They toured plantation houses and cruised on a sailing ship at sunset. Edie thought it would be fun to go snorkeling or even deep-sea diving, but Milo had an aversion to going beneath the surface of the water, and so they lay out on their beach, beneath the umbrellas positioned for them by the villa's obliging staff. Edie's new bathing suits were the colors of hibiscus and of guava. Milo wore trunks that gave his majestic, furry stomach ample room. Edie was delighted with the ocean and kept peeking out at it to make certain it had not gone anywhere.

On their third night in the villa, Edie stood at the open patio door to watch the beach, which had turned a radioactive white in the moonlight, and the dark restless water beyond. "Let's go for a walk," she suggested to Milo, who was reading an absorbing book about the Crimean War, one of several he had brought along with him.

Milo made the "Mnn" noise that meant he was too deep in the pages to respond further.

"Okay, well, I'll be back in just a bit," Edie said, stepping out of the door and closing it behind her. She hadn't gone ten steps before she heard Milo scrabbling to get the door open.

"What are you doing?"

"Going for a walk." She guessed he had been too occupied with his reading to hear what she'd said before.

"What are you thinking, heading out there by yourself? Good Lord."

He looked both anxious and indignant. Perhaps he'd thought she'd announced she was going to peel off her clothes and go for a naked swim. Although there wasn't any real harm in that either, was there?

"It's not safe. I really can't allow it."

Edie began to explain that she didn't intend to go in the water, if that was what he was so worried about, trying to ignore the word "allow," which was not something she was used to hearing, either from Milo or anyone else. Milo said that there were criminals, organized gangs who preyed on unsuspecting tourists. She could not be expected to know this since she had never been to the islands before, but he had, he'd heard the stories. "I'm sorry to sound so alarmist, but please understand, I feel responsible for you, making you give up so much, dragging you all the way here . . ."

Edie said that she had not given up anything she missed, and she hardly considered herself dragged anywhere. "Come on out with me, then," she coaxed, and Milo did so, although with a backward glance at his book.

They walked down to the edge of the water, which at that point was an almost equal mingling of Atlantic and Caribbean, and Edie thought she could stand there forever, watching the frill of breaking waves and the vastness of sky and water, and Milo said, "Whatever would I do if anything happened to you? How could I go on?" Edie considered that he must be especially sensitive to the prospect of loss, given his marital history. "Humor an old man," he murmured, reaching for her hand. For the rest of their trip she made sure to complete her beach walks by sunset.

Back in New York, they had a spur-of-the-moment civil wedding, witnessed by two of Milo's friends who were classical musicians and who serenaded them with violin and oboe. They had a merry wedding brunch at the neighborhood deli, with champagne brought in from around the corner. Edie's ring was an emerald set between two diamonds, and it was a little large for her finger but Milo said it could be sized. Since Milo did not wear rings, Edie's wedding gift to him was an old-fashioned pearl-headed stickpin for his tie. It seemed to Edie the very best way of getting married: charming, unfussy, making it up as you went along.

Edie's parents were hurt, of course, that she had "eloped," as her mother put it, and with this much older man who wrote the kind of books they got along very well without reading. Who knew what dire things Anne had already told them. "Baranoff. That sounds Jewish. Is he Jewish? Honey, it all seems so sudden. How many times has he been married before?"

"That doesn't matter. It's just something that happens to

people, all right? Milo's really looking forward to meeting you," Edie said, although that was just a way of speaking. Milo had not gotten around to expressing such anticipation.

"Edie, honey? Now, I don't want to offend you, but it's possible to get an annulment within the Church if there's what they call lack of due discretion, or psychological incapacitation, or some other things the priest will ask you about. I'm going to put your father on—"

Edie hung up the phone. Everyone in her family was a very conventional person. They already thought of her as peculiar and overeducated, lonely and unwomanly. Well, they could add Milo to the list of her disappointing accomplishments.

Meanwhile, she had this whole new life to get under way. She arranged her little shelf of books in one of the many spare rooms. It was understood that she would take up some serious writing of her own, once she had a chance to knock a few ideas around. Edie mentioned, shyly, that she might like to find herself some sort of job, something that took advantage of her extensive and prolonged training in the language arts, and Milo said he would ask around among people he knew. Meanwhile, he encouraged Edie to let him know if she wanted to "fuss with the curtains, anything like that around the place." Edie had not yet decided. The apartment needed updating, surely, but it was so ornate and oversized and dowdy, you couldn't just tackle a little piece of it, as witness the room with the peculiar modern furniture. She hesitated to start in just anywhere.

As for Amparo, the near-invisible maid? Edie got used to seeing her slipping in and out of rooms, a small, wizened Filipina of indeterminate age. Her face was brown and folded in on itself, her hair, where it slipped out of its kerchief, a coarse and patchy gray. It was Milo's habit to leave Amparo's paycheck in the kitchen on Fridays, along with a note indicating any requests for the coming week. She understood English, then, although Edie seldom heard her speak. Was she exploited, should Edie feel any sort of useless guilt in her presence? Or was Amparo grateful for the work? Edie didn't know. There was so much that she did not know, and about so many people.

When Edie offered, as a wifely gesture, to take over some of the cooking from Amparo, Milo asked her why she would want to do such a thing, and Edie had no very good answer.

Milo worked mornings in his study, then went out to clubby, man-about-town luncheons. Edie attended some of these, but it was a strain to keep up with so much conversation by and about people whom she had never heard of although it was assumed she had, authors and columnists and producers and writers of art reviews. In the evenings she and Milo either stayed home for quiet dinners or else went out to receptions or parties with the same sort-of-famous people, as well as some alarmingly decorative young women whom Edie studied for clues as to how she should (or should not) dress. Everyone knew Milo, of course, and everyone was anxious to claim his attention, chat him up, ask him for favors, which he parried with polished ease. There was a reason he made his living by talking. Edie stood next to him and practiced smiling out at the room in an unfocused way. She was not beautiful enough for people to pay her court in her own right. She had an unhappy vision of the fashion-model ex-wife at similar parties, maybe even in the same rooms, every lovely inch of her drawing attention and admiration.

In the cab on their way home that night, Edie asked, "Did Ondaate like going to parties?"

Milo turned to look at her, although in the patchy darkness she could not see his face. "Why do you ask about her?"

"No real reason, never mind," Edie said, backpedaling. "Just wondering."

"You need to understand, I have a great many painful memories."

"Of course. Sorry."

"You are my fresh start. My way of putting certain things behind me."

"Of course," she said again, feeling bad because she had made him unhappy. Still, it would have been a good thing to know what the problems between them had been, if only so that she could avoid repeating the same mistakes. As if Edie would have ever been able to imitate, either by accident or intention, such an exotic creature. Ondaate, or her image, was always turning up somewhere, in the way that people did when you wished to avoid them. In a billboard perfume advertisement, or dressed as a cowgirl in a fashion magazine, or gracing a charity event to promote reforestation. Did she still live in New York? Paris? Africa? It didn't seem to matter. High-visibility people like her were everywhere and nowhere, like the deity.

Edie begged off going to Milo's lunches, saying that she wanted to get her own work done, although she spent most of her time writing amusing e-mails to her old friends back at the university. The rambling, spooky apartment depressed her. Often she went out and just walked, or sat in coffee shops so she could see the sidewalk stream of people coming and going in all their unimaginable richness and oddity. It was like the ocean, she could watch forever. She had only just begun to stick her toes in it.

Edie couldn't help notice that, although when he was home, Milo kept his study door open and she was free to look in and chat with him, when he left the house, the door was always closed and locked. She couldn't decide if she should be offended by this, if it had anything to do with her at all. Maybe it was just habit, the way some people locked their cars no matter where they were. She asked Amparo—that is, she pointed to the locked door and made infantile, encouraging faces. Amparo just shook her head. "Secret," she said.

Edie didn't think she could ask Milo about it. He wasn't a man who liked questions. She'd hoped to learn a little about his two sons, the grown men who were now, technically and ludicrously, her stepsons. A couple of times she'd mentioned them on the borders of conversations, as in, she supposed his sons were every bit as smart as he was. Or, she knew it was early to be making plans for the holidays, but maybe he and his boys were in the habit of spending them together, and he should just let her know.

Milo, of course, saw right through her inexpert fishing. They were eating breakfast in the dining room. One of the mild domestic reforms Edie had instituted was sitting at an actual dining table for meals. Milo put down the knife he was using to spread jam on his croissant. Surely he would be better served by healthier eating habits, Grape-Nuts, say, but she was saving that suggestion for later.

"I've told you I was not the best sort of parent. It was a difficult time for us all."

Edie began to say how she certainly understood this, but Milo held up one hand, silencing her. She had seen him make the same magisterial gesture on the television shows, to good effect. "My sons and I are, for most intents and purposes, estranged. They chose different paths in life, mostly to show their contempt for me. Benjamin is a karate instructor and lives in California with his wife. Jacob joined the military. I don't know if you'll have any occasion to meet them."

Edie would have said how unfortunate this was, how she hoped that in time the breach would be healed, but Milo's traffic-cop hand still silenced her. "The truth is, my dear, that you have a tendency to pry, with all your oh-so-innocent questions. It's not an attractive habit. I don't wish to keep bringing it up, so I hope you will do your best to control it."

Edie said nothing. She felt her face flame with heat. Milo was being unfair. As if it was her fault that he'd done a bad job at fatherhood. She was only asking the most ordinary questions, the kind of thing people asked when they first met you. And she was so very much on his side, so well disposed toward him! So anxious to help, to be of use, to soothe!

Milo must have realized that he'd gone too far. That evening he brought her an intricate braided bracelet made of opals and gold, in its own little red leather case. Edie exclaimed over it and put it on, and their dinner that night was an exceptionally fine one that Milo had delivered from an Indonesian restaurant that had recently opened to great acclaim.

But Edie still felt the sting of her grievance. It nagged and nudged at her. She should have said something, argued back instead of sulking. She knew better. She knew all about cultural conditioning and the danger of female passivity; she'd read all the books. If she had been a bit starstruck by Milo, if marrying him had been entering into a more traditional relationship than she might have imagined—she had even changed her name to Baranoff—it was because women now had a multitude of options. No longer trammeled by expectations or judgments, they could follow their own road. Like those young women who

wrote freely about behaviors that might be regarded as degrading if they had not been matters of personal choice.

This line of reasoning did not entirely console her.

The next day she did Internet searches for Benjamin and
Jacob and found nothing. She took what inventory she could of
Milo's shelves and closets, looking for . . . she wasn't even certain, but she didn't find it. Some remnant of the personal history
that he excised from his book jackets—even, it seemed, from
websites. She found any number of online pictures of him and
Ondaate, of course, gleaned from different publications. What
an odd pair they made, Milo stout and bearded, like a bear turned
into a professor. Ondaate in a tangerine-hued halter dress, taller
than Milo by a head, her long arms draped around his shoulders,
her amazing hair glowing like a moon wrapped in clouds.

Edie shut her computer off and went out into the hallway.
The weather had turned hot and the building's air conditioner
was on, though it labored and fretted and didn't quite keep up
with the heat. It made her feel headachy, out of sorts. Milo had
left for the afternoon. He was taping an interview for National
Public Radio about the cultural history of leprosy. Some of the
things he knew about, the things he wrote about, simply confounded her. The distant mutter of the vacuum cleaner told her
that Amparo was busy elsewhere in the apartment.

Edie stood at the door of Milo's study and tested the doorknob. It was locked, as she expected, but it had a little bit of give
in it. She'd locked herself out of enough apartments to know a
trick or two. She went back to her study and extracted a credit
card from her wallet. She worked the card between the latch
and the door frame until the latch slipped and the door nudged
open. If Milo already thought of her as someone who pried,
well, what did she have to lose?

Nothing in the room looked that remarkable to her, nothing out of the ordinary, certainly nothing worth locking up. Only Milo's usual mess of books and papers, as if genius and creativity required disorder. Edie took a few steps inside, careful not to touch anything. On the desk's surface was a yellow pad scribbled with Milo's notes, his thicket of pen marks. She bent over it and read what seemed to be a denunciation of someone Milo took issue with: "absolutely puerile thought process," "pitiful need for validation," "lack of any real rigor or discipline." Edie was familiar with this sort of diatribe. Intellectuals of Milo's caliber seemed to engage in regular public blood feuds, defending and attacking, choosing words as if they were pins in a voodoo doll.

Edie made a slow circuit around the room. Books and more books, like every room in the apartment. Many of the ones here were copies of books Milo had written himself. Edie felt her headache tighten. What a strange sort of life it was, this production of ideas, this herd of words. You respected it, of course, as you respected any sort of accomplishment, but there was something wearying in it also, something deadening and futile.

With great caution and delicacy, she teased open the drawers of Milo's desk and found nothing more interesting than bundles of old canceled checks. All this while she tried to avoid the computer's black and silent screen, but finally she pressed one finger to the on button, and it chimed and glowed.

Of course he used a password. The screen presented her with the blank window and waited, with mechanical patience, for her to type it in. She had no idea what it might be. She realized that she no longer heard the noise of the vacuum cleaner. Hastily, she shut the computer off and left the room, pulling the door shut, the lock tight, behind her.

The next day, Milo announced he had to make an unexpected trip to Australia, a last-minute opportunity to speak at a seminar on the workings of the International Criminal Court. Unfortunately, they were only able to extend the invitation to Milo. He'd inquired, of course, but the cost of airfare, of the accommodations . . .

Edie said she understood, although she didn't entirely. She thought that Milo might have paid for her airfare himself. Milo was excited at the prospect of the trip, and Edie told herself not to make such a big deal of it. This was what Milo did, after all, travel from one plummy opportunity to another, arranged by people who paid him to lend star power to their enterprises. She'd go with him next time. Milo said, "It's only for a week. Amparo will take care of the house, no worries. And we can talk on the phone, just like old times!"

There was a great deal of dry cleaning and packing and arranging of itineraries, and Edie was "invaluable," Milo said, in helping him. They were especially fond with each other, as if the idea of separation was restoring some of the energy of their original courtship. And maybe, although you might not want to think it, there were people who managed better if they did not contend with the daily fact of each other at close quarters.

On the morning he left, Edie went downstairs with him, helped supervise the loading of his carefully prepared suitcases, kissed Milo goodbye, waved until he was out of sight, then went back to the huge, empty apartment. There was really nothing here for her to do. Although she had reminded him of it a time or two, Milo had not yet called any of his notable friends who might have provided her with employment. She took inventory of how she felt. Forlorn. Restless. The life she'd imagined for herself had not yet begun. She was at low tide.

Milo would be on a plane for hours and hours. Edie went

out for a walk to try to lift herself out of her discontented state. When she came back, Amparo was waiting for her just inside the apartment door—she had never done such a thing before—her face knotted and furrowed even more than usual. She plucked at Edie's sleeve. "Missy, Missy!"

"What? What's the matter?" Edie pushed past her. A man stood in the main room, hands behind his back, examining the bookshelves. He was wearing a blue military uniform, his hat on a chair. His dark hair was cut short. He turned toward Edie and she had the sensation of recognizing him without knowing him. Surely this was one of Milo's sons.

"Excuse me," she said. "I wasn't expecting anyone."

"And who are you?" He had Milo's voice, but a couple of tones lighter. Milo's big forehead and dark eyebrows, but with everything smoothed and straightened.

"I live here. You don't. I'm Edie Baranoff."

He looked her up and down. "You're kidding."

Amparo was still crouched in a corner of the hallway, ready to flee or sound the alarm. "I didn't catch the name," Edie said.

He pointed to the name patch on his chest. "Bialosky, United States Army."

Edie frowned. "I'm sorry, I thought you were . . . Isn't Milo your father?"

"Legally. Biologically. Occasionally." Edie shook her head, not getting it. "Obviously, there's some information he hasn't shared with you."

Edie ignored this. "Well he's out of town. He just left."

"How disappointing," he said, not sounding particularly disappointed. "So, what happened to the big tall goonybird girl? The previous Mrs. Baranoff?"

"I'm sure I don't know. How did you get in here, anyway?"

"People tend to trust a man in uniform."

"They shouldn't. I don't."

"But you're curious. Did you say Edie? Jake."

She didn't offer to shake hands with him. They stared at each other. Edie said, "Why do you have a different last name?"

"Curiouser and curiouser."

Edie turned to Amparo, and, pantomiming and nodding, tried to convey that things were all right, all right, and that she should bring them some coffee. Amparo wailed and fled. They watched her go. Jake Bialosky raised an eyebrow, inquiring. "We don't have much company," Edie explained.

"Good thing, that."

"Why don't you sit down. Are you a sergeant or a captain or something?"

"Lieutenant. Or something."

Edie waited until he chose a seat, then took one opposite him. There was a space of silence that felt like a competition. Then Edie said, "I'm afraid that Milo hasn't told me much about you."

"A shocking oversight." He was enjoying himself, all jaunty hostility.

"How long has it been since you've seen him?"

"How long have the two of you been married?"

"Never mind that. Why did you want to see Milo, anyway?"

"I need a reason to see my own dear pappy?" It was the strangest thing, looking at him. Like viewing Milo's baby pictures. "I was in New Jersey, visiting my mother. This is a side trip. A whim."

"Your mother. I'm sorry, I thought . . . I thought she had cancer." And died. Milo had said so.

"That was a long time ago, when I was a kid."

"So . . . she's all right?"

"Any reason she shouldn't be? No thanks to Milo. He bailed on us. Of course, he wasn't Milo back then. He was Myron Bialosky. You didn't know? Just one more thing, I guess."

"That's ridiculous."

"He underwent a convenient transformation."

"Prove it."

"I didn't bring documentation." He shrugged, Milo's habit of moving one shoulder, then the other.

"Uh-huh."

"It drives my mom crazy. 'Milo? Why Milo? He wants to be classy? Why not Maurice?' She took to calling him 'Milo the Magnificent.' The name kind of stuck. I think he actually likes it."

"That's some story," Edie said. People could say anything.

"You don't believe me. Okay. Here's the rest of it anyway. We lived in Bayonne, my mom's still there. Just your ordinary, one-generation-up-from-the-ghetto immigrant life. Myron was working for his father-in-law, my grandfather, painting houses. Can you imagine that? But Myron's an ambitious guy. Smart too. You may have noticed, we are never allowed to forget how smart he is."

He was watching her for some reaction. Edie wondered if he was here for money, if he'd get around to asking about money. "Go on."

"I guess he wanted a brand-new shiny life, not a sick wife and two little kids. He started spending time in the city, he said he was working there and taking night school courses. And maybe he was. Along with making sure he met some useful people who could help him out. We saw him less and less. He sent money for a while. He talked my mother into a divorce and married this rich Canadian woman. Oh come on. You didn't think he earned all this by the sweat of his brow." Bialosky nodded to the room's compass points.

Edie heard a faint rattling that meant Amparo had delivered the coffee cart to the next room. Edie got up and wheeled it in to them. "A Canadian. That's a nice touch. I'll make sure to ask Milo about her."

"You do that. Cream, please. No sugar."

"So where is she?" Edie asked, pouring his coffee. "This Canadian?"

"She died."

"Oh come on," Edie said, scornful now.

"You're very loyal. I'm sure he likes that."

"It's in really bad taste, having her die. It's piling on."

"Rather unexpectedly, I believe."

"So now he's a murderer."

"I didn't say that. But there are different ways of killing somebody," Bialosky said. "I see that your ring doesn't quite fit."

Her left hand curled into itself, a reflex. The emerald slid around to her palm. "It needs to be adjusted. I haven't taken it in yet."

"I expect it's recycled."

"You hate him and you want me to hate him too."

"I wouldn't say it rises to the level of hatred. More like, loathing."

"Maybe you're just some kind of con man."

"Maybe Milo's the con man." He drank some of the coffee and set the cup down, reached into his jacket pocket, took out a card, and scribbled on it. "Here. Call me, we can keep up with the family news." Edie didn't reach for it, so he put it on the table.

"Shouldn't you be overseas somewhere? Shouldn't you be off fighting a war?" She thought that anybody could go out and rent a uniform, anybody could pretend to be anybody.

"I'm stateside now. Fort Drum. Milo will be so pleased to hear it. Where did he find you, anyway? You look, I don't know, more wholesome than his usual."

"Perhaps," Edie said, "you wouldn't mind seeing yourself out."

Bialosky stood, tucked his hat under his arm, and left the room. The front door closed behind him. Edie's nerves jingled and jangled. At that moment what seemed important was not even the truth of the matter, but what she chose to believe. Was she really loyal? Did she want to be? It seemed as if she had been given a choice as to exactly which of two ways she wished to be stupid.

That evening, after Amparo left to go home, Edie stood again in front of Milo's study door. Once more, she used a credit card to ease the latch open, and sat down at his computer. When the password window appeared, she typed in, *Milothe-Magnificent*.

The screen changed to its home page, open for business. Edie tried his e-mail account. His mailboxes were tidy and disappointing, as if he'd cleaned them out before he left town. A couple of messages had come in, one from a charity foundation and one from someone hoping that Milo would blurb a book about the coming environmental apocalypse. And a one-line message sent just last night from someone with a screen name of re-markablelady: *Have you forgotten?*

Before she could talk herself out of it, Edie typed in a reply: *Remind me.* And sent it off.

She closed the computer and left the room. Oh goddamn

Lieutenant Something, scratching the itch of her neglected-wife grievance, sending her peeping and prying in what was certainly a bad idea.

But there was also something thrilling about it.

Milo called from Australia in the middle of her sleep. The connection was tinny and his voice had a filtered quality. Still, he sounded in excellent spirits. Everything was going very well, very well indeed, and he hoped Edie was getting by all right, and wasn't it funny to think that here, Down Under, it was already tomorrow!

Edie sat up in bed, listening to him. She said she was fine, and she was glad to hear that he was enjoying himself, and he said he would let her get back to sleep now. "Goodbye, Myron," she said, and there was an especially long, filtered pause before he said goodbye to her.

In the morning she called her sister Anne. "What if it turns out that somebody might have told a few fibs about their past? Would that be a big deal? A mortal sin?"

"Somebody like a spouse? I don't know, I guess it would depend on if the person married to them felt like they were being played. What's going on?"

"I'm not sure." She didn't want to tell Anne about Jake Bialosky, if only because it would make everything seem more real. "I guess I'm having trust issues."

"Has he been screwing around on you?" Anne asked, too avidly.

"No, that's not it." Edie was indignant. But then, what about remarkablelady? And once you allowed yourself to doubt, everything began to unravel. If Milo wasn't Milo, what else might be false? She hid Jake Bialosky's card away in her copy of *The Foucault Reader*.

She knew she wasn't going to be able to stay away from Milo's computer. She was curiouser and curiouser. She was bitten and smitten. This time Edie went through his address book. There was no entry under Bialosky. But here was Edie, along with her old campus address. There were also a great many female names, but most of these were only first names, Suzanne or Maeve or Helena, with just a phone number attached. And here, although she had not been expecting it, was Ondaate, complete with phone, e-mail, and Manhattan address.

Reckless now, she dialed the number. It was answered on the third ring, surely by Ondaate herself. Who else would speak with that peculiar intonation, that combination of lilt and purr: "Halloo?"

Edie had not thought about what to say. "Oh, hi, you don't know me, but my name is Edie Baranoff."

"Baranoff? What does the little patoot want from me?"

"Nothing, he doesn't even know I'm calling."

"Who are you, Baranoff?" Suspicious now. "Some other family?"

"No, Milo and I got married." Edie waited a beat. "Recently."

"You want what, congratulations? Or advice? Or where I hid his Viagra? I did that. Hid it so he would not distress me."

Edie decided to pretend this was humorous. "Oh ha ha. No, that's okay, I guess I just wanted to say hello, you know, ahead of time, in case we should ever see each other, around town."

"If I am seeing Milo, I am running the other way. He is a terrible snob man. No one is ever good enough for him. He is always pick, pick, pick at me. I am too thin, too stupid, too foreign. He marries me just to tear me down! Hateful man! I have no time for this!"

"Wait, could I just ask you, do you know anything about him being married to another woman, a Canadian? A woman who died?"

"If she died it was because he bored her to death with his big talk. I have other problems, I am hanging up. I have cut off all my hair and now my head is very tiny. Goodbye."

Edie was still at Milo's computer. The e-mail bell chimed. The message was from remarkablelady. Edie opened it. It was a picture of two enormous breasts, globe-sized and tipped with spreading brown nipples, distorted by the camera angle. The breasts were thrust forward and filled the entire screen, the body behind them invisible. Edie deleted the picture and shut the computer down. Milo was due back home the day after tomorrow.

He called from Sydney, where he had a night's layover, still jazzed up from his week of oratory and glad-handing and dining well. The conference had been a great success. Everyone said so. But of course he was looking forward to getting back home, he'd missed her so!

"I expect you'll be jet-lagged," Edie said. "I'll try to let you sleep in when I get up. I have some job interviews the next morning."

Milo said he must have misheard her. Something about interviews? "Yes," Edie said. "I called around to a few of your friends." She mentioned their well-connected names, the editors and columnists and producers who held the keys to so many kingdoms. "I'm hoping one of them can come up with something for me."

There was the gravel sound of Milo clearing his throat. "I'm not sure this is such a good idea, sweetheart."

"Oh? Why not?"

"Well, when you get hired through the back door, so to speak, you enter the workplace with other people resenting that, you know, and that's a burden you don't want to have."

Edie pretended to mishear him. "Yes, it's exciting, isn't it? The pay probably won't be much for an entry position, but there's tons of potential. You have a good flight!"

Milo arrived home late the next evening, cranky from travel and with bloodshot eyes. Right away he started in on the job search. "I really wish you hadn't made those calls. It could put me in a very awkward position. Conflicts of interest, that sort of thing."

"But you said you were going to call them. And when you didn't get around to it, I thought I could do it myself and spare you the trouble." This was not entirely untrue, only mostly.

"And what makes you think you have the qualifications to do the sort of high-end work we're talking about here? I'm sorry, my dear, but I believe you're confusing your very ordinary liberal arts education with the kind of advanced knowledge and sophistication these positions require."

They stared at each other. Milo rubbed at his eyes, inflaming them further. "I don't want to talk about this anymore, I'm too tired right now. But I don't think I can sleep yet. I might catch up on e-mail. It was so difficult to get Internet access."

Did Edie imagine that he gave her a particularly searching look when he mentioned e-mail? But that was nonsense; he'd been halfway around the world when she'd done her snooping. Edie said solicitous things about the wearying effects of crossing so many time zones. She went to bed but she couldn't sleep either. The two of them had entered some new phase. Milo might not be exactly who he said he was, or who she had believed him to be. But then, it was possible that she was not the person she had believed herself to be all this while.

By the next day, when she looked at Milo's study, he had nailed new and sturdier pieces of wood trim around the door frame.

She went out and got herself a job in the office of a company that developed television shows for different cable outlets, shows that featured makeovers and competitive weight-loss derbies and battling families, all her old trashy favorites. She had missed watching television. Her job was "production assistant," and it involved a lot of fetching things and answering phones. The office was a hectic place where business was transacted at top volume. Edie would make herself indispensable. She saw that right away. She would learn the ropes and anticipate needs. She would unpack some of her old hanging-out clothes, jeans and T-shirts and boots so that she'd look like everyone else there. Milo would hate it.

And he did. "I can't imagine what you were thinking. These are vulgar people who make a vulgar product. I can't be associated with any of this."

Edie said that he was not associated with it. "I'm not using Baranoff. I'm on the payroll as Edie Gordon. And you never have to watch any of the shows."

"Why couldn't you work somewhere more"—Milo raised his hands and let them fall to his sides—"suitable?"

"You told me I was too badly educated and commonplace to do anything important," Edie reminded him.

"I didn't mean you should do something ridiculous! Why do you need to work anyway, don't I provide for you?"

"Now Milo, please don't be prehistoric. Oh! I forgot to tell you, your son Jake stopped by while you were gone."

"Jacob? What did he want?"

"Just saying hello, I expect. He didn't stay long. He seems like a very nice young man. And good-looking! Takes after you."

Milo gnawed on his bottom lip, considering her. His eyes looked even worse today, puffy and with drooping, blood-red rims. At least he'd stopped going on about her job. Edie said, "Would you like me to call the pharmacy and see if they have any kind of salve, you know, cream they could send over? In case you picked up an infection."

"What are you saying? What infection?" He tried to stare her down but he was too bleary.

"Your eyes, silly. Conjunctivitis. Very contagious. Try not to rub them. I can call and they'll run right over with some medicine. The kinds of services you can get in New York! It's really . . ." Edie paused. ". . . remarkable."

Milo went to the eye doctor, who diagnosed an infection and prescribed antibiotics and a green eyeshade that made him look like an irradiated frog. He sat in the main room and brooded, unable to read or write. Edie suggested books on tape, or voice-recognition software, or even a television, but Milo would have none of it. She was glad she had a reason to leave.

It was her second full day of work. She had a blast. Already she could tell who among her fellow employees would become her friends, who would be a pain in the ass, how she'd navigate among them. There would be opportunities, possibilities. She would prosper.

She was walking home, enjoying the mild chill in the air, the blue and lengthening shadows, the preposterous fall fashions in the boutique windows. As she approached the apartment building, she saw Amparo standing outside, dressed in her old furry coat and clutching a number of plastic bags. Her tragic monkey face registered distress. Edie hurried up to her. "Amparo, what's the matter?"

The old woman's hands clutched at Edie's sleeve. "Quitting."

"What happened, is Mr. Baranoff all right? Amparo?"

She only shook her head and pressed a small key into Edie's hands. "Secret," she said, then scuttled away toward the subway and disappeared underground.

Apprehensive now, Edie hurried upstairs. Milo was just where she'd left him, installed in his chair with a litter of Kleenex, coffee cups, and empty plates surrounding him. "What happened with Amparo, what did you do to her?" Edie demanded.

"How telling," Milo said, "that you assume I did something to *her*. A number of small but valuable objects are missing. She removed them and sold them for profit. I can think of no other explanation."

"What objects, what's missing? How can you keep track of everything, you're practically a hoarder."

"Women," said Milo wisely, "will always steal. It makes no difference how generous you are to them. They aren't happy unless they can sneak around behind your back and pick your bones. I know what this job business is all about. You're seeing someone, another man."

Edie stiffened. "That's preposterous."

"Is it, now. You think because I'm stuck here, I don't know what goes on." The green eyeshade wagged at her.

"Ridiculous."

"You married me for my money. Now you think you can frisk around, kicking up your heels."

"I married you because you asked me to! What's the matter with you, are you having side effects from those pills?"

"This all has to do," Milo said, aiming his gaze just to the right of where she was standing, "with your pitiful need for validation. Your lack of any real rigor or discipline."

Edie gaped at him. "Incredible."

"I used to believe you were merely young and unformed. Now, strange as it is to say so at the moment, I see more clearly. There's something insipid about you, my dear. Something that feels the need to attach itself to more established personalities and ingratiate yourself. So who is he? Now that you've sucked me dry, who's your next victim?"

Edie was steadying herself now after her first shock. "I don't believe anybody thinks of you as a victim, Milo. I certainly don't."

"Some greasy actor? Cameraman?" His jowls shook with rage.

"That is . . ." she gathered her nerve, . . . an absolutely puerile thought process."

If Milo had a reaction to this, she couldn't read his eyes behind the green shade. He said, "Use caution, my dear. I am not without resources. The wounded animal is the most dangerous."

This alarmed her, but she took care not to show it. "I think you're simply in a foul mood from sitting around all day and eating the wrong things. If you're constipated, it's your own fault."

Edie went to her bookshelf and retrieved the card with Jake Bialosky's phone number. Milo was still in the living room; she could hear him coughing and fretting. Milo was keeping his study locked these days, even while he was home. Edie fit the key Amparo had given her into the lock. She let herself in and set the dead bolt. For extra protection, she propped a chair beneath the doorknob.

She used her cell phone to call Jake Bialosky. She reached his voice mail and he leapt into her ear, sudden and immediate, as if he were in the room. Edie stumbled over her message. "Hi, ah, this is Edie, ah, we met last week, how are you? Could you give me a call as soon as you get this? Your father's having some kind of a fit."

She hung up and listened for noises in the hallway, but the apartment was quiet. Her heart beat and beat. Had Milo gone crazy? Or maybe he had always been crazy. She switched on his computer. Its screen brightened. He had received a new e-mail, this one from someone with a camera held between her knees.

A light shone from beneath the door, then a darkness moved back and forth along it. Milo. He rattled the doorknob. "What's the meaning of this?"

"I need a little me time, Milo."

"Open this door." He threw his weight against it, but the lock held. "What's the matter with you?"

"Nothing. Aside from being, you know, insipid and pitiful and all that."

A pause while he regrouped and sugared his voice. "Sweetheart?" He spoke into the door's crack. "Can't we just talk? I'm sorry. I don't know what got into me. You're right, it must be that medicine, I'm having a reaction." He paused. Edie kept silent. "You know I don't believe any of those things I said, how could I?"

"Which things, exactly, did you not mean?" She was clicking through the onscreen desktop, but these were mostly the files for his boring books.

"I was feeling sorry for myself. I don't even remember. Please open the door."

"I think I'll stay in here, thanks."

"I shouldn't have accused you of infidelity." He tried the door-knob again. The chair wobbled. "Although you do like attention, don't you? You make this particular face when we're out in pub-lic, this 'Please gratify me with an admiring glance' expression. Let me in and I'll show you what it looks like."

"Go away, Milo."

"You're a modern girl, aren't you? You believe everything you read in your magazines, you want everything you see in television commercials. You dress yourselves up like tramps and then you expect people to take you seriously when you go to work and start ordering everybody around."

Edie tried his Internet history. News sites, mostly, and some that might have been escort services, and a few more surpris-ing ones that featured comic book characters and cute animal videos.

"Are you listening to me? I should have left you where I found you, out in the cornfields with the illiterate undergraduates. I brought you here, I introduced you to people you never would have met on your own in a million years, the very best artists, writers, thinkers. I hoped you'd fit in, or at least that you wouldn't embarrass me. Did you even attempt to improve your-self? To do the kind of serious, first-rate research and scholar-ship that you claimed was your life's goal?"

She didn't want to believe anything Milo said, but what if he was right about her? What if she was ordinary? All those years spent reading and studying and grinding away at her thesis. Sup-pose she had no particular aptitude or talent, no thoughts worth thinking, let alone writing down? What presumption, what a waste of time and energy, what a fool that would make her.

"Shall we enumerate all the ways in which you're a disap-pointment? You've simply traded one mediocre job for another.

Now you will produce the televised pap which your students back in Cornville gobble up. You haven't made a positive impression on a single one of my friends. They barely remember your name. And by the way, you've gained some weight."

Here was a Skype account, with a history of calls to "Brenda." Brenda? She heard Milo stamping around in the hallway, impatient because she wasn't answering. She said, "Just how many dead wives do you have, Milo? I'm a little confused."

He made a roaring noise and rattled the door again, then retreated down the hall. Edie tried Jake Bialosky's number again, and again got voice mail. She punched in her sister Anne's phone number and waited while it rang. Anne answered. "Edie? What's up?"

"Do you think I'm fat? I mean, was I fat the last time you saw me?"

"What? You're not even close to fat, if you were a supermarket chicken nobody would buy you. Can I call you back? Jenna's ready for bed and she wants me to read her a story."

"Okay." Anne hung up. Edie called Jake's voice mail again. "Hi, this is Edie again, I was really hoping to talk to you."

Jake clicked on. "Hello? You still there?"

"Oh, hi. I don't know if you remember me, but . . ."

"What's going on over there, what's the matter with Milo?"

Adrenaline was catching up with her and making her shake. "I'm not sure, well, he has an eye infection."

"And it's making him have fits? You mean, seizures? Did you call an ambulance? Do you need me to come over?"

"Not that kind of fit. More like, a tantrum. What, you're in town? Aren't you in the army? I locked myself in his study and he's trying to break down the door."

"I'm coming over."

"Wait, I need to ask you . . ." Her phone buzzed. Anne was calling. "Hold on a minute, would you?"

Edie switched over to Anne's call. Anne said, "Jenna's looking for her tiara, she won't get in bed without it. Whoever came up with the idea for princess merchandise, they really cashed in. I just wanted to say, I don't think you're a bit fat. But you could do some toning exercises, things that strengthen the core, you know, Pilates, or some of the yoga classes. You must have a gym on every corner in that neighborhood."

"I can't stay on the line. Milo's mad at me, he's been carrying on about me getting a job. And some other stuff."

Anne was asking what kind of job when Edie switched back to Jake. "Hi, Jake?"

"I'm just now getting into a cab."

"Oh, good. But listen, I need to ask you, what's your mother's name?"

"It's Friedman. Brenda Friedman. She remarried. Why? What's Milo doing?"

Edie listened. She heard noises at some distance, the sound of heavy objects hitting the floor. She guessed Milo was in her study, laying waste to her bookshelves. "He's around here somewhere."

"If I can't get into the building, I'm calling the police."

"Okay, bye." Edie hung up and typed in the number on the Skype account. A woman answered on the fourth ring.

"Myron?"

"No, this is . . . a friend of Myron's. Is this Brenda?"

"What friend, where's Myron?"

"He's busy." The throwing noises had stopped. Now he was whacking and hacking at things, most probably with the cere-

monial Japanese katana sword that was on display in the dining
room.

"You wait right there!" the woman told Edie.

A minute later the computer screen dimmed, then brightened. An old woman with unconvincing red hair stared out at
Edie, looking her over. "Who are you?"

"I'm Mi . . . Myron's wife."

"No you're not. The wife is some colored girl."

"I'm the new wife."

"Well I'm the old one. Ha." Brenda's neck and face were
powdered with some flour-like cosmetic and her red lipstick was
slightly off-center. Her head bobbed around on the screen in a
disconcerting way, as if it was severed.

"Wasn't there some other lady? After you? The one who—"

"Dead Debbie. The one who died at the dentist's, they gave
her too much gas. There was a big lawsuit. Dead Dental Debbie.
We were all very sad about it. Ha. Does Myron know you're
calling?"

"No, I was just, you know, curious. I guess he didn't tell you
about me."

"He mostly likes to call and talk about his latest too-big-for-
his-britches big deal." The head tilted and squinted into the
computer screen, taking Edie in. "How old are you anyway?
Since when did he start marrying children?" More of the squinting. "None of my business, but can he still manage a normal
married life? If you know what I mean."

"I met your son Jake. He came to visit."

"Jake is a good boy. Like his brother. I tried to do my best.
What's that racket?"

Out in the hallway, Milo was using the sword to gouge and

splinter the wood around the doorknob. Edie said, "We're having sort of a fight, me and Myron."

"Well let me talk to him. He needs to calm down, his blood pressure is way beyond stupid."

"I've been trying to get him to ease up on the red meat and butter."

"That's good, that's what you ought to be doing. He takes up with all these fast numbers who don't know a thing about feeding a family."

Edie's phone chimed. It was Anne calling back. "Excuse me a minute," Edie told the head. "Hi, did you get Jenna to bed?"

"Yes, finally. You got a job? A real job, I mean, not just teaching?"

"That is so insulting, why do you always have to devalue me? I don't want to talk about this right now." She hung up. "Sorry," she said to Brenda Friedman. "My sister. She has these attitudes."

"Is that Myron I hear carrying on?" Brenda asked. He was pounding on the door with his fists and bellowing.

"Uh-huh."

"You should let me talk to him, he knows I don't put up with that kind of foolishness."

"Here he is now," Edie said, as the door burst and gave way. Milo leaned on the door frame, gasping for breath. The sword point was broken off. His green eyeshade had worked its way up over his forehead, and his eyes were clotted with rheum. He turned his head from side to side, as if trying to find her. Edie stood, ready to bolt or crouch.

"Myron, for God's sake, look at you," Brenda Friedman said from the computer. Her red mouth made a disapproving shape.

"Get a grip! You sit down right now before you hurt somebody! What happened to your eyes?"

Milo dropped the sword and sank to his knees on the carpet. Brenda said, "Sit up, I can't see you very clear. What are you now, some man-of-action superhero type? Every new woman, it's a new you. Then you get tired of yourself. You get tired of the woman. Myron! Talk to me!"

Milo hauled himself up to rest his chin on the desk. "Brenda, I don't feel so good."

"I'm calling 911," Edie announced, as Milo clutched at his chest, turned beet-colored, and fell over backward with a crash.

"Myron, Myron!" A wailing noise from the computer. "Boychik! Why did you ever leave home?"

Jake Bialosky arrived just as the paramedics were wheeling the gurney with Milo's body through the apartment door. Milo had been bundled and zipped into a heavy-duty black rubber bag for transport. A number of the seldom-seen neighbors had opened their apartment doors to observe his progress down the hall. Jake conferred with the paramedics, then touched Edie's arm. "You okay?"

"Yes, thank you." And she was, or she would be, once she got over being stupefied. She looked Jake over. "You aren't wearing your uniform."

"I was mostly trying to impress before," he admitted.

"I guess you're like, a man of action."

"What?" Edie shook her head: never mind. "Did you need to go back in and sit down?" Jake asked.

"Not in there. I don't think I want to have anything to do with the place."

"Understandable."

She would sell it all and move to somewhere cool and modern and clean. She would keep her nifty underpaid job. She would become the person she was meant to be all along. It was as if forces greater than herself had solved the problem of her existence. She turned to Jake. "Would you think it was terrible of me if I said I really could use a drink somewhere?"

He was studying her, making up his mind about her, or maybe remaking it. "My mom called me. I should call her back."

"Of course."

"Listen, maybe you could use some help the next few days. I feel kind of bad about, well, everything."

"Me too," Edie said, although she was pretty sure that there were things she might, in time, come to feel not bad about at all.

PRINCE

"There's a dog that's seen better days," Sheila said. She was standing at the front window, eating her breakfast of peanut butter and toast. Ellen came up behind her to look. Sheila already had her coat on, and it was hard to see past her sister's thick, corduroy shoulder.

"Where?" Ellen said, but then she saw the dog. It was standing on the sidewalk as if taking the air, or maybe it had no particular place to go. It was a largish, buff-colored dog with a plumey tail that curled over its back. It did not resemble any recognizable breed, and whatever its mix of ancestry, the parts had not meshed well. Its legs seemed longer in back than in front, its chest was too heavy, and its head, with its long, upright ears and narrow black muzzle, resembled a kangaroo's. "It's a boy dog," Ellen said, pointing. "See?"

"Don't be cute," Sheila said. They watched as the dog took a few steps, then lay down on the sidewalk. "I expect it's a stray. If it's still around when it's time for you to go to work, call me and I'll call the dogcatcher. Don't go out there. You never know about a strange dog. It could have rabies, it could bite you. It could have mange. You understand? Ellen?"

"Yes," Ellen said. Every minute of every day there were things she was supposed to do and not do. That was Sheila. She'd worn out a husband and now she was wearing out Ellen.

Sheila turned away from the window and started laying hands on all the items she needed to leave the house: purse, keys, lunch sack, coffee mug. Although she took these same things with her every day that she went to work, there was always something hectic about the process, as if Sheila was afraid one of them might have escaped. It made Ellen nervous, and that made Sheila nervous, staring Ellen down with her severest eyebrows. "Did you take your pill yet?" Sheila asked her.

"Yes."

"Don't say yes if you aren't sure. Let's go look."

In the kitchen, the brown prescription bottle was still in its place in the cupboard next to the sink. Sheila took the bottle out and set it on the counter. "We've talked about this. I've talked until I was blue in the face."

Ellen understood that "blue in the face" was just a way of speaking. But it got caught in the drain of her brain, where it went round and round, blue in the blue in the blue in the

"Ellen? I have to get to work."

Ellen took the glass of water Sheila had poured out for her, and the pill she held out, and swallowed it down. "There you go," Sheila said. "Now you're right as rain. You're giving me that look again. Do not give me that look. When you get to work, I want you to talk to Mrs. Markey and the other people. I want you to make an effort. Smile. Just for practice, it doesn't have to mean anything."

Sheila was her younger sister, but she acted like she was the older one.

Ellen stood at the front window and watched Sheila back the car into the street. The dog was still there, in the middle of the sidewalk, looking around him like he was in the bleachers at a ball game. Sheila paused the car and tapped the horn, probably to try and get him to go away, but the dog just looked around some more, and Sheila drove off.

Ellen stayed at the window. She didn't have to get to work until ten, and even then it didn't really matter if she was late. The dog had its mouth open and was panting, even though it wasn't hot outside. Ellen wondered if he was thirsty. He probably didn't live around here and had been wandering around trying to find his way home, and now he was too tired to go any farther. Maybe hungry too.

Ellen filled a plastic bowl from the cupboard with water. She opened the refrigerator and took out the leftover casserole, beef and noodles. She cut a big square of it and put it on a paper plate and set it in the microwave to take the refrigerator chill off. They had lunch meat, ham, and Ellen laid some of that on the plate, along with a couple of pieces of cheese that she peeled loose from their plastic wrapping. They had never had dogs in the house, so she wasn't sure what they ate, except dog food.

She carried the water to the front door, set it down, and went back for the plate of food. Then she opened the door just enough to look out. The dog hadn't moved. Ellen waited to see if it was going to run at her and try to bite, but it just turned its black kangaroo-shaped nose in her direction, in a polite way, as if not wanting to ignore her. Ellen put the bowl and the plate a few steps out on the front walk. "Here you go."

Ellen went back in the house and shut the door. She watched

as the dog appeared to think about getting up, then scrambled to its feet and came up the front walk. It put its nose into the food and ate it in big smacking gulps. It lapped up the water, then went back to the paper plate to lick it clean. When it was done, it nosed around the evergreens beneath the window. Its curled tail stuck out from the bushes like a handle.

Ellen left the window to put the food away in the kitchen, and when she came back, the dog was gone, on its way home, Ellen hoped. It was best that it not be here when Sheila returned from work, since Sheila really was somebody who would call a dogcatcher, then call again if they didn't come fast enough.

Ellen went upstairs and lay down in bed and looked at the ceiling until she was tired of looking. The only times she could do nothing was when Sheila wasn't around. Sheila used words like "interactions" and "engaged," words she had been taught to use. Ellen was not supposed to live in her own head, since that had turned out to be a bad neighborhood. When Sheila was home, Ellen always had to be occupied with something, watching television or reading a magazine or making a mess out of her latest handcraft project. She couldn't get any of them to turn out right, knitting, embroidery, even plain sewing. She got bored with them, and sometimes she tied knots in the yarn, or put in a trail of stitches out to the edge of a pillowcase just to see what Sheila would say, and Sheila always said, "That's very nice, Ellen." The handcrafts had been Sheila's idea. The word for this was "therapeutic."

Sheila had moved back into the house after their mother died, so there would be somebody to take care of Ellen, but really because she and her husband did not want to live together anymore and the Church did not allow divorce. Sheila was not her only sister, but the others lived farther away and were okay with being married, so Ellen was stuck with her.

It wasn't like she needed anybody to take care of her. She wasn't stupid, only crazy, ha ha. It was more like, other people required explanations and reassurances.

Ellen's job was at the thrift shop run by Saint Brendan's, sorting the donated clothes. Ellen was not welcome in church itself after the terrible things she had said about Father Harvey that time, things that had not really happened, it was explained to her, except inside her head. The thrift shop was a good fit for her, Sheila said, because she could walk to it, she didn't have to dress up, and the people there were used to her, meaning, they knew she took crazy pills. It was all right being there, but it wasn't the kind of job you could get excited about.

She left the house by the back door, like she always did, and she didn't see the dog until she had started off down the alley. It must have been hanging around in the front yard and had to catch up with her. It trotted out from behind a garage and stood in her path, waiting. Ellen stopped and she and the dog looked each other over. The dog wasn't panting anymore, but its red mouth hung open, because it was either smiling or getting ready to bite.

"Hey dog," Ellen said, and it wagged its big tail. She took a step toward it and it came up to her and sniffed her legs. Was it still hungry? She'd made herself two sandwiches for lunch, one ham and one peanut butter. She opened her lunch sack and held out half the ham sandwich to it. The dog reached out and took it in its mouth, but not in an especially snappy way. More like, it would have had good manners if it wasn't so hungry.

When it finished the ham sandwich it looked up at Ellen

and wagged its tail again. It had brown eyes with light-colored lashes, and a hopeful expression. Up close, there was gray in its face. Ellen took out half the peanut butter sandwich and again the dog ate it down, coughing a little, probably because the peanut butter got stuck in its throat.

"That's all I got," Ellen said, though that wasn't entirely true. She set off down the alley and the dog trotted along at her side. She guessed the dog was all right, at least it wasn't going to bite. It didn't have a collar. Was it a wild dog? Did they have wild dogs in town? Did they live in the park? Even in winter? Where in the park? It wasn't like they had caves or anything. It was going to be winter pretty soon, and winter was cold, a time of dark and deadness. When people died they got whittled down to bones, don't think that don't think that, but not before the nasty, decomposing part. Eventually everything and everyone died, all of nature and people too, tribes nations civilizations planets the whole universe! A reverse explosion, a Big Bang of sucking nothingness!

But this was brain drain thinking or actually more of a brain blender where everything got mishmashed together and the flopping panic rose up in her throat and she just had to stop it all and breathe, and look around her, and see that she was right where she was meant to be, crossing the street on the way to work, the brown dog going along at her side like he had a job of his own to get to.

Her pills didn't always work like they were supposed to, but she knew better than to tell anyone that.

The thrift shop was in an old brick house. Ellen walked around back to the loading dock, where people dropped off their donations. The dumpster was here too, and a hose spigot but no hose. She poked around under the loading dock where some-times things ended up, and found an enamel pan. She filled this with water and set it off to one side, where there was still some of the old yard's grass. "Well, I have to go to work now," she told the dog. It lifted its nose and gave her an expectant look, so she patted it twice on the top of its flattened head. It had a good feel, a furry feel. "Bye," she said.

Mrs. Markey ran the thrift shop. She was one of those big-smile people. "Good morning, Ellen," she sang out, every day when Ellen came in, like this was something to be really happy about. Mrs. Markey wore a blue smock with a cross and "Saint Brendan's" embroidered on it. "Isn't it a beautiful day? I just love this time of year, with the leaves turning and the air all crisp. Don't you?"

"Sure," Ellen said. She didn't much notice weather.

"I should let you get started," Mrs. Markey said, as if she and Ellen had been having some delightful, extended chat.

The donated clothes arrived stuffed into plastic garbage bags or paper sacks, or sometimes just wads and heaps of them left on the loading dock. Ellen wore rubber gloves and tossed some of them into the rag bin, others into the different carts meant for children, men, and women. The carts went to the laundry room and the clothes were loaded into the giant washers and dryers and then folded or placed on hangers. Sometimes the clothes needed mending, and those were set aside. Sometimes fancy or unusual items came in, party dresses or leather jackets, and these were put on a special garment rack.

On occasion, when Ellen had found some of these fancy clothes first, she folded them up small and hid them under her coat and took them home with her. She didn't have any good clothes anymore; the pills made you gain weight, and nothing fit. But in the back of her closet she had a collection of net petticoats trimmed with ribbon, and a lace dress with a neckline in the shape of a heart, a skirt that glittered with sequins, plus filmy scarves and blouses, jeweled shoes, and a pair of long red leather gloves. Sheila would have said, "Now where in the world do you plan on wearing any of that?"

Ellen didn't think much about the dog while she worked. The pills made it hard to concentrate and there were so many things that could send you off in a different direction. These socks? These sad, busted drawers? All day long, humiliated garments passed through her hands. And while she knew that the craziest part of her crazy was believing that things meant more than they did, where did you draw the line? Did the lost, the broken, the distressed, count for nothing? Save me save me save me, each one said, as she hesitated over the rag bin. Then Mrs. Markey or somebody else poked their head in and said something that needed a certain kind of answer: prompt, cheery, yoo-hoo! Ellen mumbled and stumbled and people got that regretful, wise expression.

Ellen left at four o'clock to go home. She looked around for the dog, and right away he crawled out from underneath the loading dock, wagging his tail like they were old pals. "Hey," Ellen told him, "I'm thinking we should get you some real dog food, what do you say?" And the dog did a kind of happy dance, kicking up with his back legs and then his front legs, like he understood everything and thought it was a good idea.

So they set off down the street to the grocery, the dog staying right at her side, stopping when she stopped, then starting up again. Ellen told him to wait while she went into the store.

The grocery! Some days it was full of shouting colors and products on the shelves that reached out to you like the tentacles of seaweed but of course not seaweed. Today she was in a hurry. She propelled her cart through the aisles and bought two kinds of bagged dog food, in case he didn't like one of them, and a box of dog cookies in the shape of bones. She got a package of hamburger, because they could both eat that.

The checker put it all in two plastic sacks, and when Ellen got outside again she opened the box of cookies and gave the dog one, and then another. There was something you could enjoy about feeding a dog. They were so appreciative. "Let's get on home," she told him, and the dog was ready for that, sure.

They were still a couple of blocks from the house when Ellen saw the boys. She could have crossed the street but then they would too. They were the kind of boys who picked on people, and Ellen was always right there for that, wasn't she, fat and slow and weird. They weren't that old, twelve or thirteen, but they egged each other on and their favorite thing in life was meanness. Sheila always said to pay them no mind.

Today there were four of them. They saw Ellen too, and they lined themselves up, two on either side of the sidewalk, so she'd have to pass through them. Ellen put her head down. She had a grocery sack in each hand and she tightened her grip. Sometimes they tried to take things from her. The dog looked up at her, asking a dog question. "Pay them no mind," Ellen told him.

When she got closer, one of them said, "Hey, is that your dog?"

Ellen nodded. She kept putting one foot in front of the other.

"He sure is ugly. I guess that figures."

"Hey, what's his name?"

They'd closed in around her on the sidewalk. There was no getting past them. "Prince," Ellen said. She didn't know why she said it. It just seemed like his name.

"Prince!" They whistled and pretended to be impressed.

"So does that make you a princess?"

"I guess," Ellen said.

The boys hooted. The one who had spoken was the biggest one. He had red hair and a flattened nose. He said, "Prince and Princess . . ." And you could see him trying to come up with the meanest, snottiest thing to say . . . "Of Butt-Ugly-landia!"

"That's stupid," Ellen said.

They weren't expecting that. She usually didn't say much to them. "She just called you stupid, stupid," one of the other boys said.

The red-haired boy took another step toward Ellen but stopped and looked down. The dog had lifted a back leg and was peeing in a steady stream down the boy's pants and sogging up his tennis shoe.

The boy yelped and shook his foot and said, "Fuck! What the fuck!" The other boys hooted. The red-haired boy whirled around and made as if to hit somebody, either Ellen or the dog or the boys laughing, and that's when the dog lunged at him, barking and showing his teeth and bristling so that the hair on his back stood straight up.

"I'll get you for this, bitch!" But they were running away and taking their nasty talk with them. And then they were gone. "Nice work, Prince," Ellen said, and he sniffed at the sidewalk where the boys had been and peed some more on the same spot.

There was going to be a whole Sheila thing to get through, but she wasn't back from work yet. Ellen took two plastic dishes from the kitchen, one for water and one for food. She filled both of these and put them in the back yard right next to the porch. Prince ate the food in the bowl and then ambled over to the farthest corner of the yard and hunched himself over and pooped.

"Well I guess we had to have some of that action," Ellen said, and cleaned up the mess with a plastic bag and threw it in the garbage can in the alley. It wasn't such a big deal and you could see how people got used to doing it.

When Sheila got home, Ellen was sitting out on the back steps and Prince was resting on an old rug that Ellen had brought out for him. Ellen was wearing her winter coat, because it was getting cold and the wind had picked up. "What's this?" Sheila said. "Have you lost what's left of your mind?" She stayed in the house and didn't open the door all the way.

"He's a nice old dog," Ellen said. "His name is Prince."

"Oh is it. And what's that you're doing, exactly?"

Ellen had the small loom Sheila had bought her for making pot holders and was busy braiding yarn through it. "I'm making Prince a collar."

Sheila closed the door and went back in the house. A little while later she opened it again. "Come inside so we can talk. Your friend stays out there."

She waited while Ellen got up and dusted herself off and carried the loom in front of her so the yarn wouldn't come loose. Sheila said, "Have you considered that this dog is probably lost, that he has a family who misses him, and who's heartbroken with worry over him?"

"Families aren't always like that."

"Have you even thought about looking in the lost and found?" Sheila folded her arms and waited. When she already knew the answer to a thing, there was a space right between her eyebrows that gleamed with happiness. Ellen shook her head, no. "Well I'm going to do that right this minute. What if he has fleas? Do you want to start scratching fleas? Ellen! You have no idea where this dog came from, or if he's dangerous, or if he has some kind of dog disease."

"I'll take him to the vet," Ellen said. "I'll do all those things you're supposed to do."

"Vets are expensive."

"I'll use my Social Security money."

Ellen's Social Security money went into a bank account and stayed there, except for what Sheila called "household expenses." It was another one of those things that Sheila had put herself in charge of. Ellen kept her head down. She could feel Sheila looking at her, the beam coming out from that place between her eyes.

"We'll talk about that later," Sheila said. "Meanwhile, I want it understood, I will not have a stray dog in my house."

"It's my house really," Ellen said, but only after Sheila had left the kitchen.

When it was time for bed, Ellen cooked a hamburger for Prince and gave him some extra dog cookies. She put an old blanket on top of the rug so he'd have a warmer bed. "I'm sorry you have to stay outside," she told him. "It's because of Sheila. She's just that way." Prince licked her hand and settled down in his bed. It was like he understood about Sheila, and he'd make the best of it.

In the middle of the night, Ellen woke up to hear the wind smacking against the windows, and rain coming down hard. Prince! She jumped out of bed, ran downstairs, and opened the back door. "Prince!" she called, but he wasn't there. Rain poured through the downspout and pooled around the bed she'd made for him. "Prince! Where are you?" The air was black with cold rain. Her head and feet were already soaked. She started crying.

Then a dark shape came out from beneath the bushes along the alley fence. "Prince! Here boy!"

She held the door open for him and he trotted in, shaking himself. Water flew everywhere. Ellen knelt down and hugged him so that they were both wet. "I'm sorry sorry sorry," she told him. "Are you all right? Oh, Prince."

"Ellen?" Sheila was calling her from the top of the stairs. "You don't have that dog in here, do you?"

"If you make him go outside, I'm going with him," Ellen said, and she waited for Sheila to do one thing or the other.

"Basement," Sheila said. "And make sure he stays there." Ellen heard her go back down the hall and shut the bedroom door.

"Come on," Ellen told Prince. "It'll be okay now." She flipped on the basement light and took his water bowl and some dog cookies downstairs with them. She used towels from the laundry to dry Prince off. She found an old nightgown of her mother's and changed into it from her wet pajamas. There were two couches in one corner from her growing-up days, the smelly kind the thrift shop wouldn't take.

Ellen patted one of them so that Prince knew it was for him, and he jumped right up. Ellen lay down on the other and covered herself with an afghan. The couch had all the same lumps and bumps she remembered from being a little girl. She burrowed into them so they fit better. She reached out and patted the top of Prince's head, which was still sort of damp.

"I'll fix things up a little better for you tomorrow," she told him.

"Thank you," Prince said.

"You're welcome," Ellen said, and then because she didn't want to think about what had just happened, she squeezed her eyes shut until she fell asleep.

She didn't remember, at first, where she was, and why the dog was snuffling at her face, and then it all came back to her and she said, "Oh wow," and sat up on the couch and tried to clear her head. It was morning, and sunlight was coming in sideways through the basement windows. "Hey Prince," she said, and he wagged his tail and did a few of his sideways dance steps and looked at her inquiringly.

"Oh, I get it," Ellen said, and took him upstairs and out the back door so he could do his thing. The rain had stripped the fall leaves from the trees; they lay in heaps of colors on the ground. She watched Prince nosing around, peeing on important places, then he came up to the door and waited for Ellen to let him in.

"You have this routine down already, don't you," Ellen said, and waited to see if he had anything to say to that. But Prince only looked up at her with his openmouthed smile, wanting his breakfast. She was relieved, she guessed, but also a little disappointed.

It was late and Sheila had already gone to work. She hadn't bothered to wake Ellen up to say goodbye before she left, maybe because she was disgusted with her for sleeping in the basement with a dog. Ellen put food in Prince's bowl and watched him clean it up. When he was finished, she said, "How about I go upstairs and put some clothes on, and then I'll take you for a real walk."

"Okay," Prince said. "But hurry up."

"Oh boy." Ellen sighed, trudging upstairs. "Oh boy."

She hadn't yet finished making his collar, and she didn't have a real leash, so she used a skinny belt from the thrift shop and looped it around his neck. "I don't think you're gonna run off, it's just a leash law thing," she told him.

"Leashes, yup, I understand that."

"I knew you were a smart dog. You should probably not say anything while we're outside, people might get upset."

"Maintain radio silence," Prince agreed, butting up against Ellen's hand to get his ears scratched.

They set off down the street, to a little park where Prince could do his business without anybody getting upset. Ellen wasn't worried about the boys, because they'd be in school now. She kind of hoped that the neighbors might see them walking and think how normal and responsible she was being, a lady walking her dog. When they got back home, Ellen said, "That went pretty well. Now what?"

"Maybe a nap," Prince said, stretching out on the living room rug.

"I'm a little concerned about this talking business."

Prince yawned and rolled over on his back so his stomach was in the air and his front paws dangled. "You mean, concerned about what other people are going to think."

"If I have another bad spell of crazy, they can put me in the nuthouse again. That was a terrible place. It's like a dog pound except for humans. Were you ever in one of those, a pound?"

But Prince was already asleep. His breathing whiffed in and out through his big nose.

Ellen plopped down on the living room couch. Definitely concerned. She didn't want to go through all that again, getting the shaky shakes and talking a mile a minute. She'd started having her troubles a long time ago, when she was first out of school and waiting tables at the Chuck Wagon. It was like her head was a balloon on a string that she carried along bobbing in the air, and all of a sudden it just popped. She got very excited about things that nobody else did, and she was convinced that the food at the Chuck Wagon was being poisoned (which was comical; it was just ordinary bad food), and she couldn't stop talking for love or money. The customers were alarmed when she told them about the poison, and the restaurant owner made her sit in his office with the door closed while he called her father. Her father had been alive then—of course!—and he came and got her and drove her to the hospital. Except she had not believed it was a hospital. It was a prison where they did unspeakable things to people. She'd been plenty crazy, sure, but she still didn't think she'd been wrong about that part.

Even when she was a little kid, Ellen had always been off in her own world, as her mother said, and while it wasn't true that nobody ever paid attention to her, there were times they seemed surprised to come across her. There had been five girls—a boy had died when he was just a baby—and when you counted them off on the fingers of one hand, Ellen was the one finger left wiggling that you couldn't remember. Ellen had not been the pretty one (Cecilia), or the smart one (Brigit), or the good one (Agnes), or even the snotty one (Sheila, duh). Finally she turned into the crazy one, and then at least she was easier to keep track of. There were so many brothers-in-law and nieces and nephews and aunts and uncles and cousins and cousins' families and out beyond that, like distant planets in the solar system, the second cousins and casually connected relatives whom she might never meet, but now they had heard of her, Crazy Aunt Ellen.

Had she been possessed by demons? She used to think that. Was it her own fault for providing them with an opportunity, for having a flawed mind and soul that allowed them entry? No no no, Father Harvey had reassured her. No matter what Sister Mary Peter said, the Church nowadays was open to scientific as well as spiritual healing, and they understood that such things as brain chemistry and genetics must be given their due. Father Harvey spoke of compassion and relief from suffering and the soul's long journey to God. There was so much loneliness in the world, he understood that, because a priest was pledged to earthly loneliness. He knew that she had always been lonely. He wasn't young, and he wasn't what you'd call attractive, exactly, but Ellen was drawn to him, and when he said that they were now married in the eyes of God, she was joyful, she put shame aside and took him as her husband.

Except that none of it had happened. It had all been inside her balloon head.

Those years of living at home with Father and Mother, and then just Mother, and life had gone along, gone along, and the pills turned the crazy down like a stove burner. Well, here it was on the boil again, and it couldn't be helped.

They spent most of the day snoozing, and when Prince woke up, he yawned and said he wouldn't mind a little yard time, if she knew what he meant. Ellen let him out and once he was back inside she said, "You have to tell me, are you lost? I mean, is there someplace you need to get back to?"

"I was in transition," Prince said. He lowered his head and began licking at his private parts. Then he came up for air, panting a little. "I was in a bad situation, I really don't want to talk about it, and I chose to leave. I was pretty sore and tired and hungry when you found me, and it's a good thing you took me in. I definitely owe you."

"Quiet now, Sheila's home."

"Mum's the word," Prince said.

Sheila came in from the back door. Her footsteps thundered. Over time, Sheila had become, not fat, exactly, but big. She came into the living room and stopped. "Hi Sheil," Ellen said.

"What's going on here?"

"Nothing. Just me and Prince hanging out." Prince put his nose on his paws and kept his ears down and looked mournful.

"We talked about this. That dog does not belong here."

"You talked about it. Not me."

"Excuse me? Do we have a little attack of smart mouth going on? Ellen! You are not keeping that dog! He certainly does not belong in the living room!" Sheila talked about the living room like it was some fancy place.

"I'll take care of him. I'll take him to the vet, like I said, and get him his shots."

"And how do you expect to get him there?" Sheila asked, a note of triumph in her voice. "Because I am not taking him."

Ellen shrugged. "I guess I can drive, then. I can drive Mom's car." It sat in the garage, right where their mother had left it. It was a good enough car.

"Now Ellen. You haven't driven in I don't know how long. You don't even have a license anymore."

"Then I'll get one. Prince can get his dog license and I'll get my driver's license."

"Driving is a whole separate issue. Please get this dog idea out of your head."

"If you don't like it," Ellen said, greatly daring, "you can go home to your own house."

Sheila sat down hard on a leather armchair. It made a "foof" sound beneath her. "The only reason I'm here is to try and help you." Her voice wobbled. "I know you think I'm a big pain in the rear, but I'm your own sister, and I worry about you, Ellen, I worry all the time. There are so many bad things that can happen to people who aren't—like everybody else. I pray for you, Ellen, go ahead and laugh at that if you want to, but I pray to do right by you, like Mom and Dad would want me to. If they were here this minute, they'd be saying, 'Ellen, your sister loves you and wants what's best for you.'"

"I'm sorry," Ellen said. She felt horrible. She looked at Prince, but he was sitting this one out and wouldn't meet her eyes. "I don't want you to worry."

"All right," Sheila said. Her big purse was in her lap and she opened it and found her pocket pack of Kleenex and blew her nose. "We'll get past it. We'll rise above it. How was work today?"

She'd forgotten all about work. "That's a whole nother situation."

"Didn't you even go? Is that what you're saying? Oh, Ellen."

"I don't think I want to go to work anymore." It wasn't a thought she was thinking until right that minute, but once it came out of her mouth, she knew it for the truth.

"Lord give me strength," Sheila said. "This really is not up for discussion. I know it's hard for you to get along with other people, but you have to make the effort. You can't just sit in the house feeling sorry for yourself."

"I think it's more like it's hard for other people to get along with me."

Sheila stared at her over the Kleenex, then she put it away in her purse and stood up. "You've given me a great deal to think about, Ellen. I don't want to be unpleasant, but it's my responsibility to think of your welfare. I'm going to go upstairs and change clothes and start supper. Why don't you do whatever it is you need to with this dog, so I don't have to look at him just now."

"Uh-oh," Prince said, once Sheila was out of the room.

"Shush. I'll feed you, then we can go for a walk. You have to watch out for Sheila when she's in this kind of a mood."

"Is she ever not in this kind of a mood?" Prince wanted to know, but once his food bowl was filled, he quit talking and chowed down.

It was getting dark earlier and earlier now, and Ellen hurried to get Prince to the park and back home before the lonesome streetlights came on. Nobody was out on the sidewalks, so she let Prince's belt-leash trail, and he ranged from side to side, sniffing at hedges and windblown paper trash. She didn't see how she was going to get past Sheila about Prince. Once Sheila got a notion into her head, it pretty much set up housekeeping there and didn't budge. Maybe Ellen and Prince could run away together, and live like gypsies, which was something her mother used to say about shiftless, unprosperous people, well, that would be them.

Once they got to the park, Prince was quick about doing his business, and was just trotting back to Ellen when he snarled and looked around him at his hind end, then yelped.

"What is it, what's wrong?" Ellen asked, and then she felt something sting against her face, and another volley breaking against her coat sleeve, small and hard, like seeds or gravel. Prince

snarled again and barked in the direction of a stand of evergreens, dark and impenetrable, someone hiding there, a deeper
shadow in the trees, throwing something? Shooting something?
Horrible clawing nightmare panic, all the shapes her mind could
make, the thing in the trees coming for them, and Prince standing his ground, barking, until Ellen grabbed at the belt and
pulled him away and they ran and stumbled their way home.

They stopped just outside the back door to catch their
breath. Inside the lighted kitchen, they saw Sheila moving from
the stove to the sink and back, fixing dinner with her jaw set in a
hard shape. "What was that?" Ellen asked. "Are you all right?"

"Stung like fury, but I'm okay. You?"

"Me too," Ellen said, but she wasn't really, and she bent
down so Prince could lick her face, which was another thing
Sheila would have flipped out about, if she'd seen it.

They got through dinner without much conversation—
Sheila had turned on the silent treatment—and she didn't object
when Ellen made Prince a bed in the kitchen out of some old
coats. "Good night," Ellen told him. "You'll be fine here. I'll see
you in the morning."

"It's all good, don't worry about a thing," Prince said. He
turned around and around in the coats and settled down with
his black kangaroo nose tucked beneath his tail. Really, he was
so cute.

Ellen went upstairs and got into her own bed, where she'd
slept every night of her life except for those times in the crazy
hospital. She used to share a bedroom with Agnes and Sheila, but
Agnes lived in Ohio with her husband and kids, and Sheila had
taken over their parents' room. Ellen got halfway asleep, then
jerked herself awake. She had been on the edge of a dream, and

in the dream an evil thing with an unspeakable demon face crept toward her, just waiting for her to fall asleep.

Ellen got out of bed and went down to the kitchen. "Prince. Hey, Prince?" He rolled over and yawned. "Would you come sleep with me?"

"It would be my pleasure," Prince said, shaking himself and following Ellen up the stairs.

Fortunately Sheila was a heavy sleeper. She slept the sleep of the just, she used to joke. Still, Ellen shushed Prince and kept herself quiet. She patted the bed and Prince jumped up and stretched out beside her, his warm back to Ellen's front. Ellen rubbed his ears and then the groove under his nose and the fur of his chest. She said, "I bet they didn't let you sleep on the bed in your old place."

"There's some out there in the world who are cruel and hateful for no reason."

"Don't I know it," Ellen said. They fell asleep like that, and very early in the morning, before Sheila was stirring, Ellen opened the bedroom door and Prince padded back down to the kitchen.

The garage had been shut for so long, it took some doing for Ellen to lift the board that latched the doors and pry them open. Her mother hadn't driven much at the end. The car was a Lincoln because Ellen's father had always driven American-made cars. It was brown and boat-shaped, draped in cobwebs and twigs. Ellen used an old dishrag held in a pair of tongs to dust it off. The tires had a fat, weary look. She wasn't sure about getting the thing to start, let alone driving it. "Here goes nothing," she said to Prince. He was in the back seat, sniffing all the gratifying smells, leather and rot and whatever kind of animal lived in old garages.

She pressed the accelerator down to give the engine gas, then turned the ignition key. The car made a waa waa waa sound and quit. She tried again, a couple more times with the accelerator feeding the engine again, and finally it turned over.

"Well Howdy Doody," Ellen said. "I guess we're in business."

Prince looked into the front seat. "Can you put the window down so I can do the head-out-the-window thing?"

Ellen's father had taught all his girls to drive, and Ellen remembered everything as if she'd never stopped. She'd always been a good driver. It was just a matter of putting the hand and feet things together at the right times. She backed out of the driveway and rolled into the street. "We're not going to push our luck," she told Prince. "I don't want to run into anybody and get arrested."

"You should probably take it into a car place and have them change the oil and stuff," Prince advised.

"On the to-do list," Ellen agreed. She drove them around the block a couple of times, getting used to the way the world looked from inside a car. It had been a while. It was pleasant to watch the streets unrolling as she passed, and she enjoyed the ease with which you could go one way, then change your mind and head off in another. She nudged the car out to the main road and drove until she found a pet supply store. Prince waited in the car while she went in and bought him a real collar and a leash and some cookies in the shape of mailmen, and a stuffed bunny with a squeaker that he pretended to take an interest in, but really, he was too old for toys.

"We could go on a trip sometime," Ellen said.

"Like where?" Prince asked. He was biting the head off a mailman cookie.

"Anywhere with a road," Ellen said grandly. Possibilities crowded in behind her eyes, all the places you saw on postcards. I mean, why not? Somebody must go there. She turned the car toward home. This driving thing, she had it all knocked.

"Sheila at ten o'clock," Prince warned, as they came up to the house, and Ellen stomped on the brakes. Her heart shriveled. What was Sheila doing home early?

Sheila was standing in the driveway as Ellen drove up, looking into the empty garage. "I was about to call the police," she said. "Stop the car and give me the keys." Sheila's expression said: I take no prisoners.

"I can drive just fine," Ellen told her. "It's no big deal."

"Get out of there, and get that dog out too." Sheila reached in and snatched the keys from Ellen's hand. "When you drive without a license or insurance, it is a big deal. Out." She yanked Ellen's door open.

Ellen got out. Her legs were wobbly. Prince had scooted over to the far side of the back seat and wouldn't come closer. Sheila said, "Fine, he can stay there and I'll drive this car. I got some good news, Ellen. This dog has a home and I'm going to take him back to it."

"What are you talking about?"

"A very nice lady and her husband and little boy who lost him and they've been looking for him everywhere. They were so excited when I told them we had him."

"That's a big fat lie," Ellen said.

"Excuse me?" Sheila was still in her work clothes and her work shoes with the heels. She was as big as a statue.

"They didn't want him. They were cruel to him. He ran away."

Sheila let out her breath and put on her patient, grown-up face. "And how do you know this, Ellen?"

"Because he told me," Ellen whispered. She couldn't look at Sheila. Prince's tongue was hanging out and he was panting. Ellen wanted to touch him but he'd shrunk into the corner.

"The dog talks to you." The space between Sheila's eyebrows began to kindle.

"Yes."

"All right, Ellen. That's very interesting. When I get back, I'm going to call Dr. Gaily, because I know he will want to hear all about these conversations."

"No." She knew what Dr. Gaily meant. He was the doctor from the hospital. "I won't."

"Please don't be uncooperative, Ellen. It only makes everything so much harder, and it doesn't change the outcome."

"You've never loved anything in your whole life," Ellen told her.

Then a lot of things happened all at once. Sheila opened her mouth wide, either to say something or in outrage, and Prince in the back seat of the car barked and howled and shouted, "Ellen, watch out, watch out!" Ellen turned and saw the hedge behind them snapping and shaking and the red-haired boy stepped out of it, aiming a toy that looked like a rifle or a rifle that looked like a toy, and just at the last instant Ellen fell to the ground and the spray of shot hit Sheila right between the eyes.

Ellen was allowed to attend church for the funeral, packed between her two burliest brothers-in-law in case there were problems. But she sat quietly all through the service, and listened as Father Harvey talked about our earthly loss and the rejoicing in Heaven. He said that agents of God's grace were everywhere among us, working His will, and Ellen guessed he was talking about Sheila, but maybe you could make a good case for the red-haired boy too. Father Harvey was old now, and his face had collapsed into flabby wrinkles, and Ellen asked herself what she'd ever seen in him, though she'd known all along it had been his loneliness.

Later, back at the house, Ellen's sisters helped her set out the supper of ham sandwiches and casseroles, and bottles of beer and of whiskey were lined up on a dish towel on the kitchen counter. Sheila's husband came too, and he drank a good bit and cried, and even though everybody knew how things had been between them, they let him carry on. What was the harm?

The youngest nieces and nephews and cousins ran in and out from the yard, filling the house with cold drafts, while the older ones grouped themselves on the couches in the basement, bored. Everyone complimented Ellen on how nice the house looked, how well she had kept it up. She smiled a lot, aware that she was under scrutiny. Her sisters brought out the old photo albums and they passed them around and remembered this or that story, funny or sad, and how Sheila had her good points, you had to give her that. In the kitchen the men stood with their drinks in their hands and talked work and talked sports. Everyone was glad that the red-haired boy was not from a Saint Brendan's family, so they could say a lot of harsh things without feeling conflicted, like, they should have put him under the jail, the little bastard.

Everybody loved Prince, who went up to people with his tail wagging and his new collar tags jingling. He did all the tricks that people asked him, sit, roll over, shake hands, speak! When they got to speak! he said, "Woof!" and he and Ellen winked at each other, because it was pretty funny.

Finally the party was over, and the dishes washed and the trash bundled up, and Sheila's husband sent home in a cab, sobbing to the driver. Agnes, her nicest sister, got Ellen to one side and said, "You know you can come to us. We have plenty of room and we'd love to have you."

"Thanks, but I'm all right here. Really. I'm fine."

"As long as you're certain," Agnes began, then her youngest child locked himself in the bathroom and she was needed there.

The next night, Ellen and Prince had the leftover ham for their supper. "They sure were a houseful," Ellen said. "I mean, I was glad to see them and all, but I need a little more elbow room."

"You guys do know how to throw a funeral," Prince said. "By the way, you look really nice tonight."

"Thank you," Ellen said. She was wearing two of the net petticoats, a lavender and a yellow, one on top of the other. She twirled to make them flare out. "Crazy lady fashion. Not everybody can pull it off."

At bedtime they climbed the stairs, and Prince lay with his warm back along Ellen's front, and she rubbed his nose and his ears and the fur on his chest. Prince said, "This is going to sound strange, but I don't think you're crazy. I mean, look at everything you do for yourself, and do for me, look how you managed the whole funeral thing. I think crazy is something you outgrew."

"Huh," Ellen said. She wanted to believe it, but she wasn't so sure. She still felt the same as she always had. "Okay, but, not to be rude, you and me talking. That's not crazy?"

"No, that's just magic."

They were almost asleep. Prince's rib cage rose and fell, rose and fell as his breathing slowed. Ellen said, "Promise me you'll stay with me forever."

Prince stirred. "Every day of my forever, I will stay with you."

"Oh, yeah, that's good, okay," Ellen said, and then they both slept.

ABOUT THE AUTHOR

Jean Thompson is the author of six previous novels, among them *The Humanity Project*, *The Year We Left Home*, and five previous story collections, including *Who Do You Love* (a National Book Award finalist). She lives in Urbana, Illinois.